# NO FIXED LINE

DANA STABENOW, born in Alaska and raised on a 75-foot fish tender, is the author of the award-winning, bestselling Kate Shugak series. The first book in the series, *A Cold Day for Murder*, received an Edgar Award from the Mystery Writers of America. Contact Dana via her website: www.stabenow.com.

# DANA STABENOW

"Kate Shugak is the answer if you are looking for something unique in the crowded field of crime fiction."
**Michael Connelly**

"For those who like series, mysteries, rich, idiosyncratic settings, engaging characters, strong women and hot sex on occasion, let me recommend Dana Stabenow."
**Diana Gabaldon**

"A darkly compelling view of life in the Alaskan Bush, well laced with lots of gallows humor. Her characters are very believable, the story lines are always suspenseful, and every now and then she lets a truly vile villain be eaten by a grizzly. Who could ask for more?" **Sharon Penman**

"One of the strongest voices in crime fiction." *Seattle Times*

"Cleverly conceived and crisply written thrillers that provide a provocative glimpse of life as it is lived, and justice as it is served, on America's last frontier." *San Diego Union-Tribune*

## The Kate Shugak series

A Cold Day for Murder
A Fatal Thaw
Dead in the Water
A Cold Blooded Business
Play with Fire
Blood Will Tell
Breakup
Killing Grounds
Hunter's Moon
Midnight Come Again
The Singing of the Dead
A Fine and Bitter Snow
A Grave Denied
A Taint in the Blood
A Deeper Sleep
Whisper to the Blood
A Night Too Dark
Though Not Dead
Restless in the Grave
Bad Blood
Less Than a Treason
**No Fixed Line**

## The Liam Campbell series

Fire and Ice
So Sure of Death
Nothing Gold Can Stay
Better to Rest

✳

Silk and Song
Death of an Eye

# DANA STABENOW

# NO FIXED LINE

HEAD of ZEUS

First published in the UK in 2020 by Head of Zeus, Ltd.

Copyright © Dana Stabenow, 2020

9 7 5 3 1 2 4 6 8

A catalogue record for this book is available from the British Library.
Library of Congress Cataloging-in-Publication Data is available

ISBN (HB): 9781788549110
ISBN (XTPB): 9781788549127
ISBN (E): 9781788548977

Typeset by Divaddict Publishing Solutions Ltd.

Printed and bound in Great Britain by
CPI Group (UK) Ltd, Croydon CR0 4YY

Head of Zeus Ltd
First Floor East
5–8 Hardwick Street
London EC1R 4RG

WWW.HEADOFZEUS.COM

*For*
*the Rasmuson Foundation*
*who are such stuff as*
*Alaskan dreams are made on.*
*Thank you.*

...though there is no fixed line between wrong and right, there are roughly zones whose laws must be obeyed.

—Robert Frost

Anna was a warm, heavy weight against his side, her eyes closed, her breathing deep, her tears drying in faint silvery streaks on her cheeks. At least she was asleep now.

A shadow fell over them and he curled a protective arm around her before he looked up.

The Bad Man smiled at him and held out something. When David didn't take it the Bad Man removed the foil wrapper and held it out again. It smelled like food. David didn't want to take anything from the Bad Man but his stomach growled, and Anna would be hungry when she woke. He snatched the sticky bar out of the Bad Man's hand. The Bad Man smiled again and patted his head. David held himself rigid and waited for the Bad Man to stop.

The airplane shifted suddenly, up and down and side to side and back and forth. The Bad Man staggered a few steps, grabbing at the back of a seat to keep from falling. He looked toward the front of the airplane and shouted something. The piloto shouted something back. The plane jerked again and one of the duffel bags that they had loaded onto the plane fell from a seat into the aisle and broke open, spilling large square plastic bags everywhere. One of them *burst in an explosion of tiny white tablets like* aspirina. *The Bad Man stooped to pick up the loose plastic bags from the aisle and beneath the other seats, cursing every time the plane yanked him off balance again. He cursed again when he couldn't get the zipper on the duffel to work, and had to tuck the duffel beneath a seat so it wouldn't flop around and spill the bags again. Afterward he went forward to fall into the chair next to the* piloto.

*Something glinted from the floor and David looked down to see a* teléfono. *His heart leapt. It must have slipped out of the Bad Man's pocket when he fell. He leaned over, straining at the belt, and managed to touch it with the tips of his fingers. He pulled it toward him until he could pick it up and slip it in his pocket. He looked up at the front of the plane. The Bad Man and the* piloto *still had their backs turned. The airplane shook again, a hard up and down bump, rocking him back in the seat.*

*David hadn't known there were bumps this bad in the air. He'd only ever been on an airplane once before, two if you counted when they had to change from one plane to another in the big* aeropuerto, *and the bumps on those planes had been little. There was a nice lady in a uniform with a cart, too, who brought them little bags of treats and a whole can of Coca-Cola for each of them. There was no nice lady on this airplane. Only the Bad Man and the* piloto.

*David broke the food bar in two and put half away in his pocket for when Anna woke up. He ate the other half. It was sticky and dry at the same time, with chewy little frutas in it that didn't taste like anything. It reminded him of the bars that people had given them sometimes on the long walk north. People had given them water in bottles, too. He wished he had one of them now, but he would not ask the Bad Man. He would never ask the Bad Man for anything.*

*The plane bumped again and Anna cried out "Mami!" but she didn't wake up. They were sharing the last seat in the very back of the little plane. David made sure to sit on the outside so Anna wouldn't fall out on one of the bumps. It was what Mami had told him to do the last time he had seen her. "Take care of your sister, David. Don't be afraid, mijo. They will bring me back very soon."*

*But they had not brought Mami back very soon. They had not brought Mami back at all. David and Anna had been put in a big building inside one of many cages made of chain link with other niños from Mexico and Honduras and Guatemala and El Salvador who had made the same long walk north for the same reasons. There they were held for so long David lost count of the days. It was too hot during the day and too cold at night. There were no beds and they had to sleep on the concrete floor. There was only a plastic bucket for a baño, there were no toothbrushes or bathrooms and no way to wash their clothes. Food came once a day in foil packets, dry and tasteless. Everyone got one bottle of water a day, and after two days some of the bigger niños began taking the water from the smaller niños. Nobody stopped them.*

*Then one day big anglos in black jackets with big white letters on the back came into the cage and took away six of them: David and Anna and four other boys of David's age. Outside the building the sun was bright and David couldn't see very well at first. The four boys went away with two anglos and another two took charge of David and Anna. "Are you taking us to Mami?" David said, and one of them smiled and nodded and said, "Si, Mami."*

*First they were in a big blue van, which took them to an aeropuerto that had too many airplanes to count. They got on the big airplane with the pretty lady with the cart and flew to another, bigger aeropuerto where they got on another airplane. This time when they landed the sun was gone and it was cold and the ground was covered in snow. David knew what snow was from the picture book about the little boy in the red suit. He scooped up a handful and showed it to Anna and she had laughed and for a moment both of them forgot about Mami and where she was and why she wasn't with them.*

*But then the big men, who had changed from their jackets into regular clothes, put them in another big black car and drove them through city streets beneath a full moon to a house. The man who lived there gave the big men a black briefcase and they left David and Anna with him and drove away.*

*It was a big house with windows all around. There was a big lighted star that glowed against the snow on the hillside that made David think about the tin stars Mami decorated the house with, back when they had a house, back before the bad men came and killed Papi and hurt Mami, and Mami took them to make the long walk to* el norte.

But there was no feliz *about this* navidad, *because the big house was where the Bad Man lived. He locked David in a room and he hurt Anna. When the Bad Man let David out Anna was crying, her skirt sticking damply to her legs. Did he make you take a bath? David said.*

*He hurt me, she said, sobbing, like* los pandilleros *did Mami, and then he washed me.*

*The Bad Man came back in the room and gave Anna a bag of candy. David took it away from her and threw it in the Bad Man's face as hard as he could. So then the Bad Man hurt David, too. For the first time David was glad Papi was dead so he would never have to tell him the things the Bad Man did to him and Anna. The one thing, the last thing Mami had asked him to do, protect his sister, he could not do. Sometimes he wished* los pandilleros *had killed him, too.*

*They were nine days in that big house on the side of the mountain with the light from the star shining through the windows. He looked at the back of the Bad Man's head where he sat in the seat next to the* piloto *and wished he had a gun like a* pistolero *in the* narcocorridos. *He would shoot the Bad Man dead, and then he would take Anna and find Mami and together they would find a safe place to live where there were no* pandilleros *and no Bad Men.*

*This evening for the first time they had left the house on the side of the mountain and driven to a place where this small plane was parked. They went inside and the* piloto *started the small engines on the wings that sounded like the big engines on the big airplanes and they had taken off and flown for about an hour to a tiny place somewhere else. It was snowing and David didn't see the airstrip through the window until just before they landed. They parked next to another airplane almost exactly like the one they were in and the Bad Man opened the door and the other airplane's door opened and someone came down the steps carrying two big duffel bags and handed them to the Bad Man and then went back to his airplane. The Bad Man closed the door and the other plane took off and they took off afterward into the deepening dark and the wind-driven snow.*

*The airplane jolted again, more violently this time. The piloto shouted something. The Bad Man shouted back. The roar of the engines seemed to change. David looked over Anna's head and outside the window he thought he saw the sharp point of a rock, but it was quickly obscured again by the black of the night and the snow driving past.*

*The piloto and the Bad Man were shouting at each other again and the airplane was still jumping up and down and lurching back and forth and side to side and it felt like they were falling and the engines got louder and Anna woke up and started to cry. It's okay, David said, although he knew that it wasn't. It's okay, Anna.*

*And then there was a screeching, grinding crash so loud it hurt his ears and the blackness outside the window seemed to flood inside and swallow them up.*

*I'm so sorry, Mami.*

# One

MONDAY, NEW YEAR'S EVE
*Canyon Hot Springs*

"NEED A REFILL?"
"Well, sure. But who's going to go get it?"
A good question. The wind was howling, the snow was swirling, and on New Year's Eve it was already as dark as it got in Alaska to begin with. Which made cuddling with your honey in the pool closest to the cabin at Canyon Hot Springs all the more, well, delicious, Matt Grosdidier thought. There was something about being outside in a blizzard in midwinter and not being lost or cold. And not in the process of responding to a scene of medical mayhem in the middle of one. That work was left to his three brothers this evening, as he had won the coin toss. It didn't hurt that he was the only one of them with a steady girlfriend, especially in the woman-poor Park, and was the subject of their manifest envy. He sighed with pure happiness.

"What?" Laurel Meganack narrowed her eyes at him. She, too, was naked and submerged up to her neck in the steaming pool.

He gave her a winning smile. She remained unimpressed, drained her wine and handed him her empty glass.

He laughed and kissed her. She responded with enough enthusiasm that he gave some thought to going for a two-fer before rather than after, but she stiff-armed him. "Did you think you didn't have to work for it? Go."

He sighed to let her know how he suffered, and on purpose splashed her good when he vaulted out of the pool and ran for the cabin door. The blowing snow stung his skin with a thousand tiny needles. There was significant shrinkage but you couldn't blame a guy for that. The wind chill had to be thirty below. He could hear her laughing over the sound of the storm. He was moving pretty fast by the time he hit the door.

The cabin had been built by hand the previous summer by Kate Shugak, whose property this was and who, when Matt asked if he and Laurel could spend New Year's Eve there, had rolled her eyes and said, "Ah, to be young again." Which Matt had, correctly, taken as tacit permission and had loaded up his sled forthwith with various eatables and drinkables and an entire box of condoms. Safety first.

The cabin was solidly built and snug, with a sleeping loft over the door reached by a ladder, a small but very efficient cast iron wood stove, and an outhouse just a few steps outside the back door that had an actual toilet seat. Alaska

Bush luxury defined. He grabbed up the open bottle of red from the counter and before he could think twice about it trotted out the door and splashed Laurel again leaping back into the pool.

She laughed again, fortunately. "My hero."

He refilled her glass. "Always," he said, and was a little surprised to realize he meant it.

The pool was one of seven of varying sizes that rose from a seep beneath the one they were marinating in and overflowed one into the other down the bottom half of the narrow canyon. Old Sam Dementieff had homesteaded the canyon and the surrounding one hundred and sixty acres back in the Stone Age—well, before World War II, anyway—and had left it to Kate. It was the place where she had spent the previous summer recovering from being shot in the chest at point-blank range. Building a cabin seemed an excessive way to go about the job of recovery, but then Kate Shugak was a law unto herself and Matt Grosdidier was not the man to second-guess her. He liked his balls right where they were. Suffice it to say that Canyon Hot Springs was Kate's hideout, her bolthole, the place she went to to get away from it all. Her happy place.

He looked at Laurel, who was regarding him over the rim of her glass with an expression that could only be described as smoldering. His happy place, too. Without breaking eye contact he took her glass and set it down in the snow edging the pool, and put his own next to it. She came easily into his arms, swinging a leg over his and settling down on top of him, everything lining up with what could only be described as perfection.

She nuzzled at his neck in the spot just below his ear that seemed to connected directly to his cock. "You're like the Coast Guard," she said, her voice a low and excruciatingly sexy murmur.

"How's that?"

"*Semper paratus*," she said. "Always ready."

He fumbled in back of him for the condom he'd brought out with the wine, and jumped when she bit him. "Hard not to be around you."

He felt her smile against his skin. "Hard is the word." Her hand dropped below the surface of the water and he caught his breath. He grabbed her by the hair and pulled her head back to get at her mouth again—god, how he loved her mouth—but she pulled away. He went after her blindly and she grabbed his head and said, "Matt. Wait."

"Why?"

"Listen." She shook him. "Matt, listen!"

He pulled back and stared at her. "What? It's the wind, it's—" And then he heard it, faintly, over the sound of the gale whistling and wailing up the canyon walls, the scream of a jet engine, faint at first, growing rapidly nearer and louder.

"What the—"

The sound of the engine increased to a roar as it passed overhead and then as suddenly ceased. A second later a booming crash made them both jump. Even above the wind they could hear tearing metal screaming in loud, abruptly truncated protest.

Five seconds could not have passed. To Matt it felt like an hour and even as he was up out of the pool he was cursing himself for his slow reaction. The door banged open and he tore into his clothes, yanking on everything from the skin out including his down bibs and parka. Next to him Laurel was pulling on her own. "Do you think anyone could have survived that?"

"Won't know until we look. Not likely, though." He stuck foot warmers to the bottoms of his socks and made sure she did, too, before stamping into his Sorels.

"Still have to look, I get it. Can we take the sled?"

"Not very far, but we will as far as we can." He put hand warmers into his down mitts and pulled them on.

"We brought the snowshoes, right?"

"On the trailer. Part of the survival kit." Although he doubted either the terrain or the weather would allow their use. Bulked up to twice their natural size by their Arctic gear they lumbered out of the house and went around to the side where the sled and the trailer were parked next to the woodpile. He yanked off the tarp while she climbed on and pressed the starter. That blessed engine came to life at a touch and he sent up silent thanks to Yamaha engineers. He clipped the first aid pack to an eyebolt screwed into the inside of the trailer. Laurel scooted back and he climbed on the seat in front of her. They slipped goggles over their parka hoods. Matt took one precious moment to run over everything they'd done since they'd heard the crash, trying to think of anything he'd forgotten. It was always the one thing you didn't bring that you desperately needed at the scene.

The skis had frozen into the snow but they only had to rock the snow machine a few times before it came loose. Matt gave it some gas, a very little, and they left the negligible shelter of the cabin and crept slowly but purposefully into the center of the canyon, the wind howling into their faces. It increased in volume and in noise and seemed to be trying to shove them off the sled and the sled over on top of them. "Hold on!" Matt said, and stood up to lean forward, shifting his body weight out over the skis. The light cast by the sled's lamp was obscured by fine, dense snow blowing horizontally across their path, only briefly and sporadically illuminating the homicidal rocks, ridges, and outcroppings that obstructed their way. Matt kept their speed at just above a crawl, hoping to minimize the damage if they did collide with a chunk of Quilak granite. All too soon the canyon narrowed and the ground rose so steeply that the snowmobile's engine rose to a protesting whine. Matt was just about to put it into neutral and break out the snowshoes when Laurel said, her voice faint against the wind, "Look!" Her mitt pointed over his shoulder.

For a brief lull the snow cleared and revealed what he had taken for another small outcropping but was in fact the vertical stabilizer of an airplane. It loomed up momentarily out of the darkness and then the snow closed in again. He goosed the gas and the sled's engine yowled in protest but it moved forward far enough that the headlight caught the one thing that was not like any other in this roaring wilderness. From what he could see, which wasn't much, the rudder had more or less survived the impact. One of the horizontal stabilizers was pretty chewed up while the other was completely gone. The fuselage forward of the tail extended maybe eight feet. The snow was coming down so hard that in another ten minutes they might have passed it by if the wreckage hadn't partially blocked what was left of the little canyon before it turned into a mountain ridge.

"Scooch back!" She did and he didn't step off the sled as much as roll off it, trying to spread out as much of his weight as possible. He didn't know how firm the snow here was, he didn't want to posthole through it if he didn't have to, and he didn't want to break out the snowshoes until and unless he absolutely had to. He rolled over until he was just below the wreckage, and then he squirmed forward on his elbows and knees until he bumped his head against the fuselage. In spite of all his Arctic gear, in spite of the hot pads in his boots and mitts, the cold was beginning to make itself felt. He paused, trying to snatch some of the oxygen going by him at what felt like the speed of sound. He couldn't smell any fuel so the wings were probably not nearby, which was at least a relative mercy. The very last thing he wanted to have to deal with in this blizzard was a fire. He turned over and used his heels to push himself to where he could grasp the ragged edge of the fuselage where it had torn itself from the rest of the aircraft. He pulled himself alongside it and around it and then through it, with the stray thought that he wished the sadist who presided over his annual fitness certification could see him now.

The fuselage seemed to be pretty well wedged into the cliff face, and he walked his elbows forward until his head was partially sheltered from the storm and squinted around. It was dark inside and fast filling up with snow. A headlamp. Yeah, he sure could have used a headlamp about now. There was a flashlight back in the first aid kit in the trailer instead of in his pocket, too.

By some freak of physics the floor of the fuselage was almost level. He could make out the vague outline of a single remaining airplane seat. Wires and strips of interior laminate dangled from places where the bulkhead had ripped open and what looked like stuffing, probably from one of the seats. He wiped the snow from his goggles. And there, in the back—

"Fuck!"

He tested the edge of what was really just some ribbing sandwiched between a couple of pieces of aluminum. It seemed steady enough, like maybe it wouldn't shift beneath his weight and roll down the side of the canyon and over himself, Laurel, and the sled, in that order. And Kate Shugak's cabin, let's not forget that possibility, the one that might actually get him killed. He got his feet beneath him.

The wreckage held steady, wedged between the snow and the rock. He duckwalked forward, one cautious hand and foot at a time.

They were kids, belted together into the last seat remaining on the aircraft, which astonishingly had remained bolted to the floor. Let's hear it for the FAA and strict aviation safety regulation enforcement. They were both limp, hanging from their seatbelt, and frost was already forming on their faces and clothes. He stripped the mitt from his hand and felt for pulses. Faint, but there.

The boy was wearing a T-shirt and shorts, the girl a sundress with a cardigan over it. Neither of them was packing much in the way of body weight. He had to get them down to the cabin and into the warm.

He took one precious moment to clear his mind and think it all out before moving into action. He stripped off his parka and laid it out on the floor. He cut the seatbelt with his belt knife and rolled them inside the parka side by side. He cut lengths from the dangling wiring and used it to tie the parka tightly around them, and then more to fashion a rope which he tied to the wiring around the parka in a makeshift three-point harness. He shoved them and the parka and the wiring harness out of the fuselage and into the weather. All he had on beneath the parka was a T-shirt and the bib of his Carhartts and the snow stung his exposed skin with a fury that made him feel like it was drawing blood. Yeah, should have put his hoodie on under his parka, too.

The wind was blowing so hard that it pushed the parka full of kids sideways over the slope of snow instead of straight down to the sled, but Laurel had seen what he was doing. She had put on her snowshoes while he'd been inside the wreck and she stepped out and snagged the edge of the parka as it went by. He wiped his goggles again and let himself down onto the snow, too tired now to be careful. His foot promptly sank in up to the hip.

"Fuck." He knew his fatigue signaled the onset of hypothermia, but he managed to pull himself out onto his belly and more or less swam over the surface of the snow to the sled. Laurel helped him put the kids in the trailer and shoved him in after them. She climbed on the sled and they started to move. He realized that during the time he'd been inside the wreck she had also turned the sled around so that it was pointing downhill.

I'm so keeping her, he thought.

The journey back was quicker than the journey up, and they got the kids into the cabin in short order. Matt collapsed into the single chair and started to shake. Laurel jammed as much wood into the stove as it would hold, rolled the kids in front of it and then went back outside to shut off the sled and tarp it up. Back inside she stripped off her Arctic gear and then had to find a pair of wire cutters to get the kids out of the parka.

"N-n-no unnecessary m-m-movement." His teeth were chattering so hard he could barely get the words out. "Are-are-are their clothes wet? Is the p-p-p-parka?"

She felt them, and shook her head. "The snow is fine and dry. None of it stuck."

"L-l-leave them on the p-p-parka. Get out the h-h-hot p-packs and t-t-tuck them in around them. C-c-cover them up with b-b-blankets."

She did so, working quickly and efficiently, and then emptied a bottle of water into the tea kettle and put it on the Coleman with the burner on high. While she waited for it to boil she got his boots and bibs off and pulled a sleeping bag up to his chin, working the zipper around so his hands were free. A few minutes later he was sipping gratefully at a steaming mug of chicken bouillon, steadying it with both hands so he wouldn't spill most of it down his front. After what felt like a very long time his shivers began to abate and he relaxed against the back of the chair with a long sigh. Her expression, which had been looking a little pinched, began to smooth out. She nodded at the children. "Should we wake them up and try to get something hot into them?"

"No. They're warm and dry. I'll check their body temps in a minute but I think we got to them in time."

There was a murmur from one of the children. Laurel was at their side a moment later, smoothing the hair back from the boy's forehead as he blinked up at her.

"Why, they're beautiful, Matt," she said. "And they might be twins they look so much alike, although the girl is smaller."

Matt heaved himself to his feet and shuffled forward,

mug in one hand and holding up the sleeping bag with the other, until he could watch over her shoulder.

"Hey, guy," she said gently. "Don't worry, you're okay, you're alright, everything's fine. You're safe."

He muttered something they didn't catch. "What did you say?" The boy's eyes widened and he struggled to sit up. "No, no, don't do that. You need to stay where you are and get warm. What's your name?'

He struggled against her hands. "*Mi hermana! Mi hermana!*" Tears filled his eyes.

"What?"

"Your sister?" Matt said. "Buddy, she's right there, right next to you."

Laurel, catching on, patted the girl. "Right there, see?"

The boy turned his head and saw the girl unconscious next to him and grabbed her shoulder. "Anna! Anna!"

"Buddy, no, stop that." Matt knelt down awkwardly and put his hand on the boy's forehead. "She's okay. *Ella es* okay. Let her sleep and get warm. You'll be okay, too. All okay. Okay?"

Something about Matt's slow deep voice was reassuring to the boy. He rolled over on his side, wrapped his arms around the girl, and was out for the count.

Matt shuffled back to the chair. Laurel got a mug of her own and climbed into his lap, drawing up her legs and snuggling into his shoulder. He gloried in the shared warmth of her body. Those moments out in the storm were the single most vivid reminder of his mortality he'd ever had.

"'*Ella es* okay?'" Laurel said finally.

He had just enough energy left to shrug. "One year of high school Spanish. I only took it because Crystal Topkok did. I was hot for her big time."

She raised her head and they looked at each other.

"What the actual fuck?" he said.

She knew what he meant. What was anyone doing in the air in this weather? At this altitude? Anywhere near the Quilak Mountains, a sharp-toothed array of dedicated plane killers on a good day? "Pilot error?"

He snorted. "You think?" He looked at the kids. "At least we got them out. At least they're alive." He leaned his head back against the chair and closed his eyes. "Good work."

She looked at his face, drawn with exhaustion and the delayed beginnings of exposure. He hadn't hesitated after the crash. He had moved immediately to respond even though the chance of survivors was next to none, and he'd taken it for granted that she would help, no questions asked, no matter what it took.

She snuggled her head back into the hollow between his shoulder and his neck. His heart beat strongly and steadily in her ear, and she closed her eyes, letting the warmth of the fire and his body seep into hers.

I am so keeping him.

# Two

## TUESDAY, NEW YEAR'S DAY
### *The Park, Kate's homestead*

"TWO PACKAGES OF YEAST? REALLY?" Vanessa peered over Kate's shoulder. "You put barely a teaspoon in that rustic loaf of yours."

"Ah, but this is fry bread. It's not sitting overnight in the refrigerator, we're making it today. We want the dough to come up fast." Kate stirred the yeast into the warm water and nodded at the saucepan. "Test the milk."

Vanessa dabbled a finger. "Baby bottle warm."

"Perfect."

Vanessa turned off the burner. "What next?"

"Oil, sugar, salt, add the milk, stir it all together, and then let it stand for fifteen minutes. Meantime get out the big cast iron frying pan and put it on the big burner." Kate put the dirty dishes in the dishwasher and set the kitchen timer, and for the umpteenth time in the last four years made a mental bow of gratitude toward the Park, which had hand-built her a new house with all the modern conveniences. She still missed the cabin her father had built, burned down by an asshole too nearly related to the young woman now sharing a bed with Kate's adopted son, but a dishwasher, a clothes washer, a flush toilet and a shower went a long way toward alleviating any lingering nostalgia. "Coffee?"

"Sounds good."

They sat down at the table. Kate added half and half and sugar. Vanessa gave the requisite shudder, to which Kate gave the requisite response, as in none.

"How long have you been making fry bread?"

"Can't remember a time when I wasn't elbow deep in dough of some kind." Kate smiled. "This recipe comes from a friend, Joyce White, who lives in the Valley. It's better than Emaa's. Although I never would have said that out loud while she was alive."

Vanessa was a slender young woman with chin length dark hair in a fashionably asymmetric cut, large eyes with impossibly long, thick lashes, and a solemn expression.

"I like the haircut, by the way," Kate said.

"Thanks."

"We haven't had much chance to talk. How was your first semester?"

Vanessa shrugged. "All right, I guess."

"Wow. I'm drowning in your enthusiasm over here."

"I don't know, Kate." Vanessa turned her mug around between her hands. "I don't know if I'm cut out for college.

It's just one kegger after another, and who's hooking up with who. I thought I'd seen people drunk in the Park, but..."

"I remember," Kate said. "College isn't about drinking, it's about swilling. Find the ones who don't."

"Where?"

"The library, maybe?" Kate was absurdly pleased when a smile, however fleeting, crossed Van's face. "What about your classes?"

"Please don't ask me if I've declared a major."

"Okay. Any good teachers?"

"There's a journalism teacher I like."

In her senior year Vanessa had been the editor of the *King Chronicle*, the Niniltna High School online newspaper. "So, that's good."

"Yeah, but he's old and he can barely email. The future of news is online. I don't think the guy even knows what Facebook is."

"I thought Facebook was only for old folks nowadays anyway. What about your other classes? Any joy there?"

Vanessa shook her head. "Getting the required stuff out of the way. It's all just a rehash of high school." She drank coffee and looked at Kate. "The good teachers are watching Juneau. They know what's coming, and they're looking for jobs somewhere else, and you can't blame them. We'll be lucky if there's a University of Alaska left after this legislative session. I don't want to go to school Outside. And college isn't cheap, Kate."

"I'm begging you, tell me you didn't take out a college loan. We talked about this—"

"Oh god no. My grandparents had an education policy that matured when I was eighteen and with the stickpicker job over at Suulutaq during the summer, I'm fine for spending money. But…" She shrugged. "It just feels like I could be spending that money better somewhere else."

Kate thought about it. "Okay," she said, "I get it. College isn't for everyone. I went because my grandmother insisted and she was a lot older and tougher than I was. And it helped me get a job in Anchorage." Unconsciously her fingers traced the white scar that bisected her brown throat nearly from ear to ear. It had shrunk a good deal since the pedophile had come at her with a knife at the end of the case that proved to be the last in her career as an investigator for the Anchorage DA. "But consider this." She leaned forward and caught and held the young woman's eyes. "Once you get a degree, you can't lose it, it can't leave you, it can't divorce you, it won't die on you, it's yours for life. Damn few other things in life will ever achieve that kind of permanence. And remember that it's never about the major to future employers. It's that you proved you finish what you start." She sat back. "What does Johnny say?"

"Johnny's different." Vanessa sighed. "He knows what he wants to do. He took fifteen credits last semester and he's taking twenty this one. Mostly I see him when he's sleeping. He'll probably have his degree in three years, if not sooner."

"You haven't said anything to him? About how you're feeling about college?"

Vanessa drank some more coffee. "What about you? How are you doing?"

Kate took the change of subject without protest. You never got the truth when you tried to force a conversation. First rule of interrogations, too. "Some days I feel like I got shot in the chest six months ago. Those days are becoming fewer, though." She looked over at Mutt, sprawled out in front of the fireplace.

"She's fine, too?"

"She raced us on the snow machine on our way back from Mandy and Chick's the other day. By the time we got back she was sitting at the top of the steps. Jim swears she was laughing at us."

Mutt's ear twitched but the comment wasn't worth waking all the way up for. Besides, it was true.

"And there is the incomparable benefit of living in an Erland Bannister-free world, which makes up for any amount of other drawbacks. So when I say I'm fine? I mean I am soooooo fine."

Vanessa watched Kate drink her coffee and, well, marveled. Five feet nothing and a hundred and twenty pounds, all of it muscle. Hazel eyes tilted up at the outside corners, high, flat cheekbones, a broad brow, a wide mouth with full lips, skin like bronze in the winter and dull gold in the summer. She had thick, raven black hair worn in a pixie cut allowed to fall from a natural, off-center part. No gel for Kate Shugak. No makeup, either, as her skin was wash-and-wear perfect and her lashes were already thick and black. She was what, thirty-eight? Thirty-nine? She looked thirty at most. She had to be cordially hated by all of her contemporaries.

She was dressed in jeans and T-shirt, with thick socks for slippers. No rings or jewelry. It was practically a uniform, accessorized by windbreaker and sneakers in summer and parka and Sorels in winter. Vanessa tried to think if she'd ever seen Kate Shugak dressed in anything else, but if she had couldn't remember when, so probably not.

When Kate moved it was with a rough kind of grace and all the self-assurance of her place in the world that Vanessa longed for and didn't have. Kate made her living as a private investigator, solving crime and catching criminals all over the state of Alaska. More than that, she was everyone's go-to whenever there was any kind of trouble—personal, political, friend, family, local, state, federal—as she was related through her grandmother to half the state and had howdied and shook with most of the rest of it, in particular the law enforcement community.

A fixer, Vanessa thought. Kate Shugak was everybody's fixer. Not always without cost, however, as witness the shooting the previous July that had left both Kate and Mutt at death's door. She thought about how close the Park had come to losing both of them and repressed a shiver. A world without Kate in it was not a world she cared to inhabit.

Kate looked at her and Vanessa reddened at being caught staring. "What do you love?" Kate said.

"What?"

"What is it that you love to do?"

"Well." The color fading from her cheeks, Vanessa considered. "Talking to people and finding out their stories, I guess. The best part of high school was the year I edited the *Chronicle*." She became animated. "Did you see that story I wrote about Niniltna's history, as told by the elders?"

"I did see that," Kate said. "A solid piece of work." Although the aunties had dressed up their parts of the stories considerably, she thought. Which was only to be expected. The aunties would never tell all the truth to anyone.

"I loved doing that," Vanessa said, glowing. "Going around to all the old folks and writing down their stories." She giggled, an attractive sound. "Sometimes the stories didn't gibe."

"I can imagine," Kate said, her voice dry.

"But following up was even more fun, even if I did get yelled at a couple of times."

Good thing Old Sam had died two years before, Kate thought, or you would have been yelled at a lot more, just on general principles. "If that's what you love," she said, "then that's what you should do."

"Yeah, but…"

"But what?"

"What does that look like, exactly? And how does it pay the bills?"

"Do what you love," Kate said, "and the money will come." Vanessa raised an eyebrow, and Kate shrugged. "All right, it's a cliché, but it's only a cliché because it's true."

Vanessa leaned back and sighed. "I can tell you what I don't love, and that's living in Fairbanks."

"Why?"

The girl shrugged. "No mountains. Too big, too many people. Only place worse would be Anchorage."

"You want to live in the Park?"

"Yeah, but there aren't any jobs. The mine's pretty much stuck on exploration with development on hold, fishing's down, the school's losing students and it looks like the state's going to stop funding education anyway." She shook her head. "Feels like the town is dying."

Kate couldn't argue the point because she felt the same.

There was the sound of an approaching snow machine and they looked out the window to see one burst out of the trees and roar into the yard. "What the hell?" Kate said. "It's New Year's Day. People are supposed to stay home nursing their hangovers while they try to remember the name of the person in bed next to them."

Vanessa laughed. Mutt, meanwhile, bounced to her feet and galloped over to the door, dancing with impatience. Well, if the visitor was Mutt-approved. Kate went to answer the knock.

It was Bobby Clark, wearing black shades that seemed to meld into his black skin. He was unsmiling and he made no move to come inside and even ignored Mutt's advances, unheard of. "We need you in town pronto."

"I'm majoring in justice." Johnny shrugged. "You know. With a minor in A&P so I can annual my own aircraft. When I save up enough to buy one. But I'm also thinking a suit and a tie is not a good look for me, and, besides, as I understand it most law is practiced indoors."

Jim laughed. "Well, you won't go hungry with A&P as your minor."

"Yeah. You ever think about going into law?"

"I was always all about the badge and the gun, and now you couldn't get me back inside a classroom at gunpoint. And like you said. There is that whole inside thing." Jim hefted a shovel full of wet, heavy snow, the only kind the Park seemed to get anymore, and did his best to toss it over the steadily growing berm surrounding the hangar doors. "Although inside does have its own attractions. I have got to get me a snow blower."

"Now, now, old man, you don't want to get fat from no exercise." With a laughing protest Johnny dodged the next shovel full of snow directed his way.

Jim leaned on the shovel for a moment's respite. The sun was a faint light behind a high gray overcast sky. There was no warmth or cheer in it, only the promise of occlusion followed by more snow. The Quilaks, a mountain range that looked like the offensive line for this year's Los Angeles Rams, huddled in the east beneath protective gear made of snow falling pretty much nonstop since Thanksgiving. The rest of the twenty million acres of the Park was an eastward tumble of foothills and glacial moraines and mine tailings cut by the frozen slither of the Kanuyaq River and its tributaries. It lay quiet and still beneath a thick white blanket, waiting for the next big one to blow in off the Mother of Storms. From the look of the slate-colored horizon to the south, it wouldn't be long.

"You think I could get into the troopers?"

"What?" He turned to look at the boy. Young man. New adult. Gen Z-er. Generation Text? Whatever.

Johnny repeated the question. He looked so earnest and so very, very young in spite of all of eighteen years to his credit. Although everyone was looking younger to Jim nowadays. And Johnny's face was beginning to take on some of the ruggedness of his father's in its hard planes and angles. "Tell me why."

"Well." Johnny looked a little embarrassed. "Serve and protect."

The idealism of that response was almost debilitating and Jim had no way to immediately answer to it. It wasn't that he'd left idealism behind him with the job; it was that it had never been what had motivated him to get into law enforcement in the first place. It was fun, it took him all over his chosen home, and it was a great way to meet women. Maybe, once in a great while, you were able to help, to make a difference in someone's life, to get a bad guy out of the vicinity of decent citizens and keep him out. But it happened so seldom that you couldn't count on it as a motivating factor. Unless you were Johnny's age.

"Jim?" Johnny's manner was hesitant. "Why did you quit?"

Jim closed his eyes and replayed the scene in his head as he had so many times before. "I had my weapon out, had it aimed, had my finger on the trigger. I told Kenny to drop his rifle and when he didn't I said it again. Instead, he shot Mutt, and still I didn't get a shot off in time before he shot Kate." He opened his eyes and looked at Johnny. "I'd always been able to talk my way out of any situation. Never once had to fire my weapon in the line. So I was still talking when he shot them." He shook his head. "Johnny, if you're serious about this, one thing you have to remember above all others. It's not your oath, it's not any of that shit they teach you in college or even in the academy. It's this. You're the good guys. You serve the public, you protect the public, and it doesn't matter one good damn if that public is trying to shoot moose out of season or shoot your woman dead—you're now one of the good guys. You serve. You protect." He paused. "That's the ideal, anyway."

"You sound sad when you say that."

"I feel sad when I say that. I fell down on the job."

They shoveled more snow. The supply was endless. "You miss it?"

"Sure. Parts of it are fun. Wearing the uniform." He smiled a little. "The smoky hat was the best babe magnet ever invented. And then there's that thing ordinary citizens do when you show up at a scene. Just your appearance can calm people down, ratchet back a situation going south. Great for the ego. And, yes, sometimes you can help, just by virtue of bearing the badge. Feels good to do that, to be that guy." He looked at Johnny. "But people lie to you every day on the job. And sometimes they shoot at you, too. It can be... disheartening, and discouraging. You get your nose constantly rubbed in the worst of human behavior, some unimaginably bad. There's a reason so many cops are drunks and divorced."

"I know I want to be involved in the justice system somehow. Make it work more for people than against them."

"Well. Your first choice was attorney. You have your pilot's license, right?"

"You know I do."

"You getting much flying in? Building any hours?"

"I try to get in the air at least once a week. There's a small flight school at the Fairbanks airport." Johnny made a face. "Fuel's not cheap, though."

"You okay for money?"

"Sure, Dad left me pretty well set. But I don't want to blow it, you know? I remember '08, even if I was just a kid."

"Me, too," Jim said with feeling.

"Harsh."

Alaska had been insulated from a lot of what went down Outside but people had still lost jobs and homes and pretty much everything, and oil dropping to below $40 a barrel hadn't helped the state's budget any. Why there were only three hundred Alaska state troopers.

He pulled his thoughts away from the job and back to the conversation at hand. An idea swam in from the ether. "Huh."

"What?"

"You say don't want to work in an office. You know Anne Flanagan?"

"Sure. The Flying Pastor. She was a friend of Old Sam's. She spoke at his potlatch." Johnny pulled a wad of Kleenex out of his pocket and gave his nose a ferocious blow. It was as red as Rudolf's from the cold. Jim figured his probably was, too. "What about her?"

"She got a grant from a nonprofit to buy that Cessna of hers and now she flies into all the villages in the Park, baptizing and marrying and burying."

"Yeah, so?" Johnny heaved a shovel full of snow up and over and then paused. "Oh. You mean why couldn't I run a law practice the same way?"

"Be a way to practice law, and fly, and be outdoors a lot. I don't know how much money there would be in it." Jim grinned. "Bet we could find something creative to name it. Aviating Ambulance Chasers sort of leaps to mind."

"Yeah, that'd be my very first choice."

"Soaring Shysters?"

"Jim."

"Legal Eagles?"

Johnny considered. "That's not terrible. I could put an eagle decal on the plane." He saw that Jim's attention had wandered. "What?"

Jim squinted into the gray sky at a rapidly approaching speck, increasing in volume from an irritated fly to the soundtrack of *Apocalypse Now*.

"Is that George?" Johnny said.

The Bell Jet Ranger settled down in front of the hangar, blowing half the snow back from where they'd just shoveled it. George stuck his head out the door and yelled, "Jim, you need to come with me now!"

# Three

IT WAS A FAST TRIP INTO TOWN, KATE AND Vanessa on Kate's Polaris behind Bobby on his Arctic Cat going away very fast. At least during the winter, with the road frozen under layers of ice and snow, there was little chance of picking up a stray spike from back in the day when the road was a railway lane shifting copper ore from Kanuyaq to Cordova.

Although their speed was nothing compared to George and the boys in the Bell Jet Ranger. It buzzed them about five minutes after they turned from the driveway onto the main road and disappeared into the horizon like it had been launched from the USS *Enterprise* at the Battle of Midway.

"I feel like I've been scalped!" Vanessa shouted over Kate's shoulder.

Or skinned, Kate thought. The tag on the Arctic Cat was getting harder to read and she hit the gas. Behind her

Vanessa whooped, and on the trailer behind Mutt woofed. It didn't sound like a protest.

The two sleds roared across the hard-packed surface of the Park road, watched by a disinterested group of moose lying under a shelter of willow. A flock of Bohemian cedar waxwings were frightened by the noise into a susurrating cloud of brown fluff and yellow tail feathers, the snow stained by a scattering of red drops like blood from the mountain ash berries they'd been feeding on. A female lynx shoved her kits off the road at their approach, the heads of each kit popping up one by one and wide-eyed in a made-for-Disney moment as they flashed past. The air was still and the sky was gray and pregnant with menace.

The road wound back and forth from the banks of the Kanuyaq to the beginnings of the foothills, through stands of dark green spruce and bare-limbed aspen over a roller-coaster of a route that had their asses floating above their seats at least half the time. Wearing his prostheses always upped Bobby's MPH and they might have set the land speed record between Kate's homestead and the village of Niniltna that morning. He slowed down and let inertia set a more decorous pace through town, a collection of old and new buildings from log cabins to prefabs lined up on the north side of the Kanuyaq River where road, town and river met. The surface of the river was frozen solid with cracks and crevices and ledges and ice sinks everywhere except straight down the middle, where the blade of the communally owned antique Cat 10 bulldozer kept one lane smooth by being in constant motion from December to February. It used to be March and sometimes even April and Kate remembered the first week of May from when she was a kid, but those days were no more.

The town was buttoned up tight in advance of the coming—or continuing—storm and they saw no one as the two-sled caravan made its decorous way through the village from one end to the other. Bobby pulled in in front of a large frame house on the river side of the village and Kate stopped next to him. "Inside," he said, and they followed him in, Mutt padding behind. The four Grosdidiers and Laurel Meganack were sitting around the table in the kitchen, nursing mugs of coffee and unnaturally silent. Laurel's eyes were red and none of the boys looked much better.

Mutt went around the table and pushed her head between Matt and Laurel, and automatically Matt's hand came up to knot in her mane. She rested her chin on his knee.

Kate went to the coffee pot and filled mugs and set them on the table. She rummaged in the cupboards until she found a box of Thin Mints and another of Tagalongs and arranged them on a plate. She put them in the center of the table and sat down. Bobby leaned against the counter with his arms and ankles crossed. It was still odd to see him walking around on two legs.

The coffee was hot and strong and welcome after the self-created wind chill of the trip in. She waited, and Van and Bobby took their cues from her and waited, too. It was silent in the kitchen for a long time.

Finally Mark noticed the cookies and took one from the plate and ate it slowly, one bite at a time. "What do you know," he said, "these are still good."

"Probably made out of the same stuff they make McDonald's milkshakes from," Luke said.

"I remember that," Peter said, lightening. He took a handful of Tagalongs and crammed most of them into his mouth. Around them he said indistinctly, "We brought all that Mickey D. takeout home from Ahtna and the milkshakes were still, like, thick a hundred miles later. Hadn't melted at all. Scary."

"Better living through chemicals," Matt said.

Even Laurel smiled.

Caffeine and sugar, a one-two combo that never failed. "Tell me," Kate said.

Matt sighed. "We were up at your cabin at the Springs. We heard the sound of this aircraft coming scary close, especially with it blowing and snowing the way it was. Whiteout conditions, Kate. I wouldn't have gotten on my sled last night, never mind got on a plane. And then the sound stopped, and a second later we heard this just hellacious crash, even over the storm. Sounded like it came from just up the canyon, so we suited up and took the sled up for a looksee." He shrugged. "I know what it looks like around there on a clear day. I sure didn't expect to find any survivors—hell, I didn't really expect to find any wreckage, and at that we almost missed it."

"What did you find?"

"The aft section, maybe six, eight feet forward of the tailplane. What was left of the horizontal stabilizer had somehow wedged itself into this crack in the rock. There was still a seat left in the back, unbelievably, and the two kids were belted into it. I got them out and Laurel got us back to the cabin and thawed out. This morning we figured we'd better take advantage of the break in the weather and get them down here." He turned his mug in a circle between his hands and spoke without looking up. "We checked them out once we got them here. They've got belt contusions across their waists, and other bruising consistent with being in a high impact crash. They haven't woken up yet so we haven't been able to do a complete assessment. But..."

Laurel shoved back from the table and left the room. Matt's eyes followed her until she was out the door. They listened to her footsteps going up the stairs and a door open and close.

"They've been sexually abused, Kate. Both of them, the boy anally, the girl both anally and vaginally. I can only guess, but I'd say it only began recently, say, within the month. The injuries look..." He took a deep breath and let it out slowly. "Fresh."

Peter clenched his fist and hit the table hard. All the mugs and the plate of cookies jumped. "MotherFUCKER."

Mutt walked around the table and settled next to him, her head on Peter's thigh. He stroked her gray head and her yellow eyes narrowed to slits.

"No identification?"

Matt shook his head. "I didn't see anything in the wreckage. Well, I didn't really look. It was blowing like a bitch and snowing like a bastard and all I was focused on was getting them in out of the cold. But—"

"What?"

"He, the boy, he woke up for a few seconds after we got back to the cabin. He spoke a few words." Matt raised his head and looked at Kate. "They were in Spanish, Kate."

"Man," Johnny's voice said over the headset, "I see the attraction of helo as opposed to fixed wing. Pretty cool, Mr. Perry."

"You can call me George now, kid."

"Then you can call me Johnny now, George."

George chuckled. Jim closed his eyes and swallowed hard.

George was a good pilot, possibly the best pilot Jim had ever flown with, helo or fixed-wing, prop or turbine (he had almost as many aircraft certifications as he'd had divorces, and the former might have had something to do with the latter). Nevertheless, Jim's sphincter tightened up as George put the Ranger into a hover that Jim considered to be far too close to the peaks surrounding Hot Springs Canyon.

"I don't see anything," George said, sounding pretty calm as the right-hand skid came awfully close to touching down on a tooth of rock that looked purpose-made to rip men and helo into teeny-tiny pieces. Jim swallowed again and adjusted his headphones, pulling the mike in closer to his lips. "Can you push it a little farther up the canyon? You said that Matt said the wreckage was above the Springs."

Smoothly, steadily, they inched up the canyon, their wash kicking up a swirl of snow. The pools showed briefly, and the roof of Kate's cabin crept beneath them and vanished.

"Do you see anything?"

"No."

"Nobody here but us Koberians, evidently."

"Look!" Jim pointed.

"What?" George stood the Ranger on its nose. Through the Perspex they could see the tailplane of what might have been a small jet crammed backwards into a narrow crevice. It was almost completely covered in snow, only the tip of the vertical stabilizer visible, and that only just.

"Can you set her down?" Jim said, already knowing the answer.

"It was one thing slinging in supplies last summer when Kate was up here building the new cabin," George said. "Setting down, forget it. You'll have to come back up on sleds."

Jim looked at the unpromising southern horizon and grimaced. "Goody."

George made quick work of the trip back to Niniltna and put the helo next to the hangar. Jim and Johnny helped him roll it inside. "I'll give you a ride to the clinic," George said.

"Let me pick up the mail first?"

"I'll do it," Johnny said, and jogged across the strip to the house slash post office. He emerged a few moments later with an armful of envelopes large and small and a stack of magazines. George got a small garbage sack out of the office and Johnny stuffed it all in and tied off the top.

The 4,800-foot airstrip sat on a long, roughly rectangular flat-topped bluff that sat above Niniltna village proper. They set off down the hill, passing the Niniltna Native Association's building, the trooper post, and Auntie Vi's. When they came to the intersection with Riverside (there was an actual street sign now, Jim saw, and marveled), George paused. Jim looked at him. "What?"

"I checked with Anchorage ATC, Jim, and here's the thing."

"What thing?"

"No aircraft has been reported missing. From anywhere."

Jim stared at him. "What?"

George nodded. "I know. Weird, right? Not from anywhere in the system."

"Well..." Jim was at a loss. "Where'd it come from, then?"

"Good question."

"What's the range on a small jet?"

"Well, hell, Jim. You know as well as I do it depends on the jet and the load."

"Ballpark it."

George shrugged. "Say a thousand to fifteen hundred miles."

"So Whitehorse is as easy as Anchorage or Fairbanks from here."

"Depending on the aircraft, Vancouver or Seattle is just as easy from here." George nodded across the intersection at the shop and the house across and just down the road. "Did you hear about the Topkoks?"

"Herbie and Sarah? What about them?"

"They're dead."

"What?"

Johnny leaned forward from the back seat. "What? Herbie Topkok is dead? What happened?"

"They went to Hawaii for Christmas vacation, took a tour of the volcano on a boat, the volcano erupted, and a giant gob of magma landed on the boat and killed them."

Jim looked at him.

"What?"

"I'm waiting for the punchline."

"No punchline, because it's not a joke." The pilot's eyes were, for a change, serious.

"Christ," Jim said. "If I didn't know them I guess it'd be funny."

"Yeah, everybody in town is worried about who'd going to fix their sleds and boats now."

"Heartless bastards."

George shrugged. "Practical. Herbie'd get it. Hear tell none of the kids want to move back to Alaska, so they'll put the shop up for sale and hope for the best."

"Good luck with that." No property in Niniltna and environs had changed hands since the feds put the Suulutaq Mine on hold.

"Man, that sucks," Johnny said. "Herbie was a good guy. Whenever you needed a bolt or screw, he always had it right there. He was like the Alaska Industrial Hardware of the Park." He sat back. "Man."

George took his foot off the brake and stepped on the gas and pulled into the intersection, turning left. "Unless I miss my guess, that tailplane is off a small jet. Might be an old Cessna Citation I've seen on the strip here a couple of times this past year."

"Do you know who it belongs to?"

George shook his head. "No tail numbers, and they always parked down the other end, and never overnight. Most of the time they were on the ground for a couple of hours, if that. I always assumed they were people coming to take a look at the mine."

They drove to the clinic and pulled in behind Kate's sled. "That's not even the best part, though."

Jim stared at him. "There's more?"

"This is the Park. Of course there is more." He grinned.

Goaded, Jim said, "You should have been an actor, George. What more? What?"

George's grin faded. "I'm pretty sure that jet landed in Niniltna a little before midnight on New Year's Eve. I'm pretty sure I heard that turbine whining up outside." Most experienced pilots—hell, most experienced passengers—could identify different aircraft by the sound of the engine and Jim didn't question it here. "It was snowing so hard it was dark outside all day. I wouldn't have dreamed of going anywhere near an aircraft. When I heard the engine I got up and took a look out the window, but it was total whiteout conditions. I couldn't see past the window frame on the other side of the glass."

Jim frowned. George had an apartment over his hangar, with windows looking south-southwest, right over the strip.

"And." George said, who looked, just a mite, as if he were secretly enjoying himself.

"Oh for crissake. And what?"

"And while I can't swear to it, because whiteout, I'm pretty sure I heard two of them."

Jim felt his jaw drop. "Two jets? In that storm?"

George nodded. "I think we know where one of them ended up. But what about the other?"

Kate was standing in the clinic's one patient room, looking at the two sleeping children. The boy was a little older but they otherwise might have been twins, and they were heartbreakingly beautiful, with thick black glossy hair and features that looked cut from smoky topaz.

She felt someone beside her and looked up to see Jim. She looked back at the kids. "Did Matt tell you?"

"Yes."

There was something infinitely comforting in his deep, steady voice, and when he put his arm around her shoulders she let herself lean against him, just a little. She swallowed. "We don't even know who they are."

"We'll handle it," he said.

"We don't even speak their language."

"We'll find someone who does."

"Where are their parents, Jim?"

"We'll find out."

Anger would come later, but all she felt now for these children was pain. "Who did this to them?"

"We'll take care of them, Kate."

There were two ways to take his statement, and she found that comforting, too. "Let's go home."

But the weather had decided to sock in again and they decided they had tempted fate enough for one day. They went to Auntie Vi's B&B, where this time of year there was always a free bed and dinner waiting.

There wasn't much Viola Moonin Shugak hadn't seen in a long and storied life. Occasionally homegrown birthers took bets over the bar at the Roadhouse as to just how long that life had been, but it was never conclusively settled because birth certificates weren't always issued to Alaskans born in what was then only a territory, and almost never to Alaska Natives born in the Bush at that time. Auntie Vi certainly wasn't saying.

Auntie Vi was shorter than Kate, with snapping black eyes set in a face like a Shar-Pei's and had thinning, defiantly black hair that she had lately been encouraging to grow into a skimpy braid that snapped around like a bullwhip when she was in motion. It lent a great deal of emphasis to whatever she was saying at any given time.

They told her about the plane crash and the two survivors and she broke a Pyrex measuring cup and a mixing bowl while cooking dinner. Kate thought the breakage had more to do with rage than with age. Auntie Vi had a lot to say, too, fortunately most of it in Aleut as Vanessa and Johnny were sitting right there, bright-eyed and inquisitive and Vanessa looking as if she were prepared to take notes for future reference. Mutt, no fool, had taken refuge on the couch in the living room. Fortunately, there were no other guests. Everyone intelligently maintained a prudent silence until the pot of adobo slammed down in the middle of the kitchen table next to a platter of fry bread still sizzling from the pan. Bowls and spoons were dealt out like cards in an especially pissy snerts game. A blessed silence descended over the room as the wind howled outside and snow stung the glass in the windows.

Jim had seconds and with great restraint resisted thirds. It had been a long time since breakfast. He pushed back from the table and stretched. "Man, that was good, Auntie. Thank you."

Auntie Vi glared at Kate. "Every bite a gustatory delight," Kate said.

Auntie Vi's eyes narrowed, and Vanessa said, "Auntie Vi, has there ever been a newspaper in the Park?"

The glare switched targets. "What's that you say? Of course we had newspaper. Back when mine was going."

"Was it daily?"

Auntie Vi shook her head. "Once a week only."

"What was its name?"

Auntie Vi ruminated. "I remember that thing," she said, triumphant. "The *Pick & Shovel*."

"Obvious, much?" Van said, rolling her eyes. "When did it go out of business?"

"Quits when last track pulled up behind the mine." Auntie Vi snorted, which was her default expression and used to denote everything from disgust to disgust.

"Huh. Does anyone have any old copies tucked away anywhere?"

"Ask old-timers. Some peoples save anything."

Auntie Vi had been taught proper English at the Indian Residential School she'd been forced to attend Outside, so every time she used her childhood pidgin it was an in-your-face reminder of her roots. Sometimes Kate thought the old woman used it to remind everyone else of theirs, too. She said mildly, "Has anyone cleaned out Auntie Edna's house?"

Auntie Vi's glare dimmed. "No."

"She collected everything," Kate said to Van, "and so far as I know never threw any of it away."

Van brightened. "Really?"

"She was a serious hoarder." Kate looked at Auntie Vi. "Maybe you could take Van over there and take a look."

The glare was back full throttle. "Maybe."

Van and Johnny excused themselves and disappeared.

"You."

Kate looked up to see Auntie Vi giving her the evil eye. "Me what?"

"You fix," Auntie Vi said again.

Kate met Auntie Vi's beady black eyes for a long moment, her own face expressionless. Jim wondered if he should whistle the theme to *The Man With No Name*. "I fix, Auntie."

Auntie Vi gave a sharp nod, and got up to clear the table.

"You caved," he said. They'd moved to the living room, rousting Mutt from the couch.

"Yeah. Well. It's Auntie Vi. What're ya gonna do."

"What does she expect?"

"Learn to speak Spanish overnight so I can talk to those kids, find their mother, and reunite their family. And while I'm at it broker world peace and fix climate change."

"Piece of cake, then."

"It's what I do." She leaned her head back against the sofa and closed her eyes.

He studied her face. "It's those two kids."

Kate opened her eyes and looked at him. "How could it not be? Auntie Vi's not wrong. Somebody has to do something, take care of them. They're just kids." Her voice broke a little on the last word. "Babies, really."

He was too wise to offer false comfort, but he did link his fingers with hers. Her hand closed convulsively over his. She looked at him. "I just realized we've never had the conversation."

"What?" he said, alarmed. "You mean birth control? Because I distinctly remember—"

She almost smiled. "Not that conversation, but I admit it was nice to see you squirm there for a second or two."

"What, then?"

"The kids conversation. Did you?"

"Did I what?"

"Want them?"

He stared at her until he realized his mouth was half open. He closed it with a snap that hurt his teeth. "No."

"Just like that?" When he would have answered she raised a hand. "Think about it a minute before you answer."

He meditated upon his knees for a moment, and then he turned to face her fully. "I was an only child, from a not-very-loving family. I don't spend a lot of time thinking about it, but when I do, it's pretty obvious that I ended up here because I wanted one."

"A loving family?"

"Well," he said ruefully, "a family, anyway. You know already, I've told you, I was drawn here since I was a kid and saw *Nanook of the North* on some old movie channel on TV. I started reading about it, everything I could get my hands on, and watching all the movies, even the bad ones." He shuddered. "John Wayne and Fabian. Jesus."

She laughed and he was ridiculously pleased. "But I wanted law enforcement and I wanted Alaska and I finally got here by way of the troopers. You know what John Barton said to me when I got off the plane in Sitka, on my first day at the academy? 'Don't pick any fights,' he said. 'You pick a fight and inevitably six months later you'll be working for him or she'll be working for you. In Alaska, everybody's related to everybody else.'" He shrugged. "Keep your head down, he said, do your job as best you can, and stay away from politics."

"What's all this got to do with not having kids?"

"You asked," he said, pointing at her. "I'm getting there." He was smiling but there was a quality of introspection, of gravitas, even, behind the smile that she didn't remember seeing before. "So I graduate at the top of my class and swear my oath and get my badge, and I do my probationary period in the Valley."

"And then?" she said when he paused.

"And then I shipped out to the Bush. Kateel, then four hundred people, which had an on again/off again police force, and was surrounded by villages averaging fifty to a hundred people you could only get to by air, unless you wanted to hike. Hiking would have drastically cut down on my response time so I learned to fly."

He fell silent again. She waited.

He looked up. His smile was faint this time, a faded memory from long ago. "It took a while to sink in."

"What? What took a while?"

"That I was a triple threat." He thought. "A quadruple threat, really. White, male, rich—comparatively, at least—and an officer of the law. Sometimes the only law they ever saw. The only representative of government they ever saw. Other than their postmaster."

She had a sudden memory of Max Maxwell, that quintessential Alaska old fart on a par with Abel and Old Sam, who had been a Territorial Policeman back in the day before Alaska was even a state. He had said much the same thing and sixty years ago it would have been even more true then than it was when Jim took his badge into the Bush.

"The poverty in some of those places—Jesus, Kate. And they're so far apart, and so far away from the larger towns and cities where all the services are, health, welfare, law. A village loses that one capable elder and right away the substance abuse, the child and spouse abuse start ramping up, assault, rape, murder. Teen suicides are always the worst. They can be infectious, spread to other villages. It can destroy a village, Kate." He was silent for a moment.

"And they are so very, very Native," Kate said softly.

"Yeah."

"And you so, so weren't."

"Nope. Other than the fun factor of somebody new flying into the village, they mostly tried to ignore me. It took me a while—too long—to realize that I was always going to be other." He sat back and brought his legs up on the couch. She mimicked him and rested her legs on top of his. "I don't think there were five thousand people all told in my entire post. I don't know what it is now. A lot of the villages are losing population."

"Like Kushtaka."

He thought about the village that murder had decimated, not only in death but in diaspora. "Yeah." He sighed. "I did the best I could, tried to be fair, but it was slow going trying to get any cred with those folks. Some of my villages those fucking northwest Jesuits had relocated their asshole abuser priests to. They had no reason to trust another gussuk Outsider."

"What if you had been a Native yourself?"

"I don't know that'd be any better. If he or she had been Inupiaq themselves, chances were they'd have been related to everybody which meant they couldn't arrest anyone. If they were Aleut or Tlingit or Athabascan—" He shook his head.

"Did it ever change?"

"About seven months into my tour, they had a gathering to hash out some political stuff. Representatives from the regional Native corporation and AFN and the legislature flew in. So someone decided to stage a demonstration, which would have been okay if someone else hadn't started throwing rocks."

"Oh, dear."

"Yeah. So I stepped in, and it all came down to this one kid. Hell, Kate, he was barely old enough to vote and he didn't really know what he was protesting other than life as he knew it, which was pretty damn bleak." Jim shrugged. "So I asked the elders of his village to step in, and they tore him a new one, you know, in that calm, measured way Native elders have of ripping your liver out without ever raising their voices."

She laughed. "I know."

"They made him promise to pay restitution, which was mostly a couple of broken windows in the school where the meeting was taking place."

"Kid have a job?"

"Of course not."

"Then how—"

Jim scratched behind his ear. "Well, I didn't have anyone to clean the post and it was getting pretty ratty, so—"

"So you gave him a job so he could pay his fine." Jim shrugged. Kate bet she knew who had paid the kid and it wasn't the Alaska Department of Public Safety. "And then?"

"Well, it wasn't like I was adopted or anything. But every now and then someone would drop off a fillet of char or a piece of caribou backstrap at the post. When I landed in the villages they'd come out to say hi instead of holing up waiting for me to knock on the door. One time—" he smiled "—one time they'd lost power and the lights were out on the strip so the whole village lined up their sleds on both sides of the strip and turned on their headlights to illuminate the runway so I could land."

"Pretty cool."

"Yeah. It was."

"And from there to Tok?"

"Yeah. I didn't ask for it, they just moved me. They said I was such a hell of a fellow that they wanted me to straighten out another trouble spot." He paused. "It's beautiful out there, Kate, in its own way. Miles and miles and miles of flat tundra, stretching out into the horizon. There's a national monument up there, a desert made up of yellow sand dunes, about twenty-five square miles. You look out your window from a thousand feet and that shows up on the horizon and you think you've been teleported to another planet. And then more tundra, no trees except maybe some stunted spruce and alder, but mostly it's just thick brush and berry bushes and wildflowers and salmon rivers as far as the eye can see. A few rolling foothills here, the tag end of the Brooks Range over there, and this unending sky overhead. And during the winter the aurora just all over that sky, every color, and they talk, Kate, I don't care what the scientists say."

"Little buzzing sounds when they dance. I've heard them, too." She'd never heard him talk like this before. "You really did like it up there."

"Like I said, it wasn't my idea to leave." He looked at her. "I think your grandmother might have had something to do with that."

"Emaa?"

He nodded. "She was at that meeting where the kid broke the windows. And then, a couple of days into the job in Tok, she came to the post, introduced herself, and said that if there were any problems in the Park she should be my first call."

"Wow."

"I think she might have had something to do with me being posted to Niniltna, too," he said.

"Emaa was dead three years before you opened the post here."

"I think she had it in mind from the time she got me moved to Tok."

Kate thought it over. "She did take the long view." She rubbed the sole of her foot against his leg. "I'm glad to know all this, but you've kind of wandered from the point."

"In the Park I did all over again what I'd done in Kateel, only more people, many of them as always behaving in the worst possible ways." He shrugged. "And you respond, and you take corrective action."

This time she laughed. "Sounds like parenting, all right."

"On a massive scale. And there you have your answer. I think I'm kinda done with that." He caught her foot in both hands and started massaging it. She groaned. "Yes, yes, yes, just like that."

"Ew," Vanessa said from the door. They looked up simultaneously to see her grinning.

"You're interrupting a private moment here, brat," Jim said.

"Then you should have locked the door," Vanessa said. "Johnny and I are staying in town for a couple of days."

"What about—"

Van rolled her eyes, a leftover from her annoying teen years. "It's almost a month until classes start."

"A month? Geeze. When I was in school classes started up again the second week of January."

"It's not all bad." Jim waggled his eyebrows at Kate. "Just think. You and me and no kids in the house. Whatever shall we do to fill in all that empty, lonely time."

"Ew," Vanessa said again, and retreated.

Across the room, still pissed that they'd evicted her from the couch, Mutt was lying with her back to them, her head on an enormous bone Auntie Vi had produced from the freezer. Kate watched as her chest rose and fell. "What's on your schedule tomorrow?"

He was looking at his phone, and turned it so that she could see that he'd pulled up the NOAA app, which, miraculously, sported a sun for the following day. "The forecast is clear for a day, maybe even a day and half.

George and I are going to run up to the canyon on sleds and see what we can find of the wreck, if anything. You want to come with?"

She suppressed a shudder. "Sure. Three sets of eyes will be better than two. And let's not forget Mutt's nose."

"I would never forget Mutt's nose," he said. "Hey, I forgot, I picked up the mail. Let me go grab it."

He returned with the bag and they sat next to each other on the couch to divvy it up.

"Oh great, some law firm wrote me a letter. This'll end well." Kate picked up a white legal size envelope and ripped it open. She unfolded the single sheet of paper inside.

Jim was reading the most recent statement from his account at the brokerage that handled his inheritance. Money was very odd. If you had a lot of it, it seemed almost to breed in the very best Christian tradition, going forth and multiplying in the most amazing fashion. There didn't seem to be a single bank or brokerage big enough to hold the estate his father had left him, and his assets and their holding companies made for a thick stack of paperwork. He wondered if Beverly's jointure was doing as well, and hoped so. He had no wish ever to hear from his father's widow again, and he was certain to if she ran out of money. It all depended on who she chose as her second husband. It might already be that gigolo who'd been chasing after her when Jim left California, in which case hearing from her in the future was a Nostradamus-level prediction.

He had a card from his half sister, a pediatrician with Doctors Without Borders currently serving in Côte d'Ivoire, which made for an interesting stamp, and another from his half brother, a cop with the San Diego Police Department. They had yet to meet in person but he called his birth mother, Shirley, once a month. Those conversations were building a relationship that he hoped would one day lead her and her husband and their two children to visit the Park. He wondered if Kate would let him build a guest cabin.

Families, he thought. He'd take the one he'd created in the Park over the one he was born into any day. Especially if that meant he could share his bed for the rest of his life with the woman sitting next to him.

Who, he realized, had become preternaturally still. "Kate?"

She looked up, a dazed expression in her eyes. "Read this," she said, handing him a letter.

He read it. "What the hell?" And then he read it again. "Erland Bannister made you the trustee of his estate?"

Voices woke David up. He held very still, listening. He couldn't hear the Bad Man. That was one good thing, but who did those other voices belong to? Some men, and one woman. They were talking in English, like on the television at the Bad Man's house. Was he back in the Bad Man's house? And where was Anna?

He fought to open his eyes. The first thing he saw was Anna on a bed next to his. There were people standing over her. A woman, the one he must have heard talking, was pulling a nightgown over Anna's head. Anna's eyelids fluttered and she muttered something but she didn't wake up. The woman, she looked a little familiar, had silent tears slipping down her cheeks. The man next to her, he looked familiar, too, like David knew them both from somewhere. Was he one of the Bad Man's friends? The woman pulled the sheet up and tucked it beneath Anna's chin. Anna rolled over on her side, still sleeping. The man put his arms around the woman's shoulders and she turned her face into his chest. Her shoulders were shaking.

Three other men, younger than the first man but who looked a lot like him, stood in the doorway speaking

*English in low voices. He could tell they were angry about something. He held very still and watched them carefully through his lashes.*

*He was in another bed in the room, covered by another sheet. The beds stood high on metal frames and the room was painted white and there were* instrumentos medicos *on the walls like at* la clínica *at home. Did the Bad Man bring them to* el doctor? *Why?*

*He tried to remember. There was the big house, and the star on the mountain, and the men who took Mami from them and sold them to the Bad Man. They were with the Bad Man and then—*el aeroplano! *He remembered now. They were on the plane and it was dark outside and the plane was bumping around and then... then what? He had a confused memory of a cabin and a stove that burned wood and—he looked across at the man holding the crying woman. They had been there.*

*They turned to look at him and he shut his eyes. He heard footsteps and gentle hands tucked the covers under his chin like Anna's. The woman whispered something and the man whispered something back, and David opened his eyes a crack to see them tiptoeing out the door. It closed behind them with a soft click. He didn't hear a bolt thrown or a lock turned. He knew what those sounded like well enough by now.*

*David sat up and when the sheet fell back he saw that he had a nightgown on, too. That was bad. They would need clothes if they wanted to get away and get back to Mami.*

*He looked around and saw their clothes folded on a chair against the wall.*

*And the phone. Where was the Bad Man's phone that he had stolen on* el aeroplano? *He cast a wary look at the door. It was still closed. He slipped from the bed and padded to the chair. His jacket was on the bottom. He felt in his pocket and was relieved when it slid into his hand. They hadn't found it. He pulled it out and thumbed it on. There was no password. He smiled.*

*Mami had made them learn her number over and over and over every night before they went to sleep, all the way from Tegucigalpa to* el norte, *every single night, over and over again. She had bought them both phones before they left and put her number in David and Anna's but she said if they lost their phones they would need to know her number.*

*David and Anna hadn't lost their phones. The big men in the blue jackets with the big letters on the backs had taken them. They might have taken Mami's, too.*

*But they might not have.*

*He took a deep breath and pressed the green phone button and tapped in the numbers. He held the phone to his ear. It was ringing. It rang. And rang. And rang and rang and rang and rang. He let it ring twenty, twenty-five times.*

*Slowly, he lowered the phone and ended the call. Maybe Mami had turned her phone off. He would try again later.*

*He felt very tired, and his stomach ached. He pulled his nightgown up and looked down to find a wide, ugly bruise across his waist just below his belly button. There were more bruises on his arms and legs, too, and his neck hurt. He was glad he didn't know how he'd come by the bruises but he didn't want any more of them.*

*He looked around the room, at the closed door, at their clothes folded on the chair. They were clothes the Bad Man had bought them, beautiful clothes, and new, the first new clothes they'd had in a long time. He hated them. But at least they were clothes. They had something to wear when they had to run.*

*He tried one more time to call Mami, letting it ring even longer this time. Still no answer, even though he was straining for it with every sore muscle in his body.*

*The spurt of energy was strong but brief, and suddenly his neck couldn't hold his head up for one moment longer. He took the phone and climbed into bed next to Anna. She sighed and curled into him, clean, and warm, and safe, for at least this one moment. The last thing he saw before he fell back to sleep was her thick black lashes fanned out against her cheeks, and the last thing he heard was the steady sound of her breathing in his ears.*

*Take care of your sister,* miho.

*I will, Mami. I promise.*

# Four

"KATE SHUGAK," KATE SAID. "WE SPOKE on the phone earlier this morning."

"Ah yes, Ms. Shugak. Eugene Hutchinson." He cast a quick look around Kurt's office and without changing expression in the slightest seemed to lift his lip in a slight sneer. Kate bristled inwardly and Kurt outwardly but they maintained a similar stony silence. Mutt, sitting next to Kate, fixed her unblinking yellow eyes on the attorney she could tell Kate already disliked and gave her usual impression of preparing to repel boarders in the event it was necessary. What Mutt deemed necessary was fluid, as was who she cared to designate as a boarder.

Eugene Hutchinson, the author of the letter Kate had read the night before, was in his late fifties or early sixties and attired in a gray three-piece suit carefully tailored to disguise his paunch. His hair was a thin white tonsure, his eyes were a sharp if watery blue, his nose long and inquisitive, and at rest his lips formed a single line that no matter how hard he stretched them into a smile still looked like a noose someone had yet to put around the condemned's neck.

After a moment, he extended his hand. After a moment, Kate took it. His skin felt like it belonged to someone who had a regular spa day on his calendar and the muscles beneath it felt like they never did anything more strenuous than pull the knots tight on his shoelaces. She let go as soon as she could and sat down. "All right, Mr. Hutchinson, what is all this about?"

He settled himself in the second visitor's chair, crossed his legs and fussed a bit with the crease of his elegant trousers. He smiled at her, and then generously extended his smile to Kurt. Kurt stared back, unsmiling.

"This is Kurt Pletnikof. He is a trusted associate," Kate said. "I've asked him to sit in on this conversation." She smiled thinly at Hutchinson's moue of displeasure. "If you wanted me to welcome you with open arms, Mr. Hutchinson, you shouldn't have used Erland Bannister's name to get my attention." She glanced at the clock on Kurt's wall and wasn't the least bit covert about it. "Now what is this all about?"

He sighed and recrossed his legs so he could fuss with his other crease. "Very well, Ms. Shugak. I represent the living trust of the late Erland Bannister, which was filed in probate shortly before he died in November. As such it is my duty to inform you that he named you his primary trustee."

"Holy shit," Kurt said, startled out of his imitation of the Sphinx.

Hutchinson ignored him, watching Kate. There was a trace of amusement in his expression, but no uncertainty. He was for some reason sure of her acceptance.

Kate looked back at him and found absolutely nothing to say. Or to think, for that matter. Her mind was a complete blank. Until this moment she had thought the letter an elaborate joke, but there was something about Hutchinson, as much of a caricature lawyer as he was, that told her this was anything but. She knew a sudden and fervent wish that she and Mutt were sledding up to Canyon Hot Springs to help Jim and George search for body parts in the snow.

Hutchinson opened his briefcase (it was lined with black silk, Kate noticed) and extracted a file. He held it out to her. "This document contains the particulars, Ms. Shugak. I've included my card. Please call with any questions you might have." He shut the case and stood up.

"Wait a minute," she said.

"Yes?" He appeared to be enjoying himself. It made her distrust him all the more. "Did Erland discuss naming me as his trustee with you?"

"I'm afraid that comes under the heading of attorney–client privilege, Ms. Shugak."

Kurt snorted.

"I don't know anything about being a trustee," she said, "but I know enough to know that I don't want to be Erland's trustee."

Hutchinson cocked his head. His expression didn't change but she thought he was disappointed. "That is of course your prerogative, Ms. Shugak."

"I can refuse?"

"You can," he said. "Personally, I wouldn't blame you. It's a great deal of work for often ungrateful people. No person of means ever leaves their property in such a way as pleases everyone they leave behind."

Kate could hear the relief in her own voice. "Then I refuse."

"As you wish." He turned to go.

"Wait," Kate said.

Hutchinson paused, and took just a fraction of a second too long to turn back to face her. "Yes?" There was an underlying tension to the word, faint but there if you were paying attention, and Kate was. There was an expression in his eyes of what looked like triumph, like he'd just won a bet.

A bet with a dead man?

"Kate," Kurt said, a warning note in his voice.

"What happens if I refuse? Is there another—a secondary trustee named in Erland's will?"

He looked down and tugged at the hem of his vest. "Are you refusing to serve as the trustee for Erland's estate, Ms. Shugak?"

She thought it over. "Ah," she said after a moment. "I see. If I refuse to serve as trustee, you have no responsibility to inform me of any provisions Erland made."

A small smile curled the corners of his mouth.

Kate got to her feet. "I imagine I have some time to make up my mind. I'll be in touch."

Something changed in the atmosphere of Kurt's office then, nothing she could put a name to, but she saw by Kurt's expression that he felt it, too. It was as if someone had opened the window and invited the winter inside. She heard Mutt stand up behind her. She didn't growl, but then she didn't have to.

To his credit Hutchinson kept his eyes on Kate. Only a moment passed before he extended his hand again. Again Kate took it. This time he stepped in, close enough that she could feel his breath on her face. She looked up at him and smiled. From the corner of her eye she saw Kurt flinch and this time Mutt did growl.

"You're in my space," Kate said, her voice very soft. "Back up." She helped him by using his hand as a lever to physically push him. He stepped back before it became obvious that his moving was her idea, and then fell back another pace to allow her to pass.

"You are everything Erland said you were, Ms. Shugak."

"I don't take that as a compliment, Mr. Hutchinson."

When the door closed behind her and Mutt he gave a low whistle. "That is one no-bullshit woman." He grinned. "I like her."

Kurt studied him for a long moment. "Yeah. Just tell me where to send the flowers for your funeral."

Hutchinson laughed.

Kurt did not.

Agrifina Fancyboy was sitting at her desk, attired in a magenta two-piece button-down suit that beat Hutchinson's for tailoring. Her hair was pulled back into a neat chignon, her makeup was flawless, her manicure fresh out of the box, and she looked like a cross between Awkwafina in *Crazy Rich Asians* and Lauren Bacall in anything. "I'll be right back," Kate said, because truth to tell Kurt's secretary slash fiancée intimidated the hell out of her.

She stepped out into the hallway and headed for the ladies room, checking both stalls before she got out her phone. She dialed a number. It picked up on the first ring. "Brendan?"

"Kate Shugak, as I live and breathe! And I see you are doing both, which always makes my day. What can I do you for?" His voice sank into something dangerously close to a purr. "Or just do you?"

"Something weird just happened and I need your advice. Can I buy you lunch?"

He definitely purred this time. "You do speak my language, Ms. Shugak. You downtown? Good, Simon's, ten minutes."

"You need an estate attorney for the real skinny," Brendan said, digging into his first order of a dozen oysters on the half shell and washing it down with the best Sauvignon Blanc on offer. Of course, that was after he lectured the server at length on the iniquity of not having a muscadet on the wine list. It was going to be an expensive consult, she could see that, and Brendan was going to need a clean tie afterward, and possibly a clean shirt as well.

"I don't know an estate attorney," Kate said. "I know you. Tell me what you know. If I need more, I'll ask for a referral."

He sprinkled Tabasco with a lavish hand and gulped and grinned. "Fine by me. A trustee, you say?"

"Yes. Which office it appears I have the right to turn down."

"Nearly lost to the mists of One-L but not quite, a properly written trust will in fact have named a successor trustee, someone to step in in case of the death or incapacity of the primary trustee."

"What are the duties of a trustee?"

"The trustee has a fiduciary responsibility to manage the trust properly." The tiny seafood fork was dwarfed by his enormous hairy hand as he pointed it at her. "They are liable for criminal prosecution if they're caught not doing so, and there are about a kazillion cases I could point out as examples, but how nice that I don't have to because you've had recent personal experience of one such case yourself."

It took her a moment, and then her face cleared. "The Hardin trust." A case of suspected murder had taken her to Newenham almost exactly a year ago this month.

"A slight difference exists in that the writer of this trust is dead—Erland is dead, isn't he? And someone drove a stake through his heart before they put him in the ground just to be sure?"

"And Alexandra Hardin was alive but mentally incompetent," Kate said, ignoring him, "and her trustee put her away in an old folks' home in the Caribbean and embezzled her funds."

He waved a valedictory fork and dived back into the oysters.

"Guys like Erland, it's never about how much money they have. It's about how much more money they have than anyone else."

He was willing to play. "What do you think this charitable foundation is about, then?"

"Damn if I know. Expiation? Atonement? The price of entry into heaven?"

"Erland never struck me as a believer in anything other than his own omnipotence."

"True dat." She sighed. "This makes no sense, Brendan."

"No shit, my delectable friend. Erland Bannister hated your guts." He summoned his inner Admiral Ackbar. "It's a trap!" She smiled reluctantly. More soberly he said, "Here be dragons, Kate. I think you should stay very far away from this. Hand it off to whoever the successor trustee is. Move to another state if you have to." He paused, fork suspended, as he examined her expression. "But you're curious."

It wasn't a question. "Wouldn't you be? And who's to say the successor trustee isn't a bad guy?"

Brendan shook his head. "Hawaii, is what I'm thinking. Alaska Airlines flies there direct nowadays, and you've never been, have you? And wasn't the guy you're shacked up with some kinda surfer dude in a former life? Go. Now. Swim with the fishes in reality before, you know, someone makes you swim with the fishes metaphorically."

Kate's eyes narrowed and he waved his fork again. "What? You're the one who busted Erland in bed with the Chicago mob. Just saying."

The server brought him another order of oysters and Kate's fish and chips. They ate in silence, Kate brooding and Brendan manifesting oyster-induced ecstasy. "Actually," he said, after spending a few moments considering another order and rejecting it with regret, "I'm glad you called." He saw her look and grinned. He had a great grin, did Brendan. It was big and went well with his broad face, his messy, badly cut hair, the blue eyes that crinkled at the corners, and the body that was nearly as broad as it was tall. He wore off-the-rack from J.C. Penney in a dried blood brown and a tie of psychedelic hue that was only improved by his breakfast and lunch. He was as far from Eugene Hutchinson as a lawyer could get. Kate had known him since her days with the Anchorage DA. He was still there, fighting the good fight.

"Why is that?" she said.

"You're not even the first Shugak I've heard from this year."

She sat up. "Who?"

He flapped a hand. "Relax." He grinned again, this time with a little of the shit-eater in it. "Auntie Vi."

"Auntie Vi!" Kate sat back. "Why on earth did Auntie Vi call you?"

He blew his nose with an almighty honk on the cloth napkin and crumpled up the results and left it on his plate. Kate spared a moment of pity for the restaurant's laundry. "She was calling on behalf of the Park elders, or so she gave me to understand. It seems a busload of Park elders wants to drive to Haines and take the ferry to Juneau for the Gold Medal."

The Gold Medal was an annual basketball tournament that had been going on for longer than the NBA had existed. Once a year male and female town teams from all over Southeast and a few points north met in Juneau in March for a ten-day series. Most teams were accompanied by a significant portion of the population of their towns and the competition was as fiercely cheered as it was fiercely fought. "Man, I always wanted to go to that," she said. "Okay, so far so good. What's the problem?"

"Well." Brandon smoothed his execrable tie and quirked a bushy eyebrow. "Under the new rules, the elders need passports to drive through Canada, which won't let them cross the border without one."

"They don't want to apply?"

"Oh, they applied. But the Department of State, it seems, is loath to issue them passports because none of them have birth certificates." He scooched back his chair a little, in case of flying debris.

Kate could feel the color rise up into her face and took a long, calming breath. "Why did they ask you for help?"

"It turns out I'm the only lawyer they know."

She nodded. "Of course." And of course he would be. He'd been Jack's best friend, and had visited the Park with him many times. The Niniltna Native Association had a battery of lawyers but of course none of the elders would imagine bringing this kind of problem to them. This was personal. "Were you able to help them?"

"I thought I'd talk it over with you first." Her flush was fading. He thought it was a pity.

"I'll call Pete Heiman."

"Our illustrious congressman? Kate, you know he's as crooked as a dog's hind leg."

"Yeah, but he's our dog, and if he's going to be crooked he might as well be crooked on our behalf."

"He's probably game fishing in Florida."

Kate showed her teeth. "That much closer to DC, then."

The server brought the bill and Kate managed to not look directly at the tab while signing it. They sat for a few minutes over coffee, because Brendan had to get in a little digestion before going back to keeping bad guys off the streets. "Kate?" he said.

"What?"

"Do you ever think about Jack?"

She looked at him in surprise. "All the time."

"I miss him. I miss him more with every half-assed, wet-behind-the-ears child the DA hires on as an investigator." He paused, and said heavily, "I miss my friend."

"I miss him, too," she said softly, watching the coffee swirl around inside her cup. She raised her eyes and looked across the table. "And then I remember that we had a good, long run, and that he died saving my life, and that we got to say goodbye." She blinked back sudden but not unwelcome tears. "And I'm grateful. So many people have so much less."

He nodded. "And Jim?"

She looked out the window. Moments passed. Brendan obviously wanted an answer because he actually held off on the smartass remarks. She looked back at him. "Jim is— more. More than what he seemed to be at first. Right now, he's going through some stuff."

"I heard. I want to buy a plane and learn to fly just so I can land at that Cadillac of an airstrip of his everyone's talking about."

She grinned. "He says first thing when the snow melts he's putting a big black X at both ends."

He grinned back. "And you?"

"He's—growing on me."

"Treating you right?"

"So far so good."

"If that ever changes—"

"Yeah, yeah. And Mutt loves him."

"Mutt loves anything walking around on two legs with dangly bits between."

They walked outside, where a few people had gathered in an admiring circle around Mutt, all with their phones out. Mutt was sitting in sunlit dignity, her tail curled around her feet, radiating the royal We in every hair of her gray coat. She saw Kate and stood up, and if her subjects didn't quite bow in obeisance there were expressions of dismay at her departure.

She trotted over to Brendan and got a good head scratch out of it. Brendan walked them to the Subaru and saw them both inside. "You gonna turn it down?" he said, holding the door.

She turned the key and closed the door without answering.

"What I thought," he said as she pulled out into traffic.

At least Mutt was back in the saddle, he thought as he watched them head down L Street. She had been known to save Kate's ass a time or two.

# Five

THE SUN WAS A FAINT, DESPAIRING PRESENCE overhead as they drove the Step Road from Niniltna to where the trail veered off over the foothills to the east and through the spruce thickets and over the bald knolls and around the doglegs. The sky was the palest possible blue, as if all the snow that winter had leeched the color from it. The Quilaks looked somehow flattened against it, as if rendered in 2D instead of 3D, their peaks a lifeless white instead of the more nuanced shades of blue and white and charcoal of a normal winter day. The effect made the mountains appear similar in height, instead of Angqaq as one mount to rule them all, one mount to bind them, with wings arrayed like subservient courtiers to the north and south. Jim thought the scene looked a little anime, black and white and shades of gray, and fixed in time and space when he knew damn well everything about the Quilaks was subject to radical change, instantaneous and dramatic. This new persona was unsettling to say the least.

It was a relatively quick run, George in the lead setting the pace. George used the same skills on the ground as he did in the air, an uncanny sense of situational awareness, a positively supernatural hand–eye coordination, and a penchant for pushing any vehicle to its maximum speed. Jim had been flying since he was twenty-five and he had over five thousand hours in fixed wing, far less in helo. He paid attention to the weather, and didn't take off unless and until he was sure he would get where he was going. If he flew every day for the rest of his life he still wouldn't be as good as George. Damn few were. He knew for a fact George had stopped counting his hours when he reached ten thousand, and that was even before he'd bought his first single Otter turbo when the Suulutaq Mine started up.

George leaned way out, pulling his sled up on one ski, and took the last dog leg without braking. The angle of the leg was so acute that almost everyone missed the entrance and was the reason most people never found the canyon behind it, even with explicit directions. Yeah, Jim wasn't ever going to be as good a sled driver as George was, either. He slowed down and followed in much more sedate fashion and then picked up a little speed once he was through to the narrow canyon behind it. The hot springs, a series of seven pools that remained unfrozen throughout the coldest winters, smoked in a steadily descending line down the center of the canyon. Behind them stood a small cabin with an outhouse behind it, both buried to their eaves. Behind the outhouse the canyon climbed and narrowed, the gradually inclining sides of the foothills becoming steep mountainsides.

Jim coasted to a stop next to George and raised the shield of his helmet and pulled down his balaclava. The cold stung his face but the unfiltered air felt good as he gulped it in. "What do you think?"

They stared up toward the head of the canyon, which at first sight seemed to be wholly filled in with snow.

"I think," George said, "that to find anything up there we'd have to airlift in an excavator."

"Or two. What about avalanches?"

"Dan O'Brian's better at avalanche prediction than I am. NOAA says the temp is holding." He looked up at the sky, framed by the ridges on either side of the canyon. "But I'd as soon be out of here before we test their forecast. The Mother of Storms has gotten so bitchy lately I wouldn't be surprised if she decided to change things up with rain and then we would be fucked."

"In January?"

"Ask the folks in Shaktoolik if they think it's unlikely."

They flipped down their shields and proceeded slowly up the canyon, in which the level of snow rose drastically higher as they went and whose walls pressed inexorably inward in an increasingly claustrophobic way. There was a moment when Jim thought he could almost see into Canada over the top of one crag. He found it hard to catch his breath.

They were at, what, nine thousand, ten thousand feet? Big Bump was over thirteen thousand feet, he remembered that much. His fingers and toes seemed to be going numb, and he knew that had to be wrong because he'd stuffed almost a whole box of HotHands into his mitts and boots before he'd ever put them on.

He was so intent on keeping to the track George was laying down that he nearly ran into him before he realized the other man had stopped. His sled crunched to a halt inches short of George's right boot as it hung over the edge of his seat. He flipped up his shield and tried to look like he had meant to do that. George was pointing to their right and Jim followed his finger to a jumble of rocks whose sharp edges were dulled by drifts of snow.

He squinted. One of those things was not like the other. "Is that the tailplane Matt was talking about?"

"I think so. Can't be sure unless we dig down and I'd just as soon wait until spring."

"Me, too," Jim said with feeling.

"Those kids are damn lucky Matt and Laurel were at the cabin and heard the crash."

"Yeah," Jim said hollowly. "Lucky." The fragment of fuselage leading down from the tip of the tailplane had to be filled with snow, probably packed hard by the wind. If the kids had still been belted into their seat, they wouldn't have had a chance.

George looked around. "What the hell were they doing?"

"And where the hell were they going?"

"Only a couple of things would have got me out in the middle of a storm like that one. A medivac."

Jim nodded. "And money."

"Have to be a hell of a lot of money. Unless somebody's discovered diamonds in the YT and they're smuggling them over the border." He looked at Jim. "Heard anything like that?"

"No. Heard a lot about drugs, though."

"Yeah. Me, too."

George jockeyed his sled as close to the tailplane as he could so as to brush off a bit of snow and confirm that it was in fact the tailplane. "Like I figured," he said. "Small private jet. Maybe even the Citation I mentioned." He tried to break a piece off to take back for identification purposes but the snow immobilized everything and it was frozen hard anyway and he gave up.

Jim drove his sled past the tailplane as far up the canyon as he could before the incline became so steep he was likely to tip the sled back over on himself. He came down again crisscrossing his previous route back and forth, slowly, painstakingly. About halfway down he nearly ran over a boulder and swung hard uphill, letting gravity slow him down. When he pulled right up next to it he discovered it wasn't a boulder at all but a human head staring up at the sky. It looked like a yeti, hair frozen into spikes, eyes wide open, mouth agape, skin frosted over.

His hand closed convulsively on the brake and the sled lurched so suddenly to a halt that even as slowly as he was going he bumped hard up against the sled's windshield. He was motionless for a few seconds, conscious only of his heart thudding in his ears and the bridge of his nose hurting where it had hit his helmet shield.

He heard George shout, and pushed himself slowly back onto the seat and waved George up the slope.

It took them nearly an hour to dig out the body, in part because they kept sinking into the snow up to their waists when they stepped off their sleds. They'd both brought collapsible shovels and rope, which helped. It also helped when they discovered that the bottom half of the dead man's body had been sheared off in a diagonal cut that had removed his left arm below the elbow, all of his left leg and half of his right leg.

"Jesus," George said.

"Count your blessings," Jim said. "At least he's frozen so he doesn't smell." When George made a noise Jim said, "Don't puke right on him if you can help it."

"Jesus," George said again, and swiveled quickly to rolf into a snowbank that had never done him any harm. He wiped his mouth on his sleeve, and looked back at Jim. "You just had to say something."

"Sorry." And he was, in the few moments he had to spare in levering this fucking dead weight piece of evidence out of a treacherous landscape where he could find no footing and where every moment he was afraid of bringing the entire fucking mountain of snow down on top of them.

"You're not puking, you cold-ass son of a bitch."

"Not my first body."

They shoveled snow from around the deceased and got a rope under its arms and tied it off to George's sled. He started it up and put a steady strain on the rope and the body finally popped out of the hole like a cork out of a bottle. The flesh of the abdomen tore across where it had stuck to the ice and revealed a lot of frozen intestine, and George threw up again.

They muscled the body into a couple of black garbage bags and then onto the trailer hooked to Jim's sled, not without inventing a whole new class of profanity. Jim hauled himself back up on his sled seat and lay back, panting.

"Jim?"

"What?" he said. Was it his imagination or had the sky turned completely gray again over the past hour? Probably just felt like it.

"What's that?" Jim turned his head to see George pointing in the hole in the snow left by the body. He struggled to sit up as George slipped back down into it. He bent over and stood up again, a bulging gallon Ziploc bag in one hand. It was packed with what had to be thousands of small white tablets.

Jim stared at it for a long moment, and then he laid back down on his seat, much preferring the farther prospect no matter how gray and threatening.

"A helluva a lot of money," George said.

"Yep," Jim said, staring up at the merciless sky. "Shit."

On the door of a bland office near the top of a tower in a glass-and-steel wilderness thousands of miles to the south there was a discreet knock.

"Yes."

"Sir?"

"What is it?"

"We've located the phone."

A brief silence. "Where is it?"

"At the transfer point."

Another silence, punctuated by a long, heartfelt sigh. "God. Damn. It. I warned that asshole not to go himself."

"There's more, sir."

"Of course there is. What?"

"It appears there were survivors after all."

"What? He made it out alive?"

"No, my source says both Mr. Curley and the pilot were killed in the crash."

"Good. Who then?"

A clearing of throat. "It appears there were two children on board."

"What the—oh, you are fucking kidding me. Curley

83

brought his toys with him? He couldn't do without his underage pussy for the length of a goddamn freight run?"

"It appears not, no, sir."

"Motherfucking, moronic ASSHOLE."

"As you say, sir."

A brief, fulminating silence "How did you locate the phone?"

"Someone made a call from it, sir, to a cell phone bought in Honduras."

"Honduras?"

"Yes, sir, from a small electronics store in Tegucigalpa. One of ours is already en route to see if the store keeps records of phone sales. It is my belief that one of the children has the phone, sir, and made that call."

A longer and considerably more fraught silence. "You will deploy whatever resources necessary to do whatever has to be done to find that phone. Curley ran his part of the operation on it. It cannot be allowed to fall into the wrong hands."

"I was under the impression that those phones defaulted to factory setting if anyone unaware of the code tried to access that particular file."

"That's what the nerds tell me, Jared."

"Yes, sir."

"Do I look like the kind of man who believes anything told him by people who wear Ewok T-shirts to work?"

"No, sir."

"And, Jared?"

*"Sir?"*

*"This stays in-house. No word of this leaks to our Russian friends. The last thing we need is the Bratva fucking things up. Those assholes have no boundaries. It's our mess and we'll clean it up. Clear?"*

*"Yes, sir."*

*"One more thing."*

*"Sir?"*

*"You'll remember the little problem we had in the same area last fall?"*

*"Very clearly indeed, sir."*

*"There was a woman—"*

*"A private investigator, sir."*

*"Yes, well, that might be what she files her taxes under, but she could be more accurately described as a wrecking ball. I don't want her anywhere near this."*

*"No, sir."*

*"I mean it, Jared. If she's sniffing around, I want her discouraged. Or disposed of. I really have no preference as to which. Discreetly, of course."*

*"Of course, sir."*

# Six

HOWEVER ENJOYABLE THE JOURNEY, there is nothing like your own bed. Especially one with your own Jim in it. Kate smiled her way out of sleep and rolled over to take advantage of her own Jim, and woke all the way to the realization she was not in her own bed, she was in Anchorage, and Jim was in her own bed in the Park.

She got up, dressed, and stamped downstairs. Mutt looked at her from her sprawl in front of the fireplace and her jaw dropped in a lupine laugh. "Oh, shut up," Kate said, and went into the kitchen to make coffee. When the sky began to lighten she bundled up and went out to check on the status of the Coastal Trail, around Westchester Lagoon and through the tunnel to where the trail followed the eastern edge of Knik Arm. The air was still, the sky was a hard, gray shield overhead, and the Knik was filled with shards of sheet ice that tinkled against each other on the outgoing tide.

She settled into a rhythm of walking and running, counting her steps with one part of her mind while the rest of it worried over what she had learned the day before. Mutt loped in front of her, making occasional forays into the brush on either side to frighten the living hell out of the occasional Arctic hare. She was probably mentally marking the places she'd started them from for snack time later.

Kate's breath left white clouds hanging in the air behind her as her muscles began to warm up and her legs settled into a rhythm. Erland Bannister, a man of great power and influence, had hated her with every part and fiber of his being. That he'd tried to have her killed more than once, and, worse, that he had failed would have set his hatred in concrete. And let's not forget the little matter of her being the proximate cause of him being jailed for it. That sting would not have lessened when he'd managed to weasel his way out of jail on a technicality with the help of a corrupt judge.

The trail was hard packed and turning to ice in places, especially the cross-country ski tracks set into the left-hand side. She came around the corner into Lyn Aery Park and found Mutt dancing delightedly around a skier sprawled across the trail, skies and poles and legs and arms twisted into a knot of Gordian complexity. "Help!" came a high, thin, panicked voice from inside the knot. "Help me! There's a wolf attacking me!"

"Only half!" Kate leapt over him in one smooth jump. "Mutt! Leave that poor guy alone and come on!" A moment later Mutt shot past her at full gallop and crashed into a leafless stand of elderberry, from which immediately a panicked crow took to the air in a blur of black wings, leaving a lone feather floating down to the ground behind.

Erland had hated Kate, no doubt of that. She had cordially returned the sentiment. Brendan was right. The only reason for Erland to name her his trustee was for him to have planted some kind of poisoned pill within his estate, something that he would have orchestrated very carefully to do her the maximum damage at the most opportune moment.

Or maximum damage to someone she loved.

She thought that over for another half a mile, and came to the conclusion that, no, Erland wouldn't have bothered with a secondary target, he would have aimed straight at Kate in an attempt to totally trash her credibility and blacken her name. It had always been personal between the two of them. He had never forgotten and never forgiven being taken down by, one, a woman, and two, an Alaska Native woman. He had been the fartiest of old farts, first among equals in the Old White Boomers Club. They had built the state up from what they regarded as nothing, expropriated it from the Native peoples they regarded as less than nothing, and done their level best to shape Alaska's future into a statehood with themselves in power and a resource extraction model of capitalism with themselves as the primary beneficiaries. The Alaska Native Claims Settlement Act in 1972, where the federal government had been forced to pay the Alaska Natives land and money in exchange for a right of way over tribal lands for the TransAlaska Pipeline, had started the state down a road leading to at least a partial equality of the races, but guys like Erland were not known for elasticity of thought or acceptance of those previously determined to be other or lesser. And when they were crossed or flouted, they got mad and they got even.

But Erland would have known that that would be the first thing she thought, so he would have also known that her first instinct would have been to refuse.

So what trap lay in that direction?

A cow moose crashed out of a thicket and pounded down the trail, saw her, and veered back into the brush. A moment later Mutt appeared in her wake, tongue lolling out of the side of her mouth. "Shame on you," Kate told her severely.

Mutt sneezed, tail wagging furiously, and dropped down on her forepaws, hairy butt in the air.

"Oh no, you don't," Kate said.

Oh yes she did, and she pounced, snagging the hem of Kate's jeans in her teeth and tugging enough to break Kate's stride. She stumbled and just barely caught her balance before she faceplanted on the trail. "Mutt! Dammit!"

Mutt yipped, spring-loaded a couple of nearly vertical

bounces to land ten feet away, and looked over her shoulder, tail wagging furiously.

"All right, you asked for it," Kate said, and gave chase, which lasted until Earthquake Park when Kate cried uncle and turned around to head back home. The city looked good from here. Bound by Knik Arm on the west and Turnagain Arm on the south, the glass sides of the cluster of tall buildings that formed downtown reflected images of the Chugach Mountains lined up behind them. They were unlike the Quilaks not only in elevation, being in general only a third as high as any single Quilak, but in geological personality. The Quilaks had a tendency to cluster together in disdainful rebuff. In contrast, the Chugach Mountains, while standing near together, were distinctly separate and much more welcoming. Almost none of the Quilaks were named other than the tallest, Angqaq or Big Bump. The Chugachs were named for everyone from Billy Mitchell to Rachel Carson.

This morning, the faintest hint of alpenglow receded up the peaks as the winter sun rose in the southeast. The star on the mountain was diminished, too, by the morning light, as were the exterior lights from the homes that climbed the lower reaches of the mountains to the east. Exhaust from everyone's furnaces, home and business, streamed straight up into the still air, a forest of opaque plumes pierced by air traffic, Piper Super Cubs from Merrill, 747 cargo jets from Ted Stevens International, and F-22s from JBER. There was always something of interest in the skies over Anchorage.

They returned to the townhouse an hour later, Kate with red cheeks and a runny nose, jeans soaked all down the front, and missing her hat and one glove, with Mutt looking exactly the same as when they'd left. The neighbor, a burly man with tufts of gray hair sticking up all over his head and wrapped in a fuzzy brown robe, straightened from picking up the paper on his doorstep and watched as they came up the walk. "So you're back then," he said.

"We are," Kate said cheerfully.

"Could you keep the drivebys down to a minimum this time?"

"We can but try."

He shook his head and went inside, and they did the same.

She showered and dressed in dry clothes. She'd hit Safeway yesterday and sat down to a breakfast of eggs, bacon, and sourdough toast made from store-bought bread that was barely worth biting into. Mutt gnawed on the jawbone of an ass excavated from the chest freezer in the garage. Supplies there needed replenishing if Mutt was going to be kept from free-range foraging, which had led to some mild unpleasantnesses during past visits. Anchorageites were such tender little flowers.

She made more coffee, pulled the curtains back in the living room, and curled up on the couch and disposed herself to think.

Erland had named her his trustee. Brendan said that

meant she was legally and morally obligated to see to the distribution of his assets as he had set down such distribution in his will.

She and Erland weren't friends, which meant there was some ticking time bomb implanted in his assets, set to go off at some point so as to cause her harm.

But while Erland had hated her, she was fairly certain he had also respected her, which meant that the twisty old bastard would have known that she would realize this. She didn't consider herself paranoid, and she didn't want to give Erland more credit than he was due, but that could mean that there was another giant man trap in her refusal to act as his trustee.

She sighed. There was only one way to find out. She got her phone and googled his charitable foundation. She clicked on the phone number.

It rang once, and Jane answered.

Kate recognized the voice at once. "Jane Morgan?"

"Yes." A pause. "Kate Shugak?"

"Yes."

Another pause. "I've been expecting your call."

"Have you."

"Erland named you his trustee."

"So I hear."

Another, much longer pause. Jane cleared her throat. "Perhaps you'd like to come into the office."

The offices of the Bannister Foundation were in a building still under construction in a business park in midtown. The building consisted of five connected cubes of two to five floors each collected around a half-moon of what Kate presumed would be grass come spring, no doubt with an appropriately tasteless lump of alleged art holding down the middle of it. Scaffolding climbed one side of the farthest right cube and a power tool was making a statement from somewhere inside the visqueen wrapping the scaffolding. A workman in a pair of disintegrating Carhartt's bibs ducked out from under the plastic to rummage in a toolbox. Builders wore paint stains and nail holes on their bibs like badges of honor. It conferred even more cachet if they hadn't been washed since the Truman administration. Call it the Carhartt swagger.

She parked in what would be a parking lot one day, and looked at Mutt. "Stay or go?" She opened her door and Mutt answered with a graceful leap that took her over Kate and through the opening into a neat four-point landing next to the Subaru. "Okay then," Kate said, and climbed down after her.

The main lobby occupied the first floor of the central and tallest building and brought the steel-and-glass ambience of the exterior inside in a palette of grays and, well, more grays. The walls were a light slate, the ceiling a pale taupe, the fixtures including the door handles were brushed nickel and the tiles of the floor were eighteen-inch squares of granite that looked like it had been cut out of the surface of the Knik Glacier. There were two conversation areas with club chairs and love seats in shades of gray around coffee tables painted, for a change, black. It was the *ne plus ultra* in interior design, no doubt, but it reminded Kate irresistibly of a phrase from a Tennyson poem—"dead perfection," that was it. The place felt like a columbarium.

A large counter stood at the back of the lobby, behind which sat a man dressed in a suit with an earbud in his right ear. He looked up, saw Mutt, and said, "No dogs allowed here, ma'am."

She smiled. "We're here to see Jane Morgan at the Bannister Foundation."

"There is no one by that name."

"That's all right, Mr. Sanderson. I'll take it from here."

Kate looked around to see Jane Morgan. "It's not Morgan anymore," Jane said. "I went back to Wardwell."

Jane was Jack's ex and Johnny's mother and possibly the original Kate-hater, even before that time when Kate burgled her apartment, made off with the password to her bank account and credit card, both subsequently used to great effect on a shopping spree. Which had accomplished its goal to divert Jane from fighting Jack for custody of Johnny, but which also, Kate was willing to admit now, might have been a little extreme. Not that she would ever say that out loud, or apologize for it, either.

"This way," Jane said, and led the way to an elevator containing nickel-framed mirrors that showed their reflections studiously avoiding each other's gaze. Jane looked good, if a little strained. Kate wondered if Jane mourned Erland. She wondered what Erland had left Jane in his will, if anything.

They were whisked to the top floor and the door opened onto a reception desk and half a dozen office doors behind it. They were all closed, and the reception desk was vacant.

"Where is everyone?" Kate said. "Surely you don't run this place alone?"

"Staff are on holiday," Jane said dismissively. "This way, please, Ms. Shugak."

Kate nearly looked around to see who she was talking to. Jane wasn't one to waste politesse on Kate, especially when her son had joined Team Kate at his earliest opportunity.

The office was in the corner with two walls glassed in that had a lovely view of Knik Arm and Mt. Susitna to the south. It was a distinct relief from the undertaker vibe that had continued up from the lobby. "This was Erland's office," Jane said.

A large black desk took up one corner, a suite of club chairs (gray, of course) occupied another, and a set of filing cabinets a third. Everything looked bare and unlived in. The desk didn't even have a phone on it, much less a computer. "Did you clean it out after Erland died?" Kate said.

Jane shook her head. "It was always like this."

"And Erland ran the foundation out of here?"

"He was rarely here," Jane said. She remained standing as Kate walked around to the other side of the desk. It didn't even have drawers; it was basically a lower-case Helvetica "n" in bold.

She looked up at Jane. "He had to have a laptop."

"I believe he kept everything on his phone."

"Do you have his phone?"

"I put all of his personal items in his safety deposit box at Last Frontier Bank."

"Of course." Kate came out from behind the desk and pulled open a drawer in one of the filing cabinets. Empty. She pulled another open at random. Also empty. She turned. "Do you have a laptop?"

"I do."

"Show me."

They walked to the opposite corner of the floor, furnished in exactly the same fashion as Erland's office. Instead of Knik Arm and Susitna the view was of the mountains. The star was nearer and perforce a little brighter from this distance. "What is your position here?" Kate said.

"I'm Erland's executive assistant."

"Who is the foundation's executive director?"

"Erland was its executive director," Jane said.

Kate's eyebrows went up. "He was the ED of his own charitable foundation?"

"Yes."

Not unlawful so far as Kate knew, but the optics were not the best. "Did he name someone to take over when he died?"

"You're the trustee," Jane said. She sat down at her desk, which held an actual laptop, and tapped a key. "Did you want to—"

"Hold it," Kate said. "If I'm the trustee, I'm now de facto the executive director of the Bannister Foundation?"

Jane sat back in her chair. "There is no one else." In a rare moment, she allowed a wrinkle to crease her forehead and almost immediately remembered to smooth it out again. "Have you not read the will?"

"The only representative of Erland's I've spoken to thus far is Eugene Hutchinson," Kate said with perfect if incomplete truth. "Have you seen it?"

"No, but I've been privy to Erland's business dealings since…" Jane hesitated, "since he was free once again to pursue said interests, and—"

"He hired you right after he got out of prison?"

"Yes."

"What, he put out an ad and you applied?"

Jane's expression became even more wooden. "He approached me."

"How, exactly?"

"How is that relevant? Or any of your business?"

"It's part of the Bannister Foundation's history," Kate said in her blandest voice.

Jane was six inches taller than Kate and slender, with milk-pale skin and pale blue eyes a little too small and too near together, which made her look ever so slightly cross-eyed. Her hair was so blond it was almost colorless and she was dressed in a gray (naturally) two-piece suit over a silk shirt with a bow neatly tied at the neck. The look was completed by gray pumps with two-inch heels and pearl button earrings. She couldn't have been more self-effacing if she'd gone over herself with an eraser before she'd left for work that morning.

Kate's silence was more powerful than her own so Jane said, reluctantly, "I was working at the BLM. He called and offered to triple my salary and benefits."

"Irresistible," Kate said. "Completely understandable. Tell me, were you aware of his history, and did you think the job offer might have something to do with me?"

Anger flashed briefly in the other woman's eyes but at least she didn't pretend not to know what Kate meant. Mutt, standing next to Kate and attending all this with wide eyes that seemed eerily to understand every word that was said, might have had something to do with that. "I knew it did. He told me when I came in for the interview." She cleared her throat pointedly and indicated her laptop. "Did you want to look at our books?"

"I'm guessing that my taking the laptop will be frowned upon?"

Jane took a deep breath and let it out slowly. "I— before I allowed you to do that, I'd have to check with Mr. Hutchinson. For one thing, I oversee the grant applications and implement the distribution of the grants with this laptop. It's the essential tool for my job."

Kate nodded agreeably. "Excuse me?" Jane stood up and took a step back from her desk, mostly because Kate had stepped forward into her personal space, and still more when she pulled out Jane's chair and sat down in it. She pulled out the new thumb drive Kurt had given her the day before and plugged it into the side of the laptop. The screen lit up with the password prompt. "Jane?" she said.

Jane reached around Kate with one hand and typed the password in, and the desktop popped up. The wallpaper was generic pretty blue sky with a line of folders down the left-hand side. Kate clicked on Finder, hit Command All, and sent all files and folders to the thumb drive.

Mutt's eyes popped up over the edge of the desk and sent an inquiring look Kate's way. "Almost there," Kate said to her, and shortly thereafter unplugged the thumb drive and put it back in her pocket. She stood up and walked around to the other side of the desk. "I'll take a day or two to look over the files," she said, "and then I'll be back."

"In the meantime?"

Kate smiled at Jane. "Business as usual. After all, you're doing nothing but good work here, isn't that right?"

"That is correct," Jane said. "We're funding worthwhile projects all over the state of Alaska, from women's shelters to libraries to renewable resource companies. You'll find all of the grants, awarded and pending, in the files. They're listed on our website as well."

"I'll be looking at both. Thank you."

"You're welcome." There was a brief flash of feeling in Jane's eyes, gone too quickly to identify. Defeat? Resentment? Triumph, perhaps?

Kate and Mutt retired in good order, the outer office as yawningly vacant of personnel as before. "I don't know how anything gets done around here, do you?" she said to Mutt as they stepped into the elevator.

Mutt shook her head vigorously and sneezed. They exited the elevator under the professionally suspicious eyes of the guard at the security station and escaped the grim lobby into the fresh, cold air outside. A power tool went BRAT! BRAA-AAAT! BRRRAAA-AAT! above her head and she looked up to see the guy in the Carhartts grinning down at her through a gap in the visqueen. "Hey," he said.

"Hey yourself," she said.

"Nice dog."

Mutt obligingly gave an enthusiastic wave of her tail. "Thanks," Kate said. "You look like you're about to finish up here."

He made a face. "It's been ready to occupy since October. We're just replacing some tile that blew off in the last storm." He shook his head, disgusted. "We told the architect and the builder this would happen, but of course they didn't listen."

A voice from inside the visqueen said, "You're working, aren't you, Red?"

"And getting paid for it, too, yeah, yeah," Red said, and looked back down at her. "What's your name?"

"Kate. And Mutt."

"Hello, Kate and Mutt. We're about to knock off for lunch. Want to join us?"

"Thanks, Red, it'd be great, but I'm working, too."

"Aw." He had a very nice smile and he was only about fifteen years younger than she was. Nice to know she still had it.

"Did you say this building is ready to occupy, Red?"

"Sure did."

"Does that mean it isn't occupied now?"

He shrugged. "I dunno. Only ever seen more than a couple people and the security guards going in, is all."

"Huh. Well, nice meeting you, Red."

"Woof," Mutt said, which made his smile even brighter.

"Slut," Kate said.

BBRRAAAA-AAT! BRAAAA-AAAAT!

The louder the tool, the bigger the penis.

Her phone rang as she was climbing into the Subaru and the caller started talking before she had time to say hello. "Shugak, I know you're in town. Get your ass over here, I got some questions." Click.

Kate looked at Mutt. "What do you think? Did Brillo just get around to autopsying Erland and find out that he was gruesomely murdered as he lay defenseless in his hospital bed?" A happy thought struck her. "And maybe Jane did it?"

Mutt's silence reeked of skepticism, and Kate sighed and turned the key in the ignition. "Yeah, you're right. Too much to hope for."

They drove east on Tudor until they reached the massive crime fighting complex where the good guys figured out how to put the bad guys away, or not. She presented herself at the desk and was waved through to the sanctum sanctorum, where awaited a fireplug of an individual whose energy crackled through his body and sparked off the ends of his hair, which resembled a Brillo pad, hence the nickname. He pounced. "Shugak! You took your time getting here."

"You called, like, five minutes ago."

He waved that away and regarded Mutt with disfavor. "So, you're back from the dead now, too, are you? Because the universe decided I need a four-footed lupine enforcer in my life just this minute." But he slipped her a Milkbone or three when they both thought Kate wasn't looking.

"What's up, Brillo?" Kate said.

"What's up is your bimbo boyfriend's still sending me bodies from that goddamn Park of yours. He quit, that prick, he's not supposed to be drumming up business for me anymore."

"I'll pay you twenty bucks, cash money, if you'll call him 'bimbo boyfriend' in person."

He walked over to one of the tables and whipped back the plastic sheet.

"Okay," Kate said, "first of all: Ew."

Mutt showed her teeth and went over to sit by the door in a manner strongly indicating her preference for their immediate next move.

"Be grateful, he's still partially frozen, keeps the smell down. Chopin found him at the site of that aircraft that went into your mountains on New Year's Eve."

"Where's his other half?"

"Wheeeere's the reeeeeeest of meeeeeee?" Ronald Reagan Brillo was not. "Unknown and Chopin says the weather window on finding it was closing before they even left the site."

"How'd he wind up like this?"

Brillo shrugged. "The plane hit a mountain and stopped and he kept going. Recognize him?"

Kate had thus far avoided looking at the dead man's face, but now she stepped to the head of the table and looked down. Her brow creased. "I don't—oh."

"Yeah," Brillo said. "Took me a second, too, no surprise."

"Gary Curley."

"The same."

"Well," Kate said, "I can't be sorry to see him sliced right across his groin. I just wish I could believe he was awake and aware through every excruciating nanosecond of it."

"Hard to work up much sympathy," Brillo said, nodding. "Or any. But what was he doing in the air in the middle of the Quilak Mountains in the middle of one of the worst storms in living memory?"

She looked up to meet Brillo's eyes, which blinked at her from behind lenses so thick she could see her own reflection in them, and thought of the two children in the Grosdidiers' clinic. "I couldn't begin to tell you. Why should I care?"

"Because of what else Chopin found at the site." He walked over to his desk and held up an evidence bag. Inside it was a Ziploc bag crammed to bursting with thousands of small white round pills.

Kate, did she but know it, channeled her inner Jim in a single, heartfelt, "Shit."

# Seven

## THURSDAY, JANUARY 3
### *Niniltna*

"**I**T'S A CULTURAL THING, AND I DON'T mean if you belong to a tribe or which one or no tribe at all," Jim said. "Everything is shipped into Alaska, so it follows that if you own something with moving parts you shipped it in at a tremendous expense you'd rather not repeat, thanks. Therefore you're going to learn how to make it go and keep it going. Bush Alaskans are a culture of fixers, hoarders, and make-doers."

"No argument here," Bobby said, passing the potatoes.

Jim ladled a small mountain on his plate and accepted the caribou steaks, spearing half a dozen on his fork. Bobby had done his bread-and-fry-and-finish-in-the-oven-with-wine special, and Jim could feel the drool pooling in his mouth. He'd been hungry since they came down from Canyon Hot Springs. Hard work in cold weather conditions burned more calories than anything else in his experience.

Shoveling out his hangar one day, mountain sledding the next, another day shoveling out the hangar—it felt like he'd lost five pounds since last year. He was glad when Bobby called to order his ass into town for dinner. With Kate, Mutt, and the kids all gone the house felt pretty empty.

"What we need is someone who builds snowmobiles or four-wheelers. They're for fun on the road system and basic transportation in the Bush. But then of course you're back where you started because you have to ship in all the crap you need to build them. And that's before you even start talking about fuel." He had to stop talking because his mouth was filled with food, glorious food.

"Good, huh, Jim?"

He looked up to see six-year-old Katya beaming at him from across the table, her many-braided hair standing up around her face like a dark aureole and her mouth full of potatoes. "No talking with your mouth full," said her mother for all mothers everywhere.

"Real good, Katya," Jim said.

"Did you catch any bad guys today?" she said.

"Hundreds," he said solemnly.

Katya chuckled her rich, infectious chuckle and waved her fork. "Yay! One for the good guys!"

Bobby snorted. Dinah cleared her throat in meaningful fashion and Bobby winked at her and reapplied himself to his plate.

Bobby was black and bulky with muscle, a vet who'd lied about his age to go to war and who had come home a double amputee. He looked like Denzel in *The Mighty Quinn* and he had more attitude than Kanye West and Alec Baldwin combined and it was always turned up to nine. He'd come to the Park before Kate had come home, built the A-frame and the 212-foot tower out back that mounted a dozen dishes aimed at everything between the Park and Mars. He was the NOAA reporter for the Park which provided cover for the fact that he had no other visible means of support.

Dinah had come into the Park two years after Kate had returned, one of those cheechakos whose personal history stopped at the Beaver Creek border crossing. Twenty years younger and much whiter than Bobby, they had nonetheless taken one look at each other and never looked back. On one never to be forgotten day Kate had had the privilege of officiating at their wedding, acting as Bobby's best man, and delivering their now six-year-old child. Jim had vivid memories of the event, if only because he'd had to watch Jack toss Kate over his shoulder and disappear with her into the woods, not to be seen again until morning. It had hurt like a son of a bitch and he'd only been in lust with her then.

Dessert followed.

"What is this cake, Dinah?"

"You like it?"

"It might be the best cake I ever ate."

"Olive oil lemon cake," Dinah said, preening. "I tweaked a recipe I found online. Probably be better with fresh lemons, but it's not bad. I'll pack some up for you to take home tomorrow."

He smiled at her, giving her the full wattage. "I think I'm in love."

She blushed and knocked over her mug, and Bobby snorted again. "What's with you and this fix-it craze you've got going on?"

"You heard about the Topkoks?"

"Terminated by extreme volcanic prejudice. Who hasn't? So?"

"So he ran the only shop between Ahtna and Cordova. Where are the Park rats going to go to get anything fixed now?"

"I dunno. Fix it themselves maybe?" Bobby went over to the circular console that took up the center of the A-frame's main room. He sat down and flicked some switches, turned some knobs, donned a pair of headphones, and pulled the mike down in front of his face. "Park Air coming to you live and uncensored, hoping to offend as many listeners as possible in as short a time as possible. Your host Bobby the Bandit on your six here. You know what I saw down at Bingley's today? Cheese and onion flavored potato chips! What the fuck, people? Orange in chocolate was bad enough but now they're making pumpkin-flavored Cheerios and dill pickle-flavored mints!" His basso profundo voice dropped to a register that might vibrate the A-frame off its foundations. "They're putting fruit and vegetables and sriracha in beer now. In BEER. Heresy! Sacrilege! AbomiNAtion! This. Must. END. Are you with me, Park rats? Of course you are. That's why we're all going out to the Roadhouse this Saturday to sample the beer Bernie's been brewing up in the back room. That's right, we got our very own brew pub in the Park now. Draft beer on tap! That's me in line in front of you." Bobby pushed a button and turned a knob and Ed Sheeran and Justin Bieber rose up out of speakers to blight the room. Jim, once he recovered from the shock, was fully prepared to deliver ridicule in epic proportions, and was only forestalled when Katya bounced out center stage and started dancing with an abandon Queen Bey herself could only have envied. "Come on, Daddy! Dance with me!"

Daddy did. There were shoulder shrugs and hip pops and there might even have been a little robot going on there.

Later that evening, after Katya was in bed and Dinah was editing video footage for a Chevy Tahoe commercial, headphones on and lost in communion with the pixels, Jim and Bobby moved to the couch in front of the fireplace, sipping respectfully at a very fine single malt that Bobby said he'd bought at Costco in Ahtna. Jim was pretty sure he was lying but it had never been his policy to inquire too deeply into the source of all the excellent liquor he'd been served in Bobby's house over the years. "So," he said. "Sheeran and Bieber. Who's next, the Jonas Brothers?"

Unembarrassed and unrepentant, Bobby said, "Any song that gets my baby girl up and moving and grooving is okay by me."

"And this from the man who once refused to have any music in the house that predated CCR."

"I wasn't a father then."

"Fair enough. I'm telling Kate, though."

"You, sir," Bobby said without heat, "are a traitor to the man cave. Imma have to revoke your card." They drank in companionable silence for a few moments. "Those two kids."

"What about them?"

"You heard Van got them to talk a little?"

Vanessa, whose high school Spanish proved marginally better than Matt's, had spent some time with the two children that day, trying to tease out their story. It hadn't been easy, as the boy was angry at everyone and Anna left the talking to her brother. Van at least managed to find out their names, their mother's name, and the barest of outlines of the events that had led to their presence in the Park. After that the boy had closed his mouth except to eat. When Laurel had tried to take the girl to give her a bath, the boy had attacked her. After a fraught negotiation that had brought Vanessa back from Auntie Vi's, the boy had allowed Laurel to fill the bathtub and sit on the floor of the bathroom with her back to the tub while he bathed his sister and then himself. Laurel had found jeans and sweaters of more or less the right size but shoes were proving a more difficult task and for now the kids were wearing the sandals they'd arrived in.

"What's going to be done with them?" Bobby said.

"First we find their mom."

"You gonna let them send them back after that?"

Jim leaned his head back against the couch and contemplated the firelight flickering on the walls. "No," he said eventually. "No, I don't believe we are. Not if they don't want to go, and not if Kate has anything to say about it."

They both sipped again. It was like warm honey slipping down their throats, with just a touch of cloves to spice things up.

Bobby looked involuntarily over his shoulder. "Anyone ever touch Katya, I'd—"

"I know. And at that you'd be standing in line."

*They had been two days in the room and the four men and the one woman had been very kind to them. They had been brought meals on a tray, and when Anna woke up and screamed when she saw the strangers they left the room to let David calm her down so she could eat something. They brought in a phone that spoke Spanish and tried to talk to them but David pretended not to understand until they gave up and let them watch cartoon videos on it.*

*Yes, they were nice, but he didn't trust them. Well. He didn't trust anyone, really, except for himself, and Anna, who was too young and who had to trust him, and Mami, who was not here.*

*He wasn't so sure how much he could trust Mami anymore, if it came to that. It had been Mami's idea to go north because things would be better in* el norte *than in Tegucigalpa, and the bad men at the border who had taken Mami away and the Bad Man they had given David and Anna to had proved that was not the case. There was no better here. David was not a fool. He and Anna had been sold to the Bad Man, like empanadas on the street.*

No, el norte *was not a good place. For all David knew, there were men doing to Mami now what* los pandilleros *did before they left. And for all he knew, the people they were with now meant to do the same to David and Anna.*

*They had to leave. He didn't know where, but he had to find a place where they could hide until Mami answered her phone and could come get them. He knew from the television that there were ways of finding people with their phones. He didn't know how to do that but he would find out, and he and Anna would go to meet her wherever she was. And then the three of them would figure out what came next. If they had to go back to Tegucigalpa, so be it. They would find a better place to live and Mami would get a job and David would, too, and they would be together, and he would grow up to be a carpenter or an astronaut, and Anna could grow up to be a teacher like Mami. If they stayed in* el norte, *they would do the same. So long as they were all three together. It was all he asked for now.*

*He would need to learn English, though. Mami had tried to teach them on the way but they had been so tired and hungry and thirsty at the end of every day that they had learned little and most of that he had already forgotten. One of the men of this house had brought a book, a* diccionario, *with words in Spanish and English in columns next to each other. He recognized some of the words in Spanish but his attendance at school had suffered due to the bad things happening in the town and his reading skills were more suited to picture books. They brought those, too, one with a little girl in a blue dress walking to school across Africa, and another with frogs flying on leaves, and* The Cat in the Hat, *only in English, but he could sound out the words, some of them. He would take the books with them when they left.*

*He took out the Bad Man's phone and looked at it, wondering if he should try to call Mami again now or wait until they found somewhere else. He decided to save the battery and put it away without turning it on, and went to wake Anna.*

*After three days of warmth and food and three nights of uninterrupted sleep where no one touched them and a real bathroom with a toilet that flushed, Anna was fretful when he told her they had to go. She cried, a little, but she let him dress her. They had no coats so he pulled the blankets from both beds and folded them into a kind of serape. Anna looked like a tamale. She almost giggled when he told her so.*

*They waited until the house was still. He shouldered the garbage bag with the books and the leftovers from that night's dinner and slipped out the door no one had bothered to lock.*

# Eight

## FRIDAY, JANUARY 4
### *Niniltna*

JIM ROSE EARLY AND LEFT THE A-FRAME AS quietly as possible, arriving at the Riverside Café as Laurel Meganack was making her first latte of the day. She saw him and started on a large Americano without asking. The smell of baked goods perfumed the air. "What time did you get into work, Laurel?"

She gave him a tired smile. "Baker's hours are the worst. But the good news is that I've got biscuits, scones, cinnamon rolls, and plain cake donuts for you this morning."

"I'll take a cinnamon roll for here and one of each in a bag."

"Done." She handed him his drink and he sat in a booth at the back and looked out on Niniltna's main street as the caffeine kickstarted his day.

"Here you go." A plate with a cinnamon roll the circumference of the full moon landed in front of him, along with his Americano in a soup bowl with two handles on it. Laurel plopped down across from him and blew over the top of her own soup bowl. "Heard anything about those kids yet?"

He shook his head. "No. Kate's in Anchorage. She's going to sniff around, see what can be done in the way of finding the mom. This administration, though—" Even an Americano as good as Laurel's had a hard time washing away that taste from his mouth.

"Feds going to be involved?"

"It's a plane crash, so, yeah, I'm guessing the NTSB will be parachuting in shortly. Or whenever they decide they have the best chance of not being weathered in."

She was a homegrown beauty, was Laurel Meganack, with a come-hither sparkle in her eyes and a penchant for scoop-necked T-shirts that was probably responsible for the sale of gallons of coffee and thousands of cookies. At the moment, though, the sparkle was in abeyance. "And DFYS?"

He sighed. "Probably. I don't know. I hope not."

"Those kids have been through a lot, Jim. They shouldn't be manhandled into the system, it'll just wreck them more than they already are."

"No argument here."

"Isn't there anything we can do?" There were tears in her eyes.

"They have family, Laurel," he said gently. "A mom, at least."

"Where?" she said fiercely. "Where is she? How did she let this happen to her own children? If she can't take any better care of them than this, she don't deserve them!"

"We don't know the circumstances, Laurel," Jim said, still gently. "Let's not be too quick to judge before we do."

The doorbell tinkled and they looked around to see Matt Grosdidier step inside. He looked around, saw them, and his eyes narrowed. He marched across to the booth and slid in next to Laurel. "Hey, babe." He took a closer look. "Are you okay?" He kissed her and turned to give Jim a hard stare.

With true heroism Jim did not rise to the bait. "She's worried about the kids."

"We're all worried about the kids," Matt said, putting his arm around Laurel and pulling her in close. "It'll be okay, honey. We'll make it be okay." She leaned against him for a moment, her eyes closed, and then she sat up and nudged him with her hip. "Move. I'll bring you some coffee and a pastry."

Jim raised what was left of the cinnamon roll. "I can vouch for superbity of these."

"Superbity? Is that even a word?"

"If Shakespeare can make up words, so can I."

Matt laughed in spite of himself, and Laurel returned with another soup bowl and a roll. She nudged Matt down the bench and sat down again. "Jim," she said, "what do you think of Martin Shugak?"

The roll caught in his throat and he coughed to clear it. "Little whiplash going on here, but okay, I'll play. Martin Shugak? I had a lot to do with him professionally back in the day. Pretty penny-ante stuff, mostly B&E looking for money to buy a binge. He never got sentenced to much more than time served. He shot game out of season on the reg but I never caught him at it, and—" he shrugged "— he was hunting to eat, so I never got too excited about it."

She frowned. "He do drugs?"

"Maybe a little grass, but mostly it's all about the booze for Martin. He was never into distribution, he was strictly a consumer. So far as he showed up on my radar."

"Did he ever hurt anybody? Like, you know, physically?"

"What, you want me to grade him? As lowlife as Howie Katelnikoff? Not so low as, I don't know, I can't even think of a relevant comparison. Unless it was Martin himself."

"He says he wants to be a baker."

Jim paused with his soup bowl halfway to his mouth. "Martin Shugak wants to be a baker," he said slowly, testing the words on the air. "Didn't he just inherit a whole bunch of property? Like damn near the entire Kanuyaq Mine?"

"It's in court, and it's going to be in court for years to come. In the meantime, he says the last time he was away—" Laurel waggled her eyebrows "—he was assigned to the kitchen and there was an honest-to-God baker who was inside at the same time and he took Martin on as his apprentice. Martin said he really enjoyed it and he doesn't mind going to work at three a.m. And since —" She looked at Matt. She might have blushed a little.

Matt straightened and a proud grin split his face nearly in two. "And since we're getting married and we want to have kids, Laurel thinks bringing on another employee would be a good idea."

"You guys are getting married?" Laurel was definitely blushing now, and Jim stood up to lean over the table and give her a hearty smack on the cheek. He shook Matt's hand and sat back down again. "I hear the sound of hearts breaking all over the Park, but congratulations, both of you. When did this happen?"

Matt had his arm tight around Laurel's shoulders, as if he was afraid she might get away. "New Year's Day."

Right after they'd rescued the two kids out of the wreck in the middle of a blizzard. It wasn't a situation that in Jim's opinion inspired romance but then he was coming up on forty-four this year. And then he had an extremely unwelcome thought.

He wasn't entirely sure what Kate Shugak would call a romantic situation. But how would he know? Had he ever even brought her flowers? Had they ever gone out on Valentine's Day? On a date on any day? They'd never even gone to the dump to watch the bears. Although there was that time he and Mutt had dug her out of a dump she'd been tossed into, that had to count for something. He tried to remember if he'd ever given her a gift. There was that

Christmas when he'd given her a copy of Robert's "Rules of Order". There had been a pretty big reward for that that lived on in Technicolor in his memories to this day. Last Christmas—Jesus, that was just last month, how could he not... And her birthday, when was that? He knew a moment of panic and then with a tremendous sense of relief remembered that it was in October, October sixteenth. No, eighteenth. Fourteenth?

He looked across the table at the happy couple beaming at him. He had some remedial boyfriending to do in future or he was going to be so totally fucked.

"Why?" Matt said, bewildered, and Jim realized he'd said that last sentence out loud. "Nothing," he said. "So, you're going to hire on Martin Shugak at the Riverside, Laurel?"

"I'm thinking about it," she said cautiously. "I know he might not be the best risk, but I think he's trying, Jim. And I want to help him if I can."

"Martin Shugak, baker," Matt said. "Funny he learned that in jail. Do you think they teach home ec up at the high school anymore?"

"I don't know," Laurel said with a sigh. "Any more budget cuts and we might not even have a school to teach it in."

The bell jangled and Dulcey Kineen, her three brothers and two sisters, and all three Balluta brothers, Albert, Nathan, and Boris, trooped in. Laurel got up and helped them shove two tables together and got out pad and pencil to take their orders.

Matt went back to the clinic to see if his brothers had killed anybody while he was gone. Jim finished his coffee, left Laurel a lavish tip to start her trousseau off right, and went outside to where the sled was parked. He climbed on and turned the key and let the engine warm up for a minute, thinking. Still thinking, he idled down the road a bit and instead of continuing on to the homestead turned right to climb the hill past the trooper post (at which he managed to avoid looking directly) and the Niniltna Native Association building, and arrived at the school. It was a typical Bush school, a prefab shipped in parts and assembled on site, twenty-five years old at least and getting a little long in the tooth. The gym, built entirely on site of rebar-reinforced concrete, stood a little behind, connected by a covered walkway. School didn't start again until next week so it was quiet. He'd done his share of Career Days here so he knew the way to the principal's office. Mrs. Doogan was at her desk, and looked up when he rapped on the partially open door. "Jim! Hey."

"Valerie. Got a minute?"

"Do I ever." She threw down her pen and shoved away the stack of papers in front of her. She was a middle-aged woman with a wiry runner's build. She was, in fact, a marathoner who had successfully completed the Mount Marathon race half a dozen times without bleeding, an accomplishment in and of itself. She had light brown hair cut short in an unfussy style that needed no maintenance, pale, freckled skin and steady brown eyes that tolerated no nonsense. After over twenty years teaching in Niniltna, there wasn't much that could throw her and almost nothing that surprised her, kind of like a cop with that much time in the job. "Coffee?"

He shook his head. "I was just down at the Riverside."

She got up and took her mug over to the coffee maker sitting on the credenza. "Anything new on the crash?" He shook his head. "Kids okay?"

"As good as they can be. Vanessa has managed to communicate with them a little bit. We know their names now."

She returned to her desk and sat down. "If they need a Spanish-speaking counselor—"

He winced. "We're trying to keep their presence here on the down low, at least for the moment."

"Well. When there's need." She sipped coffee. "And otherwise? Life off the job good?" He smiled. She laughed. "I see that it is. Well, I can't say we don't miss you. They're closing down the post, did you hear?"

"Just a rumor, so far as I know."

She shrugged. "Maybe. If it's true, until they find someone to replace you it'll be Nick flying in from Tok again when there's trouble." She made a face. "When he can be bothered."

"Come on, Valerie. You know that isn't fair. He's got a lot of territory to cover, and he's only one guy. We need more troopers. We always have."

"And the governor and the legislature doesn't like paying

for public safety," she said with a sigh. "I know. They don't like paying for education, either. Even less now than they ever did before."

"How are you doing for enrollment these days?"

"Almost forty, counting K through twelve. Five in this year's graduating class, god willing and the creeks don't rise. We're lucky to be so far over the limit."

She was talking about the ten-student limit. When the student count dropped below that, the state shut the school down. After that the choices for Park parents were either home schooling or moving to Cordova or Ahtna. Or, horrors, Anchorage. It was the same story all over Alaska. Some villages with shrinking student enrollments advertised Outside for families with children to move in, all expenses paid. He remembered that morning's conversation with Laurel and Matt. "Do you still have a shop class?" he said. She laughed. It was enough of an answer. "How about home economics?"

She shook her head. "Not at the moment, but..." She eyed him speculatively. "I'm hoping I can swing a grant to bring both back."

"Oh yeah?"

"There's a foundation in Anchorage that has set aside funding for education in the Bush, and they actually contacted me about it. They say that even though we have a road we qualify."

"That sounds good." Something in her expression made him say, "Doesn't it?"

"It was nice not to have to go begging, I'll say that much."
She pursed her lips for a moment. "But it's the Bannister
Foundation."

"Erland Bannister's homemade charity?"

She nodded.

"Huh," he said, and realizing as soon as he said it how
woefully inadequate a response it was.

"How big a stink do you think she'd make if I applied
and we got the money?"

If Kate really was Erland's trustee, which according to
her profanity-laced phone call last night was not a sure
thing, it might be less stinky than Valerie was anticipating.
"No way am I putting words into her mouth, Valerie. Ask
her yourself. I would point out, however, that he tried to
kill her."

"More than once," she said dryly. "I am aware, as I am
also aware he served about three and a half minutes for his
crime. But…"

"What?"

She met his eyes. "Erland Bannister himself came to
talk to me about a grant application last fall. Flew in on
his fancy jet, marched into this office and sat right where
you're sitting now, and gave me to believe that all I had to
do was apply for the check to be written. I didn't trust him
or anything he said, it goes without saying, and after he left
I wanted to clean every surface he touched with Clorox and
steel wool. But I did go to his foundation's website. There's
a list of people and organizations the Bannister Foundation

has given to. I called a few of them. On the surface it looks legit."

He looked over her shoulder. A few scrub spruces and a stand of alders had been encouraged to form a dust-catching privacy screen between the school grounds and the airport, but the ground between fell away enough that the principal's office had a fine view of the full length of the Niniltna airstrip. "Did you see him fly in?"

She snorted. "I've had a front row seat to all the air traffic in and out of Niniltna, before and after Suulutaq geared up. It felt like Seatac for a while there. When the EPA called them on their bullshit EIS, traffic slowed down some, but since we got our all! new! and improved! governor it's kicked back up again."

"Not just George, then."

"Do you know, Jim, I'd never seen a private jet until they started the prep work for the Suulutaq Mine? Since then, they've been in and out several times a month. And the weird thing is, usually if there's one, there are two. On the ground at the same time. In Niniltna!" She shook her head. "I've lived here for almost twenty years and I'm used to small plane traffic. I think I'd notice it more if there weren't any. But we're not talking Cubs and Beavers or even George's Single Otter turbo. Starting to look like Scottsdale out there."

"The private jets," he said. "You didn't happen to notice any corporate logos?"

She shook her head.

"Tail numbers?"

"Most of them don't have any. I wondered about that a little. I thought the FAA required N numbers on every aircraft."

"They've probably got them, just small enough and tucked away somewhere so you can't see them."

"Sneaky."

"I'm guessing that's the idea."

She raised an eyebrow, but he didn't elaborate. "About this grant, Jim. I don't want to go to all the trouble of writing the grant application if she's going to thunder in here and give me her best We-are-most-seriously-displeased-Ekaterina impression. Run it by her, would you?"

Well, just goody. Nothing more romantic than floating a plan to bring more of Erland Bannister's money into the Park.

He'd almost made the door when his phone erupted into the Darth Vader theme. He took a deep breath, found an empty classroom, and closed the door behind him before he answered. "Hi, John."

John Barton, the Lord High Everything Else of the Alaska State Troopers and Jim's ex-boss, let a fulminating moment pass in which Jim was reminded irresistibly of Redoubt on the boil before a full-blown eruption. "Jesus CHRIST! When were you gonna call me about what you found at the wreck site YESTERDAY?"

"What's there to talk about, John? You asked me to assist you in an investigation. I did and George brought the results into town last night. I presume Brillo's boys met him at the airport and Brillo's got custody of the evidence."

"OF COURSE HE DOES! That's what REAL crime fighters DO!"

"Yes, and I'm not one anymore, John," Jim said with enough of an edge to remind Barton that he was bellowing at a private citizen and—a faint hope—moderate his tone.

A brief silence while Barton struggled with his self-control. It wasn't something that came naturally to him. "Do you think more of that shit is up there?"

By which Jim correctly guessed that Barton was talking about the Ziploc full of pills and not the missing half of the deceased. "To justify flying it in on a private jet, I'd say there is almost certain to be. A lot more. But it's buried in about fifty feet of snow and—" he looked out the window at the threatening gray sky "—my guess is about to accumulate more. Wait until spring."

"We can't just leave it up there, Jim. Christ, every fucking tweaker in the Park gets wind of this they'll be pointing their sleds and four-wheelers north by northeast and we'll spend the rest of the winter pulling THEIR asses outta the goddamn Quilaks."

Alaska had the same problem with opioids as every other state in the union and most of the rest of the world, and Jim had seen plenty of it in his early days on the job, especially in the Matsu Valley and down on the lower Kenai. Fentanyl was the uber example of the road to hell being paved with good intentions as it had originally been invented by a doctor to manage severe pain. Now it was the illegal narcotic of choice by users and dealers alike. It was fifty times more powerful than heroin and a hundred times more powerful than cocaine and at one time had commonly been mixed with both, often without the user's knowledge, which all too often ended in their deaths. Lately it was being sold more often and more profitably straight up, and was constantly being manufactured in new analogues in illegal pill mills in China, Mexico and most recently Canada. Every time the DEA identified a new strain, another version popped up on the market. It was like playing drug Whack-a-Mole and it was never a war they were going to win.

By now the drug's use was so widespread that communities were arming librarians and teachers and even grocery store clerks with naloxone because libraries and schools and stores were becoming the front lines of the overdose epidemic. He'd been ecstatic when they'd moved on from injectors to nasal spray, but in whatever form naloxone was the one tool a first responder had to maybe reverse an overdose.

Strangely enough, the Park had thus far been spared the worst of the opioid epidemic, which was one of many minor reasons he'd welcomed the opening of the trooper post in Niniltna. The Park had its share of substance abuse-inspired human misery, but most of it was caused by alcohol. Informed by his time in the northwest of the state, he had come to the conclusion that this was the benefit of having strong elders, beginning with Ekaterina Shugak who had led by example, and extending to the aunties and the board of the Niniltna Native Association. It might be the single most essential element for a healthy and relatively sane population.

There was also the Roadhouse, the one place within fifty miles where you could buy a legal beer, and where if you became visibly under the influence Bernie Koslowski would confiscate the keys to your truck or sled or ATV and toss your ass into one of the cabins he maintained out back of the bar. He knew the birthdays of everyone in the Park, too, and bounced the underage out the door as soon as they walked in. The moment he got to hear someone was pregnant, the Roadhouse stopped serving them. Bernie, the aunties, and the board of directors of the NNA worked separately but for the same ends. He only wished that law enforcement in every community in Alaska had that kind of backup. It sure helped ease the workload, and while alcohol abuse-related crime was as horrific to deal with as any other substance abuse-related crime, it was at least familiar and treatable. It was an advantage he'd rather have done without but it was an advantage, and one he hoped would extend to marijuana, which the state had voted to legalize for the second time. Keith Gette and Oscar Jimenez had invested in two new high tunnels and were starting a crop this summer, they said for export but there were enough ex-hippies in the Park to sell to right out of their front door without the added expense of packaging and shipping. Jim expected the NNA and the aunties to have a say there as well. Bernie, he knew, was already worried about the competition.

John was right, though. The moment Howie Katelnikof heard the news he'd be en route, and he even knew the way into Canyon Hot Springs. Worse, he would probably bring Willard Shugak with him to do all the grunt work, and Jim shuddered to think what Kate would have to say about that. "How much manpower and money are you willing to dedicate to this recovery?" he said. "Keeping in mind that it's January, and it's at ten thousand feet, and the weather is crap and about to get crappier." He paused. Barton said nothing. "This isn't tenable, John. You're gonna get somebody killed."

"Then what the FUCK do YOU suggest, Chopin?"

"Leave it till spring. Hire George Perry to do regular flyovers, weather permitting. Hell, you could send up a drone to take pictures whenever it's clear. As soon as it warms up and the snow starts to melt and the wreck starts showing through the snow you can send in a team. In the meantime we keep quiet about it."

Barton breathed heavily over the satellite. "You're putting a hell of a lot of faith in our ability to do that."

Jim sighed. "There are no good solutions here, John, just bad and less bad. Even if someone does hear about the wreck and even if they do go up to check it out, they won't be able to find it. Even if they did, how many dealers and users do you know who like to work that hard?"

On his way out of town he obeyed another impulse and pulled into the driveway of Herbie Topkok's shop. It was a warehouse-sized building, not quite as big as his hangar. There was a two-story bay with an automatic door, big enough to hold a boat on a trailer and keep it and Herbie out of the weather while Herbie worked on it. The other half consisted of two smaller, single-story bays, both big enough to park Harvey Meganack's Lincoln Navigator with room to spare, and any number of Subarus of any model, as it would need to do, Subaru being the Alaska state car.

He sat on his sled, looking at the shop and the enormous house next to it. In his youth Herbie had been near enough high boat for ten years running in Prince William Sound. He'd always been frugal and he'd saved enough to build this shop and the house next to it, which was big enough to hold Herbie, his wife, and their six or seven kids. It was one of the few houses in the Park to which Jim had never been called, so it must have been a happy and well-run house. He liked to think there was at least one of them in the Park but police work inspired a jaundiced view in its practitioners and there were probably more. His own, for example. He wondered how Kate was faring in Anchorage, and didn't even try to convince himself that he didn't miss her. Lo, how the mighty have fallen.

Shop and house both were shut up tight, with no lights showing in either. There was no for sale sign out front but if

Bobby and George were right and the kids weren't coming back it was only a matter of time. He wondered how much they'd ask for it.

What he really needed to do was go to Ahtna and buy a commercial-size snow blower, so as to blast the snow berm in front of his hangar to infinity and beyond. Then he could taxi his own damn plane right out of his own damn hangar and fly to Anchorage to ask his own damn questions of his own damn woman his own damn self.

His own damn woman. Heh. There might have been a time when all his hair would have fallen out at the very thought.

He pointed the sled toward home and hit the throttle. He was going to stop at Mandy and Chick's on the way. They had a snow blower.

"*Sir?*"

"*Yes, Jared? Do you bring good news to my door? Has the entire cargo been recovered by our own people?*" *The barbed sarcasm was unmistakable.*

"*I'm afraid not, sir. I'm very much afraid that none of the product will be recoverable.*"

"*The whole shipment was lost? You're hesitating, Jared. It's never good news when you hesitate.*"

"*No, sir. One of our sources tells us one of the bags of product may have found its way into the hands of the authorities.*"

"*One of the duffels or one of the individual bags?*"

"*One of the individual bags, sir.*"

*A sigh.* "*So you're telling me that not only have we lost two weeks' worth of product, screwed our distributors, and fucked this month's P&L, but we've now also drawn the attention of the feds to our operation?*"

"*Just the locals so far, sir.*" *A clearing of throat.* "*And by locals, I mean—*"

"*Oh, fuck me sideways. Her again?*"

"*I'm afraid the medical examiner called her in to consult, sir. But as of my last update, federal law enforcement has yet to be alerted."*

*"It doesn't matter. They'll call in the marines soon enough. Any news on that phone?"*

*"No, sir."*

*A silence that seemed to build in menace, followed by a long, measured inhale and exhale. "What's the problem?"*

*"There seems to be some issue with accessibility to its location."*

*"Jared."*

*"Sir."*

*"Tell them that when I told them to find that fucking phone, I meant for them to find it or don't bother coming home. And that I don't sound like I'm joking."*

*"Yes, sir."*

*"Because I'm not."*

*"No, sir."*

*"What about that lawyer, the one in Anchorage, what's his name..."*

*"Eugene Hutchinson, sir?"*

*"Yeah, him. What does he have to say?"*

*"He says he is unable to assist us in this matter, sir."*

*"Does he? Does he, indeed?" A pause. "How well informed is Hutchinson on our Alaska operation?"*

*A clearing of throat. "I suspect that he may have been at least partially read in, sir."*

*A snort. "'Partially read in.' Stop sounding like a Harvard grad, Jared."*

"*You're a Harvard graduate, too, sir.*"

"*And don't be cheeky.*"

"*No, sir.*"

"*It may be that Lawyer Hutchinson poses a risk to our business model.*"

"*A small one, sir.*"

"*But he may pose a risk nonetheless, however small. And as you may have noticed, Jared, I am severely risk-averse.*"

"*Are you thinking of shutting down the operation entirely, sir?*"

*A silence.* "*I don't think it has quite reached the level of being a liability, not yet. I'd hate to abandon it now, given how lucrative it has grown over the last seven years.*"

"*Eight, sir.*"

"*Eight, then. And the most important part of it is for the moment at least in reliable hands. We may need to keep our heads down for a bit, until something happens to divert official attention elsewhere. Something always does. At which time we could return to business as usual.*"

"*Perhaps Hutchinson could be brought to see it that way?*"

"*Perhaps, perhaps not. Since he has not been forthcoming with aid in this trying time, I am inclined to think not. It's a risk I'm not willing to take, Jared.*"

"*Yes, sir.*"

"*I assume we still have local talent on tap?*"

"*Indeed, sir.*"

"*See to it.*"

*"Yes, sir."*

*A pause. "Perhaps expand their brief to include solving our other problem while they're at it."*

*"Yes, sir."*

*"And, Jared?"*

*"Sir?"*

*"With discretion."*

*"Of course, sir."*

# Nine

FRIDAY, JANUARY 4
*Anchorage*

THE PING OF A TEXT WOKE KATE THE NEXT morning. She fumbled for her phone and saw that it was from Kurt.

Arr Anc fm Fai Ravn 9a. Pick me up?

Yawning, she texted back a thumbs up, and went downstairs to put on the coffee. Showered, dressed, and go cup in hand, she climbed into the Subaru with Mutt and pulled out of the driveway with the neighbor looking on. Kate never saw anyone else but him on her visits into town, and he did seem to be taking up permanent residence on his doorstep wearing the same ratty brown bathrobe.

"Maybe we should get him a new bathrobe for next Christmas," she said. "I mean, if he's going to stand around on the doorstep morning, noon, and night, he could dress a little better, you know?"

Mutt looked skeptical but kept her reservations to herself.

They arrived at the curb at five minutes to nine. There was very little other traffic and no airport officers in sight. "Shall we risk it?"

They got out and went into the terminal, walking down to the Ravn gates. The Fairbanks flight was a half an hour late, of course, so Kate found a seat and sipped her coffee, Mutt sitting next to her, ears up, eyes alert, ready to rock.

A flight for Kodiak boarded while they waited, the passengers mostly young and white, fishermen, Fish and Game, a lot of Coasties since their big base was there. By contrast a flight for St. Mary's was almost entirely Inupiaq, old men, young women, every one with a baby, and mature women with sharp, knowing eyes and a no-bullshit demeanor who looked a lot like aunties to Kate. The passengers for Homer included a lot of gray-haired couples, single women, and one couple who were fighting in whispers that were getting progressively louder as they went out the door. Kate didn't envy their fellow passengers, but she was kind of admiring all the same. It took a lot of energy to work up that much rage that early in the morning. A flight full of oil platform workers left for Kenai, and another for Valdez full of the next shift at the OCC at the Valdez Marine Terminal, where the TransAlaska Pipeline ended and the oil was loaded onto tankers. Only two tankers a day now, Kate remembered hearing, where there used to be four. No wonder the oil companies were hot to punch holes in ANWR and no wonder the governor was so hot to let them.

A couple of rows over sat a tall skinny white guy wearing a cowboy hat with a paper crown from Burger King over it. He had on an NRA T-shirt and skinny jeans held up by a wide leather belt and an enormous brass buckle in the shape of a grizzly bear, but what was most remarkable was that he had a snake wrapped around his waist with its head lying on his shoulder. Every now and then the snake would open his mouth and tickle the guy's cheek with a forked tongue. There was no one within ten seats of him. Mutt, catching sight of this abomination, looked first disbelieving and then disgusted. Her ears flattened and her eyes narrowed and she started up her growl. It contained less than the usual amount of menace but it was clear she disapproved.

It did not go unnoticed. A gate agent, very young, approached and said timidly, "Your dog is alarming the other passengers, ma'am."

"My dog is alarming the other passengers? What about that guy's snake?"

"It is a fully certified comfort animal, ma'am. Please, could you get her to stop growling? Otherwise I will have to call security."

A comfort snake. Kate was so very grateful that she wasn't flying anywhere that day. They were saved by the arrival of the Fairbanks flight. Kurt was the third person through the door. "Got baggage?" Kate said.

He held up a small duffel in reply. He looked like he hadn't slept.

"Great, I'm parked at the curb. Let's go see if Homeland Security has deemed us a credible threat."

"Is that a snake?" Kurt said.

"The gate agent informs me that it's a fully certified comfort animal," Kate said.

"What the fuck?"

Humanity's cry. "To quote the late, great Dick Francis, life keeps getting steadily weirder."

"Never heard of the guy but he got that right."

At the curb there were still no guards visible, bad for the fight against terrorism but good for points on Kate's driver's license. They climbed in and headed off. "What were you doing in Fairbanks?" she said.

"Have you had breakfast?" he said.

"No."

"I'm starving."

They drove to Jackie's in Spenard and it wasn't until they were both nearly through their orders of fried spam and eggs and rice and Kurt was on his third cup of coffee that he decided to share. "That thumb drive you dropped off yesterday."

"Yeah?"

"You said you wanted me to put it on a new laptop, one not connected with our network."

"Yeah. I was afraid Jane might have loaded some malware on it. No evidence other than she doesn't like me a whole lot."

"Noted." He drained his mug and looked around for the server, who was there in a gratifying instant and smiled seductively at him as she poured. Good luck with that, Kate thought, Agrifina Fancyboy has you totally outclassed. Well, Agrifina Fancyboy had pretty much every other female on the planet totally outclassed, Kate included. "You made me nervous enough that I wanted Tyler to handle this one personally, and I didn't want to put the thumb drive in the mail so I carried it up to him yesterday."

"Tyler's your nerd? I didn't know he lived in Fairbanks."

"Our nerd now, I hired him on full time." He cocked an eyebrow, waiting on her reaction, as she was his initial and only investor as well as his silent partner in Pletnikof Investigations.

Kate was unperturbed. "The last time I looked at our financials we've got more than enough revenue to support another full-time employee, and I've seen what he can do, so excellent. I assume Agrifina is on board?" He nodded. "He moving down here?"

"As soon as he can find a house with a basement he can move into. Nerds only flourish in the dark." He was only half kidding.

"So what did he say about what was on the thumb drive?"

"First of all, there's no malware, and he dug all the way down to the bottom of every last zero and one to make sure. Then, because he's suspicious like that, he loaded it on to a laptop—" He dug into his duffel and produced it, a flat black square about one foot by two. "He has a stack of them for just this kind of job, I think he buys them a dozen at a time on Amazon. He wipes them clean of everything except the OS and in some extreme cases I think he even writes one of his own." He flipped it open, waited for the desktop to come up, and clicked on the only folder on it. The Bannister Foundation logo came up, their name in white Helvetica on a dark blue background with the gold stars of the Big Dipper fading in behind.

Kate snorted. "What was he going for, being confused with the state of Alaska?"

"When you have no legitimacy and no credibility and no track record you borrow it wherever you can. Okay." Kurt looked across the table at her. "Brace yourself. You haven't looked into the Bannister Foundation at all, correct?"

"I left my laptop at home, and the battery on my phone's dying, so no."

"So you wouldn't even know who's on their board of directors?"

A small, hard ball of apprehension was forming in the pit of Kate's stomach. "No."

"Well, don't shoot the messenger, okay?" He click on the menu, scrolled down to Who We Are, and clicked on it.

Three rows of four photographs per row, each with a brief bio beneath it. She went through it methodically.

Erland had done a good job of populating his board with movers and shakers and star power, the latter as exemplified in the person of Gabe McGuire, a Hollywood A-lister Kate had met a year ago at the same time she had helped uncover the embezzlement of the Hardin Trust. If she recalled correctly, Erland had had a piece of McGuire's FBO in Newenham, and she'd heard a rumor that Erland had been starting an Alaska production company in partnership with McGuire. Also looking smiley if less glamorous in their headshots were the president of RPetCo Alaska, two bankers, the senior partner of a law firm specializing in corporate law, the managing director of North Star Investments, two vice-presidents of Native regional corporations, and two educators. One of them was the chancellor of the University of Alaska who, given the current governor's propensity for defunding education, might be out of a job before long. Kate wondered how long he'd be welcome on the Bannister Foundation board afterward.

The eleventh board member—

"Are you fucking kidding me?" Heads turned around the restaurant to seek out the potty mouth and give her simultaneous death glares. And that was before she saw the second name farther down the list.

"Keep it down, Shugak, I have to live here," Kurt said.

She took a deep, calming breath. "So I think my day just rearranged itself."

"Yeah, well, we're not done digging into the database. I have to say that on the surface it looks pretty legit. They're incorporated in the state of Alaska, they've got their bylaws posted right there on their website, their nonprofit status checks out. Records show money coming in from donors and going out to schools, nonprofit organizations and other worthy causes."

"Dig deeper."

"On it."

Kate dropped Kurt at the office and drove south on Minnesota to take the exit for 100th Avenue. There lived her cousin, Axenia Shugak Mathisen with her husband, lawyer Lew, who was also a lobbyist for the Suulutaq Mine, and their two sons. Axenia, whose chief ambition in life as a screwed-up teen had been to get out of the Park, now returned at least four times a year as a member of the board of directors of the Niniltna Native Association. This last was at Kate's suggestion and direct machinations, yet another sin in a litany of egregious offenses for which Axenia would never forgive her.

Transplanted into the Park the house would have been called palatial. In comparison to some found on the Hillside in Anchorage, it was merely a McMansion, with one more bathroom than bedrooms and an open plan first floor in which one only needed a bullhorn to be heard between kitchen and living room. Axenia opened the door dressed in yoga pants and a Raven Corporation T-shirt, her long black hair up in a ponytail that reached her waist and absolutely no expression on her face whatsoever when she saw who was waiting on her doorstep. "Kate."

"Axenia."

They did look a little separated at birth, Kate had to admit, which might have been part of the problem. They were both short. They both had thick black hair, although Kate wore hers in a pixie cut maintained by Dinah Clark, which meant any resemblance to Anne Hathaway's was purely accidental. They both had high, flat cheekbones clad in skin a natural pale gold that bronzed under the summer sun. Axenia's eyes were brown; Kate's were an indeterminate hazel that changed with her mood, what she wore, the weather, and if Axenia wasn't quite a round eye Kate's epicanthic fold was more strongly pronounced. Kate's mouth was wider and fuller, but Axenia's thinner lips could always be attributed to attitude, not nature, especially when in the presence of her cousin.

"I didn't know you were in town."

"Could I talk to you?"

"I was just about to go out—"

"This will only take a few minutes." Kate stepped forward and Axenia perforce stepped back. "Kids around?"

"Daycare. What do you want, Kate?"

Kate removed the door from Axenia's reluctant hand and shut it firmly, leaving them standing in the foyer. "Marble tiles?" she said, looking down. "Those are new. Ritzy."

"What do you want, Kate?" Axenia said again.

So much for small talk. "I want to know why you are on the board of directors for the Bannister Foundation."

Just the tiniest flush of color washed over Axenia's cheeks. There might also have been the slightest possible air of... not guilt, that would be expecting too much. But consciousness, certainly. "I am on several boards," Axenia said.

"But you are aware of the one I am referring to nonetheless," Kate said. "How did you come to be on it?"

"I don't really think that's any of your business," Axenia said, and reached for the doorknob.

Kate shut the door a little more firmly the second time. "Oh but I think that it is. Given that Erland Bannister tried to kill me more than once, I think it's definitely my business. Did he personally invite you to be on his board?"

Axenia huffed out a breath and crossed her arms, the first sign of defensiveness Kate had seen from her in years. Whether she'd ever heard of Disraeli or not, her marriage and lifestyle in Anchorage had transformed Axenia into a "Never apologize, never explain" acolyte.

"Well?" Kate said.

"Yes, he did. What of it?"

Kate let her amazement show. "What of it? You didn't think that a guy I put in jail for murder who got out on a technicality invented by a bought judge didn't have an ax to grind in asking my cousin to be on his board?"

"Maybe he wanted to atone for his bad actions, Kate, did you ever think of that? Maybe he was looking for a little redemption, a way to give back."

"Or maybe he was looking for a way to get my cousin involved in something criminal as a backhanded way to get even with me. Whose idea was it to use your maiden name as a member of the Bannister board?" She saw the answer in Axenia's eyes. "Yeah, pretty much a given that Erland would have loved seeing the Shugak name on his board."

"Everything's not always about you, Kate."

"I'm well aware, Axenia," Kate said, her voice hardening. "This would have had everything to do with having Ekaterina Shugak's name on his board, however."

Axenia flushed. "Have you looked at all the things we've funded? For a young charitable foundation we have made a considerable impact. For the better."

"You're starting to sound like a Hallmark ad. What do you get for being on the Bannister Foundation board?"

"We meet every three months in a different location," Axenia said stiffly. "We're allowed to bring our spouses and children with us. The foundation picks up all expenses."

"Oh please, let me guess. Hawaii? Mazatlan? Turks and Caicos? Jesus, Axenia, did you even think before you drank the Kool-Aid he was passing around?"

There were definite spots of color flying in Axenia's

cheeks now. "I remember what Emaa said if you don't, Kate."

Kate's eyes narrowed. "Oh, this should be good."

"She said you had to forgive people when they were truly sorry."

It took Kate a moment to recover her power of speech. "Did you just say that out loud?"

"You can leave anytime, Kate."

"Erland Bannister was never sorry for anything he did in his life, Axenia."

"And you would know this, how? I'm the one he came to, Kate, not you."

"And there would be a reason for that, Axenia. So he told you he was sorry for trying to kill me, did he? Did he tell you he was sorry for killing his father, too?"

Axenia actually gasped.

"That's right, Erland killed his own father and let Old Sam believe he did it for the rest of his life. So far as I can tell, Erland never lost a moment's sleep over it."

"That's a lie! You made that up!"

"Axenia..." Kate sighed and looked at the ceiling. "I would ask you, for the sake of your sons and for that matter for your own sake, that you be a little more cautious in future of Greeks bearing gifts. Because that horse will split open and its contents will eat you alive, every time."

Axenia reached for the door again and this time Kate didn't stop her. On the doorstep she turned and flattened a palm against the door, preventing Axenia from closing it. "Erland named me his trustee. Did you know?"

For just a moment Axenia looked startled out of her anger and resentment. "No. I didn't know that. I don't think anyone on the board knew."

"You might ask yourself why Erland did that. It wasn't for love of me, or you, or Alaska, that I promise you."

Her phone rang as she turned onto Diamond, and she pulled into the first available parking lot to answer it. It was an unknown number. "I hate answering unknown numbers," she said to Mutt. "What?' she said into the phone.

"You sound very, ah, suspicious, Ms. Shugak."

"I know that 'ah'," she said, leaning back in her seat. "What can I do for you, Special Agent Mason?"

A smothered chuckle. "Refreshingly to the, ah, point, as always, Ms. Shugak. Are you still in town?"

"How did you know I was to begin with?"

"The medical examiner might have, ah, mentioned it."

She was silent for a moment. "You're here because of Gary Curley."

A noncommittal grunt.

"Are you telling me Curley's activities went interstate after I left the DA's office? Is that why the FBI is calling me?"

"Could you perhaps make time to, ah, visit the local FBI office, Ms. Shugak? I believe you know our location. I'll tell them to expect you."

Fifteen minutes later she walked into Special Agent Mason's office. There was no insignia on the door and the decor was the *ne plus ultra* in anonymity, like Erland's only much lower end. Special Agent James G. Mason appeared to pursue that anonymity in his own personal appearance as well. His hair and suit were both regulation cut, as was his skinny tie and Rockport dress shoes. A pair of rimless glasses slid continuously down his nose and was as continuously being pushed back up with a bony forefinger. It was a habit Kate had noticed before and one that she was certain was meant to distract from the sharp intelligence in his gray eyes. "How's Jo?" she said.

"In Shishmaref, as I understand it," he said without missing a beat, "and after that Kivalina, St. Mary's, and Barrow. As I understand it she's writing a story on how climate change is hitting northwest Alaska first and hardest." He directed his gaze at Mutt. "Hey, Mutt. We met in Adak, remember?"

Mutt took her cue from Kate and looked wary.

"Please, both of you, have a seat." He folded his hands across his non-existent belly and did his best to look benign, but neither of the women across the desk from him was fooled. "Mr., ah, Brillo told me that he had called you in to view Mr. Curley's remains."

"I believe he wanted me to confirm Curley's identity. Curley not having any family."

He smiled briefly. "I don't question his decision, Ms. Shugak, and in fact I am, ah, grateful that it put you on my radar again. So to speak. I understand you investigated Curley for child abuse back in the day."

Her mouth twisted briefly into an ugly line. "He's the reason I was hired as an investigator for the DA. The cops had been trying to bring charges against him for years and never been able to make them stick. The DA at the time got a wild hair that if he hired the department's own investigator and tasked them to go over the evidence that the investigator might find something the cops had missed. I couldn't but they brought me on permanent anyway."

"You were never able to make the case?"

Kate swallowed hard to repress the old familiar nausea and hoped Mason hadn't noticed. Mutt had, and she leaned into Kate's side, a warm, solid, reassuring weight. "He'd pay parents to let their kids live with him, no questions asked. He was essentially Alaska's white, no-talent answer to Michael Jackson."

"The kids?"

"They were always so young. Some of them barely in kindergarten. They were never going to make the best witnesses. And the parents always stayed bought."

"And always, ah, children of color."

"Oh, yes." A low growl began to rumble out of the very back of Mutt's throat, and Kate took a deep breath and let it out slowly. The rumble subsided but it did not go entirely away. "Alaska Native children were particularly at risk. Especially when Curley's Asian... providers failed him."

Mason, tactfully, let a few minutes pass before he spoke again. "What was his history?"

"He was from California originally, the Bay area. He invested in some dot-com thing before they were a thing, and it was just Alaska's bad luck he decided to take his money and come north." She hesitated. "It happens a lot. Assholes like Curley look at Alaska and see how far away everything is from everything else. Especially the authorities."

"Like Father Smith," he said, watching her.

"Exactly like Father Smith. They figure they can do whatever they want to their families and no one will ever know. And a lot of the time they're right. At any rate, we failed to nail Curley." I failed, she thought.

"You are aware that he was found with a wholesale quantity of fentanyl tablets?"

"Brillo showed me. He ID'd them as fentanyl?"

"He did. Homemade."

She was silent for a moment, thinking. "If Curley was importing them on his jet there are probably a lot more of those pills sitting around on the mountain."

"Undoubtedly."

"At present buried under a winter's worth of snow, but still."

"But still," Mason said.

She looked at him. "Not that I'm not just delighted to see you and all, but why am I here?"

He stood up and opened the drawer of the desk, from which he took his sidearm. He holstered it. "We have obtained a warrant to search Mr. Curley's house."

Kate narrowed her eyes. "Was he transporting those drugs across state lines?" Was Curley, she thought, transporting them across the international border?

Mason did imperturbable well. "Given your, ah, familiarity with his case, I thought perhaps you might like to accompany us. In a strictly advisory capacity, of course."

In spite of every effort, Kate had never managed to achieve entry into Curley's house. "Why, yes," she said. "I believe I would."

If Axenia's house was a McMansion, Curley's was the bastard offspring of a Swiss chalet and the Disney castle. There were turrets, two of them, and both had arrow slits, no doubt designed for defense in the event of an attack by Genghis Khan. The exterior was faced with stone or some kind of material made to look like it. The tops of the walls were crenelated like battlements and the front door was a massive arch of some dark-stained wood with wrought iron hinges. "Where's the moat?" Kate said.

Curley's surviving pocket had not included a key so they used a battering ram. The door was so solidly constructed that they had to call for additional help and a bigger ram. While waiting for it to arrive, Kate went around to the side—the back was actually built into the mountainside—and found the side door, which was easily breached with the smaller ram.

The inside reeked of too much money and too little taste. The furniture was all white leather, overstuffed in the living areas and suspended from chrome in the dining area. There was a wood-burning fireplace in nearly every room but the bathrooms, of which there were many, including a half-bath just inside each exterior door, of which they found four, and Kate wasn't entirely certain that was the end of it. The air was toasty warm. She saw no vents, and on a hunch bent over to place her hand flat on the floor (marble downstairs, some kind of distressed wood planking upstairs). "Radiant heat," she said in answer to Mason's questioning look. She looked up at the twelve-foot ceilings. "I wonder what the heating bill looks like."

Mutt's toenails ticky-tacked across the floor as she sniffed the corners. Someone called Mason's name and he went upstairs a broad, wooden staircase suitable only for someone in a crown or a crinoline. Kate and Mutt nosed around downstairs until she heard Mason call her name.

He was in one of the turrets, a single, round room painted a pale pink and decorated with ruffles and bows. A canopied bed sat against one wall, equidistant from a free-standing wardrobe, a schoolroom desk with attached chair, and a seating area of child-sized chairs grouped around a television mounted on the wall. The only windows were the arrow slits they'd seen from outside, filled with glass inserts that didn't open. The door had a lock on the outside but not the inside.

"And this." Mason led the way down a hallway to the opposite turret, where a similar room was painted in pale blue and decorated by Woody from *Toy Story*.

Kate thought of the two children asleep in the clinic in Niniltna, and felt the bile building at the back of her throat.

"How old were the two children, ah, recovered from the wreck?" Mason said, picking up her thoughts.

She took a deep breath. This was the first time he'd mentioned the children, and there went her hope that word of them had not made it out of the Park. "The boy, kindergarten or first grade, maybe? The girl a year or so younger. Although they're enough alike to be twins."

"There's nothing in his office," someone said from the doorway. "No laptop, no pad, no phone. I had a look around and I don't see a mailbox outside, so his snail mail went somewhere else. No landline that I can see."

"I saw a dish on the roof," Kate said.

Mason nodded at the other agent. "Find out who his ISP was."

The head vanished. Mason looked at her. "Any other ideas?"

"No way did this guy clean his own house."

"A housekeeper? Good, ah, call. We'll check."

"I didn't see any near neighbors but it's a long and winding road. Maybe a canvass of the area?"

He sighed but nodded.

She jerked her head. "Let me show you something I found downstairs."

There was a walk-in pantry at the back of the kitchen. Three walls were given over to foodstuffs, dry, canned and bagged, and a lot of that candy, sugared cereals, and cookies. But one shelf was floor to ceiling Ziploc bags, most them quart and sandwich sized. Stacked on the floor below the shelf was a pile of put-together mailing boxes of different sizes. She picked up one and displayed it. "Small flat rate box. Costs seven, eight bucks to ship, depending on how much insurance you buy. Their motto is 'If It Fits, It Ships.'"

"Bring it here wholesale, send it out, ah, retail," Mason said.

"I thought most of the fentanyl coming into the US was coming from China," Kate said.

"It is, but the Mexican cartels noticed how much money the Chinese are making at it and have begun to ramp up production and move product themselves."

"Curley didn't fly the stuff in from China."

"No. And before you say it, probably not Mexico, either."

"So we have two choices, Russia or Canada, and while I'd expect anything of Putin I have a hard time believing that a private jet could just waltz back and forth across the

Bering Strait without either the USAF or the Russian Air Force noticing."

"Agreed."

"So. Canada?"

"It is such a, ah, short hop over the mountains," he said apologetically.

"And by jet an equally short hop from Anchorage to Niniltna." She turned to look at Mason. "Have you had reports of illegal fentanyl production in Canada, Agent Mason?"

"They're called pill mills, Ms. Shugak. And yes, unfortunately. We have."

"So they make the stuff in pill mills in the YT or BC, load them on a plane and ferry them to Niniltna. Where Curley picked them up and brought them here, broke them down into retail amounts, and passed them on to... dealers?"

"That is our, ah, working hypothesis."

"It was a gallon bag they picked up at the site."

"Yes."

"Say there are, I don't know, twenty more just like it. How many doses in a gallon bag?"

He shrugged. "Say, ten thousand. We haven't gotten around to counting them yet."

Kate blew out a breath. "Yeah. Okay, then. Twenty gallon bags times ten thousand tablets each equals two hundred thousand doses." She looked up. "How often do your people think Curley was bringing in shipments?"

His answer was prompt and unequivocating. "At least twice monthly."

"So, four hundred thousand doses total. There are only about 740,000 people in Alaska." She gave Mason a considering look. "Some of it was for local customers, okay, but he was shipping the bulk of it overseas, wasn't he?"

"We believe so," he said. "Russia, Japan, and South Korea have been reporting a large uptick in street sales of imported fentanyl and oxycontin. They think it's being routed through the US. They hadn't zeroed in on Alaska quite yet." He hesitated. "And we believe it will have been more than twenty. Many more."

She crossed her arms and frowned at the floor. "I have to say, this seems awfully front line for someone like Curley. Mostly those guys don't want to get their hands dirty."

"Depended on how much money he needed how fast."

"He was loaded." She raised an eyebrow. "Wasn't he?"

"He used to be. Not so much, ah, now. He took a beating in the market downturn in oh-eight and never recovered."

Her lip curled. "And he had such expensive habits."

"Yes."

"But it's over now, right?" she said, knowing full well it wasn't.

"Until whoever is running this operation finds someone to take his place. Far too profitable to give it up without a fight. Although I don't imagine there are that many as suitable for this kind of work. Broke, a big house to maintain, money to buy, ah, sex slaves."

Kate tried not to flinch at the last two words.

"Boss?"

They looked up to see an agent beckoning, and followed him to a room in the back on the ground floor. An office with a desk, a printer, a filing cabinet containing mostly personal papers to do with Curley's taxes, living expenses, and mortgage, and on its own table, a Safescan bill counter.

Mason was admiring. "Top of the line, with a thermal printer so he'd have a hard copy to include as the shipping manifest." He looked at Kate. "That's always the problem with large drug trafficking operations. Handling the money."

Stacked beneath the table were more USPS flat rate boxes, along with a box full of rolls of mailing tape, also USPS brand. "Well. At least some department of the federal government was making money off this guy."

"I wonder how he handled postage."

Kate thought. "Be easy enough to set up a Click-N-Ship account in a fictitious name, linked to a PO box and a credit card or a PayPal account in the same name." She nodded at the printer. "Create the postage online, print it out, tape it on, drop the package off at the post office. Probably rotate the drop-offs through different post offices just to be on the safe side."

"Almost foolproof."

Mason walked out past the kitchen into the vast acreage of the living area and paused at the window. She came up behind him. It was a landscape of dull white, lead, and slate all the way across to Susitna, land, sea, and sky. On the right the mountains made an arc and on the face of one was the three hundred foot-wide star made of 350 60-watt light bulbs, lit from the Friday after Thanksgiving and which remained lit until the last Iditarod musher crossed beneath the burlwood arch in Nome in mid-March. Kate had never been quite this close to it, and until today she would have said it was one of the things she loved about Anchorage.

She stirred. "All this is very interesting, not to say alarming, Agent Mason. Why am I here?"

Mason folded his arms and contemplated the toes of his shoes for a moment. "The wreck happened in your backyard, and evidence recovered from it led directly to our presence here." He met her eyes. "If any of this speculation is correct, Niniltna may have been the transfer point in the supply chain, and you are best placed to find any witnesses to events that may or may not support our hypothesis."

Much as the vision of FBI agents en masse traipsing around the Park in their suits and Rockports provided her with no end of internal enjoyment, she had to acknowledge his point. "Please be specific, Agent Mason. Are you hiring me to use my entree into the Park to find said witnesses?"

"What are your fees?" She told him and he didn't blink. "I've been allocated some, ah, discretionary funding. As of today you're hired as a consultant—" he held up a cautionary finger "—specifically as pertains to this investigation only, Ms. Shugak."

"Understood," she said, blandly and, for the moment at least, truthfully. "I'm Kate, by the way."

"Gerry," he said. "The G is for Gerald."

They shook on it.

They were getting into the Subaru when her phone rang. It was Jim, and just the sight of his name on her screen gave her a pleasurable thrill. She shook her head and answered. "Hey."

"Hey yourself. Where the hell are you?"

She looked up at Curley's house. "Camelot. With a side of the Inferno."

"I beg your pardon?"

"I'll explain later. What's up?"

"Later is sooner than you think, babe. I'm on my way into town."

"Oh?" She sternly repressed any tendency to squeal with delight. Mutt would only make fun of her. "When will you be in?"

His voice dropped an octave. "Bedtime. Be naked."

"Promises, promises." But she hung up with a big grin all over her face. If Mutt could have raised one eyebrow, she would have. "Oh shut up," Kate told her, and was saved from annihilation only by the phone ringing again. This time it was Kurt. "What have you got?"

He sounded frustrated. "Come see for yourself."

It was getting on for sunset—or as it is known in Alaska in January, about four p.m.—by the time she got to his office. She parked and Mutt raced her up the stairs to the seventh floor. They arrived at Pletnikof Investigations out of breath but pretty pleased with themselves, Kate in particular shaking off the last of the inchoate fury inspired by the tower rooms at Chez Satan. Agrifina Fancyboy, dressed today in a charcoal suit that would have appeared right at home on the runway at Chanel, with one look brought them back to a cowed sense of decorum. They went sedately into Kurt's office and simultaneously exhaled when the door closed behind them. Kate sat in the chair across from his desk and Mutt trotted around to receive her due, in this case a strip of caribou jerky Kurt kept in his desk just for her.

Kurt looked unusually sulky.

"What's wrong?"

"Nothing," he snapped, and then relented. "Sorry. It's just that—dammit! I can't find anything wrong with the Bannister Foundation's database. He started it even before he went to prison, I think mostly because he knew if he didn't dump a bunch of his assets into a nonprofit that they'd all be confiscated by law enforcement and he'd have nothing when he got out, and he wasn't having that." He scratched his chin absent-mindedly. "He'd been planning to do it for a long time before that, though. He had his attorney write up a set of rudimentary by-laws and had him incorporate the Bannister Foundation in the state of Alaska five years before he had me left for dead—" Kate made a rude noise and rolled her eyes "— and he applied for and got nonprofit certification a year later."

"Alaska's answer to Andrew Carnegie," Kate said. "One of the rape, ruin, and run boys buying a modern indulgence, only not from the church, from the state."

He stared at her. "Kate, sometimes you sound like you're speaking in tongues."

"You had to have read Barbara Tuchman." She waved him on. "What else?"

He tossed her a folder and sat back in his chair. "He started tithing into it immediately, and evidently, from the influx of cash from other sources, was apparently convincing other people with dough it was a good idea to do it, too. Federal law says foundations have to spend four to five percent of their income every year, and the Bannister Foundation started a grant application process their first year and began awarding grants their second. Substantial grants, too, Kate." He nodded at the folder. "That's a list of the grants. All in Alaska, by the way."

"What kinds of causes?"

"A Planned Parenthood chapter in Fairbanks. A library in Unalaska. A voc ed school in Bering."

She looked up. "What's the name of that school? The one in Bering?"

"I sorted them by community."

She sifted through the pages. "Bering VoTech."

He'd been googling as she'd been speaking. "Offering

certificates and degrees in Alternative Energies, Aviation, Automotive Technology, Cosmetology, Culinary, Diesel and Heavy Equipment Technologies, Industrial Electricity, Information Technology, Mechanics, and Plumbing and Heating. Why?"

She smiled. "I might know a student there. I'll reach out. What about donors?"

"I'm just digging into the donor list now, but that's a lot harder. There are literally hundreds of small donors, twenty-five dollars here, a hundred there, but it adds up. And then there are some really humongous sums incoming, and they are pretty layered, I would guess mostly because they don't want to be annoyed by requests for money."

"So they donate to the Bannister Foundation, who removes any necessity for them hobnobbing with the great unwashed who benefit from their largesse?"

"Snide, but accurate. I'm pretty good online but tracing some of these back to the actual people who signed the actual checks is going to require Tyler-level expertise." He heaved a sigh. "I'll tell you, Kate, it's going to ruin my entire day if we prove Erland to be an honest to god altruistic philanthropist, succoring the tired, the poor, the huddled masses yearning to breathe free." He cocked an eyebrow, clearly expecting astonishment.

She laughed without taking her eyes from the list. "And I don't buy it for a New York second, either." She jerked her chin at his laptop. "Hey, can you find out where Pete Heiman is, right now?"

"Wouldn't that be DC?"

She snorted. "He's a US Congressman. Probably the last place he'd be. Somebody might put him to work."

A few taps of the keys, and he said, "Happens he's touring the provinces, Fairbanks today, and then driving down to Delta Junction and overnight tomorrow in Ahtna."

"Ahtna." Her finger tapped a name on Kurt's grants list. "The Erland Bannister Foundation gave the Ahtna Women's Shelter $250,000 last year."

# Ten

S HE STOPPED AT SAFEWAY TO STOCK UP. When she got back to the town house she put the steaks on to marinate before heading out onto the Coastal Trail. As she and Mutt went through the tunnel leading from the lagoon to the coast she wondered if Jack had bought the town house on Westchester Lagoon with her in mind because the city's trail system ran right in front of it. When she first moved to Anchorage after graduating from the University of Alaska Fairbanks Kate had found a mother-in-law apartment over a garage in one of the big houses on the hillside, owned by a Slope worker who was gone every other week and wanted a permanent on-site presence to discourage burglars. It was far enough east that it was almost in the Chugach National Forest and the roads required four-wheel drive and studs all around for three-quarters of the year. At night sometimes she could hear the local wolf pack howling. It felt almost like home. Jack would have known that she would require easy access to the outdoors if he was going to entice her off her mountaintop for sleepovers.

She smiled to herself. He himself had been enticement enough.

They were through the tunnel and she picked up speed, Mutt foraying out ahead, playing dodge ball with oncoming traffic in the form of commuters walking from downtown to Turnagain, skijorers trying not to run over their own dogs (Mutt had a high old time with them), and the occasional biker who had screwed Attack screws into their tires for traction and pumped on with grim determination and not a little fortitude, although Kate would much rather trust to her Asics, thanks. They kept it short due to increasing darkness and returned to the town house by six p.m. "Hey," the neighbor said as Kate kicked the ice from the bottom of her shoes.

"Hey," Kate said, and Mutt woofed. She barely showed any teeth but the neighbor went inside and they both heard the lock click behind him. "How many times have I told you?" Kate said severely. "Do not frighten the neighbor."

Mutt woofed again, tongue lolling out in a lupine grin.

"Yeah, yeah," Kate said, and they went inside. Kate built a fire for Mutt to array herself in front of and went upstairs to shower. Barefoot in jeans and T-shirt, she pattered back down and took a mug of coffee and her phone to the couch. Mutt, gnawing at last night's bone, barely registered her on her peripheral vision. "Priorities," Kate said. "I understand. No, really, I do, my feelings aren't hurt at all. Carry on." She found Stephanie's number in her contacts and pressed Call.

"Kate!"

Kate grinned into the phone. "Hey, Steph. How are you? Are you home?"

"In Bering? Yeah, sure, it's Christmas on Monday, don't forget."

Kate had, actually, but remembered now that the Russian Orthodox celebrated Christmas in January. "Right, I forgot. Have you found all your presents?"

Stephanie sounded a little disgruntled. "Uncle Ray is getting better at hiding them."

Kate laughed. "How is he?"

"Good." They talked for a while about Ray, a Bering elder and a very close friend indeed of Emaa's back in the day. Stephanie Chevak was Alice Chevak's daughter, and Alice Chevak and Kate Shugak had met at college in Fairbanks. They had reconnected when Kate had spent a brief time in Bering working for an air taxi six years before, which was when Kate had met Stephanie. Stephanie had been ten years old when Alice died. Kate had lost her own parents a lot earlier than that. It made a bond between them that had only strengthened as Stephanie grew older.

"Are you in the Park?" Stephanie said.

"No, I'm in Anchorage."

"Are you on a case?"

Kate grinned again. Stephanie sounded so hopeful. "Kinda sorta. Hey, remember when you told me that a school had opened in Bering that could give you the science courses you need?"

"Yeah, Bering VoTech."

"How's that working out?"

"It's kind of amazing, Kate," the girl said, sounding sober and truth to tell kind of awed. "I never would have guessed we'd have that good a school here in Bering, I thought for sure I'd have to leave home to study aviation and electrical and mechanical engineering. I mean, it's a small school and of course you can't degree here, only certificate, but the prep work the school is offering is earning me college credit that's good everywhere. If I stay on track at Bering VoTech I can slide right into pretty much any related degree program anywhere in the nation, and my advisor says I'm on track to graduate from high school a year early. I'm already working on my college applications."

"Oh yeah? Who looks good?"

"Well, MIT would be the holy grail, of course, but CalTech would do in a pinch."

"What's a heaven for?" Kate said.

"What? What does that even mean?"

Kate sighed. "They're not offering any liberal arts courses at Bering VoTech, are they."

Stephanie sounded mystified. "Why would they?"

"Why indeed."

"Anyway." Stephanie dismissed the topic with the scorn it deserved. "Will you write me a letter of recommendation for my college applications?"

"Of course," Kate said, feeling suddenly very old. "Send me the deets. Stephanie, do you have any idea where Bering VoTech gets its funding?"

"Sure," was the surprising answer. "Our teachers have all of the students write thank-you letters every time we get a grant. We got a big one from somebody in Anchorage last year, I forget their name—"

"The Bannister Foundation?"

"That's it!"

"How much did they give you?"

"It was huge, like half a million dollars or something. I remember the teachers were all walking around acting like they were drunk after the news came out."

"I can see why."

"I know, right?" Someone said something in the background. "Oh, okay, Uncle, I'll be right there. Gotta go, Kate."

"Merry Christmas!"

Kate clicked off and set her phone to play music. Larkin Poe was first up, whiplashing from wah-wah alt to ersatz heavy metal but with some of the best harmonizing since the Mamas and the Papas and maybe even since the Everly Brothers. She sang along, as much as the scar tissue bisecting her throat would allow.

She tore and washed the romaine, coddled an egg, shaved parmesan, ran garlic cloves and anchovies through the garlic press, and made croutons. There was something to be said for living in a city big enough to support a good store where you could buy good anchovies and good parmesan. It was six-thirty by then so she preheated the oven and poked and greased the potatoes. She even set the table, with a pitcher of ice water and a stick of butter on a real butter dish and everything. Another glance at the clock and she went upstairs to change her T-shirt to one that smelled less like garlic. She checked her hair and she even went so far as to put on a dab of perfume from a bottle of Chanel No. 5. It predated Jim and she had no idea if perfume went bad or not but it smelled okay so good enough.

She regarded the results in the mirror. Her nipples were clearly outlined by the fabric of the tee. It was entirely possible she had picked the lightest weight tee she could find. It was also entirely possible that dinner would be late. She grinned at herself and went back downstairs to put the spuds in the oven and set the timer. There was a monster gas grill on the back deck so the salmon steaks could go on any time, and grilling was a job best left to men anyway. Her friend Denise said it was because women were so distracted by a hundred different responsibilities at once that they always forgot and burned the food, whereas men were able to focus on two things and two things only: the beer in their hand and whatever was on the grill. She checked the fridge. Good, she'd remembered to buy a six-pack of Alaskan Amber.

She went to the living room and peered through the curtains. People were skating on Westchester Lagoon and someone had a burn barrel going and someone else had parked a food truck across the street, selling hot chocolate and empanadas. A car pulled up and Jim got out of the back seat, reaching in for a small duffel. He slammed the door and came up the walk.

She met him at the door. "You lost?"

He dropped the duffel and gave her a once-over, eyes lingering on her breasts. "No, I think I'm right where I'm supposed to be." He reached for her and she made it easier for him by jumping up and wrapping her legs around his waist. "Hey," she said, grinning at him.

"Hey," he said, grinning back. He kissed her, softly at first, and then with more determination. He nibbled, he licked, he bit, all the while adjusting the fit of their bodies so that his erection was pressed firmly into the notch between her legs.

Her heart was thundering in her ears when she finally pulled back. "Wow," she whispered.

"Wow," he whispered back.

"Wow," the guy next door said.

She laughed out loud and after a moment Jim did, too. He stepped through the door and shut it behind them, and then pressed her up against it like there wasn't a perfectly good bed with clean sheets on it upstairs. He played with her nipple. "Feels like you're glad to see me."

She slipped a hand down to cup his erection. "Backatcha."

He groaned and rested his forehead against hers. "We have a kid-free night all to ourselves. We don't have to be in a rush."

"Speak for yourself," she said breathlessly, pulling at his shirt.

"Woof," Mutt said.

Jim looked around to see Mutt standing in the doorway to the living room, great yellow eyes fixed on them.

"Back off," Kate said, "mine." She knotted her hand in his hair and pulled his mouth back to hers, all while pushing his jacket off and pulling his shirt out of his jeans. She paused for a moment to admire. "I absolutely hate to admit that I am this shallow."

His laughter sounded a little ragged. "Shallow about what?"

Her fingers skimmed lightly over his throat, shoulders, arms, chest. "Dude. I don't even know the names of the muscles you threw out over last summer. You are just flat fucking beautiful. You look like Ashton Eaton. Only, you know. White." Her hand slipped back between his legs. "Although I admit to a special liking for this particular muscle."

"It's yours to command." He flipped their positions and pushed her back against the door. "And you should talk. Hand-building a cabin from the ground up evidently agrees with you." He went on his own journey of exploration, only he followed his hands with his mouth.

"Oh," she said, her voice faint. "Do that some more."

He laughed again, more deeply this time.

Dinner was in fact late. They cooked and ate it attired in the minimum amount of clothing and adjourned to the living room with a tub of vanilla Haagen Dazs and two spoons. Kate put on a video she'd bought with the groceries. Jim groaned at the opening credits. "No way! What is this, the fiftieth rewatch?"

"No," Kate said indignantly. "It's only the tenth. Well, maybe the eleventh." The opening title crawl began with the John Williams theme trumpeting over it, and when the time came she recited the line in unison with Yoda: "'Page turners they were not.'" She glanced at Jim, who was looking at her, not the screen, a crooked grin on his face. "What's so funny?"

"Not funny, hilarious."

She pounced, shoving him down on the sofa and straddling him. "Hilarious, my ass. I'll show you hilarious." She attacked in mock ferocity, nipping, biting, and pulled back in equally mock outrage when he only laughed harder. "What!"

"A book joke in a *Star Wars* movie gets you hot. Who knew?"

She was going in for the kill or something like that when Mutt sat up in front of the fireplace and barked.

Mutt had a range of expressions, from the all-purpose sneeze meant to denote polite agreement to the "woof" that could mean anything from a deprecatory "Excuse me" to a "Would you like to rephrase that before I rip out your throat?" The growl was deployed as a threat and was never mistaken for anything else. She never whined and she rarely yipped. Her bark was deep, robust, carrying, and of a timbre that inspired the feeling that one had suddenly been sent back in time to the Cretaceous Period and not as one of the predators. She seldom barked, and almost never barked more than once because she didn't have to, as her first bark had a way of traveling directly to the amygdala and thence to the hypothalamus of anyone within earshot. Those people found their hearts beating so loudly in their own ears that they wouldn't have heard a second bark and it didn't matter anyway because by then they were breathing hard enough to send themselves into hyperventilation. There were on occasion secondary issues with their gastrointestinal tracts. When they recovered the power of thought they generally found themselves already in motion going in the opposite direction as fast as humanly possible.

In this case, her bark was reactive rather than proactive because at almost the exact same moment Mutt gave voice someone shot at the house. There was a small crunch and the drape moved, followed by a corresponding splat in the wall over their heads.

Kate and Jim hit the floor and Mutt hit the door. Kate had forgotten to throw the bolt and Mutt had long since figured out how to open a lever handle. She was outside and taking the sidewalk to the street in great leaps before Kate realized what was happening. "No! Mutt! No!" She scrambled after her and made it to the door just in time to hear Mutt bark again. The one lone skater remaining on Westchester Lagoon had to be a thousand feet away but he screamed anyway and fell hard enough to crack the ice. It sounded like another shot firing.

Kate made it to the street in time to see taillights receding rapidly down West 15th Avenue just before taking a wildly fishtailing left onto S. She didn't have a hope of reading the tag. There was no problem seeing Mutt, however, by the light of the streetlights settling into a loping, predatory stride far too close to its bumper. "Mutt! Come back! Mutt, dammit! Get your ass back here!"

It looked for a moment as if Mutt was going to ignore her and keep chasing the car, but at S she slowed and turned and came trotting back, looking very pleased with herself.

"You had one job," the guy next door said, who was of course on his porch. "No more drivebys."

"Sorry," Kate said.

He went back inside and closed the door firmly behind him. Kate followed Mutt inside and this time made sure she threw the bolt. She looked up when Jim came down the hall.

"Footprints out back, one set from where they came over the fence to the door and a second set that looked like the tracks of Usain Bolt heading out. I think they might have cleared the fence in a single stride."

"Think the shot was a diversion to get the guy out back inside?"

"Could have been the plan. Until they were foiled by our girl in gray." He bent over and grabbed Mutt's head between his hands. "She's such a good girl! Such a very good and very scary girl!"

Mutt's tailed wagged hard enough to fall off her butt and she gave Jim lavish tongue all up and down his face. Well, he'd set himself up for that.

They went back into the living room and stared from the hole in the window to the hole in the wall. "Shooting pretty high. Maybe just a random?"

"Maybe." He sounded about as convinced as she felt. "Maybe just scared shitless."

"Should we call the cops?"

"If we don't someone else will." Like the neighbor.

So they called. At that they only rated a single cruiser, Anchorage night life as lively as it was on Friday evenings, but one of the responding officers knew Jim and so their story was taken more seriously than it otherwise might have been. One of the officers dug the bullet out of the wall and promised to call him if anything developed. They all knew it wouldn't.

The door closed behind the police and they both looked at Mutt, standing in the doorway to the kitchen. She gave a modest sneeze.

"I agree," Kate said. "Not much game."

Jim's glare was pretty impartially divided between the two of them. He marched over to the living room window and pointed. "Not much game?" He twitched back the drape again and pointed at the starred hole in the glass.

"Yeah, there's some duct tape in the junk drawer in the kitchen," Kate said, and went to get it. "I have to say," she said as they were taping the hole, "I expected something like this. Just not this soon."

"What? Why?"

"Just that every time I come to Anchorage someone tries to take me out. I've been knocked unconscious, kidnapped, once someone loosened the lug nuts on the car. Why should this time be any different?"

They went upstairs. "I have to say, Shugak, that you're getting awful goddamn sanguine about getting shot at." For himself, his heart rate was just settling down to normal and he still had the coppery taste of fear in his mouth.

She shrugged without answering and slid beneath the covers. He followed and pulled her firmly into his arms, tucking her head beneath his chin and hooking his leg around her hips to pull her in tight. He remained wakeful long after she fell asleep, listening to her breathing slow and stutter in that little hiccup someone a lot braver than he was might have called a snore.

Not that anyone else was ever going to get the chance to.

He spoke at length, almost entirely in obscenities, and never repeated himself once. There followed a charged silence.

"I wonder, sir—"

"What do you wonder, Jared?"

"I wondered if perhaps it might be time to bring in Al and Kev, sir."

A silence. "Convince me."

"Well, they are both former government agents, so they can pass for DEA or ICE or FBI, always helpful in recovering strays. And you'll recall we used them to make that delivery to Mr. Curley last month, so they're familiar with the territory, as well as these particular strays."

"And?"

"Well, sir—" said apologetically "—as empirical evidence recently, conclusively, and unfortunately proves, we have no assets worthy of the name on location. The for-hire community in this area does rather trend toward blunt force."

"And?"

"And Al and Kev have proven themselves trustworthy. And didn't I understand that Al is from Minnesota? He *wouldn't be afraid of cold weather. And Kev is a pilot, which could prove most useful. They have in the past shown themselves to be capable and efficient."*

*"They have, and that's why I prefer to employ their services sparingly."*

*"Yes, sir."*

*"Still…" Another, longer silence. "Very well. Call Pappas and tell him to prep the G-2."*

*"Yes, sir."*

*"Tell Kev and Al I want them en route as soon as they can get their asses to the FBO."*

*"Yes, sir."*

*"Make sure they understand the urgency of the situation."*

*"The jet will certainly underscore that message, sir."*

*"And for sweet christ's sake, tell them to keep everything they do on the down low. This cluster does not need to be any more fucked than it already is."*

*"Understood, sir."*

# Eleven

## SATURDAY, JANUARY 5
### *Anchorage*

T HEY WOKE UP TO THE TUB OF ICE CREAM
licked clean and Mutt sitting all the way across the
living room from it with an angelic expression on her face.
"She deserved it," Jim said, "and our fault anyway for
forgetting to put it back in the freezer."

Over breakfast Kate told Jim about her meeting with
Special Agent James G. "Gerry" Mason the day before.
"Gary Curley, drug lord," he said. "I've heard him called a
lot of names but never that one."

"Mason says he lost a lot of money in oh-eight." She
described the search of Curley's house in dispassionate
terms but he was not fooled, and reached across the table to
take her hand in his. She gave him a crooked smile. "What
was that you said to me once?"

"What? When?"

"You said I never met a rule of evidence I liked."

"Oh. That. Yeah." The topic under discussion that day had been the possibility of placing a Village Police and Safety Officer in Niniltna, and Kate's unsuitability for the job.

She shook her head and squeezed his hand once more before letting go. "Those two turret rooms—you know the worst thing about them?"

"What?"

"It wasn't that they were such travesties of a storybook childhood. It was that they looked so... so well used. They've been sitting there all this time, decorated just like that, for I don't know how many children over the years. They'd written on the walls and you could see where he'd had it painted over between—" her mouth twisted "—between guests."

A heavy silence fell and wisely, he let it lie.

She raised her head and met his eyes. "In general, I like the Bill of Rights. I read somewhere that the US's most exported product isn't soybeans or 737s, it is the US constitution and I get that. You know, other than the four-hundred-year-old Native American genocide it's founded on. It's an ideal, and we'll always fall short of it, and I get that, too. But something like those two rooms makes me want to just kick down doors and the hell with whichever amendment says I can't. People knew Curley was a pedophile, Jim. Hell, they knew when I quit the DA's office and that was ten years ago. The only reason the feds got into his house yesterday is because of the drugs you found at the site of the crash.

Mason barely mentioned the two kids who might have been transported across an international border in an act of sex trafficking." Her voice trembled. "So yay us, the good guys won one, and hey, at least Curley's dead. But how many kids were cycled through those rooms, Jim? Including the two in the Park right now?"

"At least they're alive."

She sat back and sighed. "Yeah. There's that."

They were silent for a moment. "What's next?" he said.

"Kurt and our new nerd are doing their best to hack into the Bannister Foundation's records," she said. "I'm going to call Brendan, see if he kept a wish file on Curley."

"A wish file?"

"All prosecutors keep wish files, the ones they wish they could prosecute but can't because they don't have the evidence or the witnesses or what the fuck ever. He'd never give it to Mason but he might give it to me."

"George told me there was no record of Curley's plane leaving Anchorage for Niniltna. There has to be something. You don't fly in and out of Anchorage without somebody noticing. Elmendorf alone would have raised nine kinds of hell." He thought. "I know a guy. Let me call him."

He took his phone into the living room and Kate found her own phone and called Brendan. He extorted another lunch out of her the next time she was in town and promised to send her a copy of the file. "It isn't much," he said, all the humor going out of his voice. "If I coulda found more his ass would be in jail right now." He cheered up. "Still, if his ass had been in jail it wouldn't have been on that plane and he wouldn't be dead. So there is cause for celebration, Kate."

If I could have found more we wouldn't even be having this conversation, Kate thought. She hung up and noticed that she'd had three calls the night before, all around midnight from an unknown number or numbers. She went into the living room to see Mutt sitting with her chin on Jim's knee, hanging on his every word as he spoke on the phone. She was clearly suffering from a lack of attention from her favorite man. Although they were all her favorite men.

He hung up. "Buddy of mine's an air traffic controller. He wasn't on duty New Year's Eve but he'll find out who was and get back to me."

"Thanks," she said, leaning her elbows over her head on the frame of the door. The posture pulled the fabric of her tee tight over her breasts.

He recognized the look in her eye, and he smiled at her, a return to the old wide, white shark's grin of yesteryear, or even last night. He got to his feet, stepped over Mutt, and picked Kate up and carried her upstairs and back to bed. What happened there was an utter rejection of Gary Curley and Father Smith and the pedophile priests the Jesuits had hidden away in Alaska and all the rest of their corrupt, sadistic, amoral ilk. There was need and lust and pleasure, freely taken and freely given between two consenting, healthy adults. Jim took the lead, demanding her response to his hands and lips and tongue and cock and Kate allowed herself to be seduced and manhandled and thoroughly debauched. When it was over she could hear his heart thundering inside his chest. He raised his head and smiled down at her. There were no words. They needed none.

They showered together, and dressed together, paused for a touch, a kiss, a caress, and packed for home. "The Cessna's at Merrill?" she said. He nodded. "Have you checked the weather?"

"Looks worse than it is."

They cleaned away the breakfast dishes and stripped the bed and left the rest for the cleaning service. As Kate tapped the Uber app the phone rang again, and again from an unknown number. She hated answering calls from unknown numbers and she moved to tap decline but she missed and hit answer instead. She said into the phone, "If you're soliciting campaign funds for anyone other than Elmer Fudd I'm hanging up."

There was a brief silence. "May I ask who is speaking?"

"I think that's my line. I'm hanging up in three, two—"

"This is Detective Josie Branson of the Anchorage Police Department."

"Are you at the cop shop?"

"Yes, but—"

"Hang up and I'll call back." She dialed the number from memory and asked for Detective Branson, who picked up immediately. "Detective Branson? I'm the person who answered the number you dialed. My name is Kate Shugak.

I'm a private investigator, previously with the Anchorage district attorney's office. Brendan McCord will give me a reference if you'd like to call him and then call me back."

Another silence. "I'll speak with him after I've talked to you, Ms., er, Shugak. May I ask where you're calling from?"

Some instinctive sense of self-preservation kicked in. "I live in Niniltna, east of Anchorage."

"How far east?"

"Almost in Canada."

"Oh. Uh. Well, I was going to ask if I could see you, but—"

Jim made a spinning motion with his forefinger. "Detective Branson, I was just on my way out. How may I help you?" Preferably in twenty words or less, Kate thought but didn't say. Law enforcement solidarity was all, private or public.

"Ms. Shugak, are you speaking from your personal phone?"

"Yes."

"This number?" Branson read it out.

Kate's phone was set not to reveal her number to a caller unless they were already in her list of contacts. "That is correct."

"Are you acquainted with a Mr. Eugene Hutchinson?"

Jim's eyebrows went up at Kate's expression. "Yes. He's an attorney in Anchorage."

"He was," Detective Branson said. "He was found dead in his home this morning, and his cell phone shows yours as the last number he called. Three times."

Silence.

"Ms. Shugak?"

Kate drew in a long breath and exhaled slowly. "My phone was off. When I turned it on this morning I noticed I'd had three missed calls from an unknown number. Around midnight?"

"That is correct."

Kate sighed. "I'm in Anchorage. I'm on my way."

Eugene Hutchinson had died from a gunshot wound received in an apparent home invasion.

Kate digested this in silence for a moment. "I was shot at last night," she said.

Detective Branson looked surprised, as well she might. "Did you call it in?"

"We did." She gave the names of the officers, and there was a delay while Branson located the report.

"One shot," she said.

"Yes. My dog frightened them off."

Branson looked at Mutt, who sat erect next to Kate, ears straight up, yellow eyes fixed on the detective. "Woof."

She was restraining her inner dementor this morning and Kate saw Branson's lips twitch. "I can see how that might happen. The report shows that we recovered a spent round from the scene."

"Yes."

"Well. We don't yet know what caliber of ammunition Hutchinson was killed with, so we won't know until the autopsy report if there is any connection between the two incidents."

Other than the fact that he tried to call me three times immediately prior to his murder, Kate thought. "Bullets?" she said politely. "In the plural?"

Branson nodded. She was in her mid-twenties, a square, solid young woman with thin fair hair, intent brown eyes, and a serious, firm-lipped expression. She patronized the same tailor as Brendan McCord and wore black Kurus that looked well worn in. "Two shots to the chest. One to the head."

Classic mob hit, Kate thought, exchanging a glance with Jim, who was staying so far in the background of this meeting that he was practically invisible.

"What was your relationship with Mr. Hutchinson?" Branson said.

"Brief. I met him once in his official capacity as Erland Bannister's attorney, when he informed me that Bannister had named me the trustee of his estate."

It was obvious from Branson's expression that she'd heard the name. "When was that?"

"Wednesday morning."

"This past Wednesday?" Branson looked at her phone. "January second?"

"Yes. He wrote to me about the trusteeship. I received the letter on January first, and I came to Anchorage to meet with him the next day."

"Where did this meeting take place?"

"In the office of Pletnikof Investigations." She gave Branson Kurt's name and contact information and a brief summary of Hutchinson's presentation, omitting any references to her suspicions of Erland's motives in naming her his trustee. Branson made dutiful notes. "Where were you last night between midnight and one a.m., Ms. Shugak?"

"At home."

"Any witnesses?"

"One," Jim said, speaking for the first time.

Branson collected Jim's contact information and evinced no discernible surprise when it proved to be the same as Kate's own. "Well, I think that's all for the moment, Ms. Shugak. Thank you for coming in."

Kate stood up and paused. "Was there any evidence at the scene that would indicate why he was murdered?"

Branson hesitated. The correct response was to say that she couldn't comment on an ongoing investigation and dismiss them with a polite smile. Instead she leaned back in her chair and looked the three of them over, Kate assessingly, Jim appreciatively (definitely hetero, Kate thought), and Mutt with a perceptible softening. "That isn't a wolf, is it?"

"Only half," Kate and Jim said in unison.

"Oh well, that's okay then." She held out a hand. Mutt sniffed at it, thought it over, and stepped forward to allow Branson the privilege of scratching behind her ears. "I have a dog myself. A retired sled dog."

"You get him through the August Foundation?" Kate said.

Branson nodded. "Eight, neutered, raced with one of the Seaveys. He was starting to slow down so they put him up for adoption, and I grabbed him up." She smiled. "We don't go for walkies, we go for runnies. He keeps me in shape." She dropped her hand from Mutt's head. "Hutchinson's phone had been reset to factory setting. We had to pull his most recent calls, including the three to you, off the nearest cell tower. When someone thought to go further back into his records, all calls to and from his phone had vanished."

"Interesting," Kate said.

"I'll say. Hutchinson had an office in his home, but there was no laptop, no desktop, no tower, no printer. They also took his wallet, his watch if he had one, and any jewelry if he had any of that."

"Television?"

"It's a forty-three incher. They stuck to the small, portable stuff."

"Did Hutchinson have an office outside his home?"

"If he did, we haven't found it yet."

Kate wondered if Erland Bannister had been Eugene Hutchinson's only client. "How is APD seeing this crime, Detective?"

"On the face of it, and absent further evidence, my boss will write it off as a home invasion. We'll give it our best effort, but—" Branson shrugged. "We're canvassing the neighborhood but so far no one saw anything."

Everyone thought about that for a moment or two, and then Kate held out her hand. "Good to meet you, Detective Branson."

Branson's grip was firm and dry. "And you, Ms. Shugak. Mr. Chopin." She grinned at Mutt. "You, too, gorgeous."

Mutt knew a compliment when she heard one and practically pranced out of the cop shop.

Their Uber pulled up as they walked out the front door, their driver looking them over for cuffs or signs of extreme interrogation. Kate climbed in back with Mutt. "Can we go home by way of Ahtna?"

He looked over his shoulder. "I'll check the forecast again but it should be okay. It's only an hour from home and the storm is staying offshore and moving west."

Preflight and they were airborne half an hour later. "ETA Ahtna about an hour and a quarter. Also, we're going to Ahtna, why?"

"Pete Heiman's there today."

They leveled off and Jim adjusted the mixture to allow for the skinnier air at cruising altitude. "We're meeting with Pete Heiman voluntarily?"

He heard her sigh over the headset. "Pete's a member of the board of directors of the Bannister Foundation."

*They'd found an empty house almost immediately, which was good since their feet were freezing in their sandals. The front door wasn't even locked. It was cold inside but not as cold as outside. It had a kind of old lady smell, not unpleasant, like Señora Barahona around the corner, who would look out for them after school before Mami came home from work. It was filled to bursting with books and magazines and baskets of yarn and a table with tiny bags and boxes full of beads of every size and color. The walls were covered with photographs, some black and white and fading, others in color, all sizes, some framed, others tacked and taped to the wall. There was a flat television hanging from one corner of the living room with a couch in front of it that was the most worn piece of furniture in the house.*

*There was a bedroom in the back. The bed had been stripped but he found a huge stack of quilts in a closet and piled a bunch of them on the bed and settled Anna beneath them. He went around the house and locked all the locks, windows, front door and back, and then crawled in with her. It took a while to warm up the bed but they were asleep too quickly to care.*

*The next morning they woke up when it got light out but stayed in bed so they didn't have to get out from under the covers. The refrigerator was empty but the electricity was still on and David figured out how to turn on the burners of the stove. No water came out of the faucet when he turned it on but there was bottled water in the pantry and one filled the kettle. There was canned milk and Nestlé's cocoa—it was strange how many things were the same in* el norte *as they were at home—and he made them mugs of steaming cocoa for breakfast, along with some white salty crackers and butter from a round can that were also in the pantry, along with a can of meat that opened with a key and came out like a brick. It smelled okay so he sliced it up and fried it in a little frying pan he found in the drawer in the bottom of the stove. It was good, but then they were so hungry anything would have tasted good.*

*He never did figure out how to turn on the television so they spent the day on the couch wrapped in blankets reading the books they had brought with them. Anna wanted to play with the beads so David found some with holes big enough she could poke thread through and make a bracelet and a necklace. She was too little to use a needle.*

*On their second morning in the house he was just reaching for the Bad Man's phone to try to call Mami again when he heard someone at the door. He jumped down from the chair in a panic and Anna started to cry. He grabbed her hand and hauled her back to the bedroom. They hid in the closet in the back, behind the rest of the quilts. Be quiet, he said to Anna. Be very quiet so they don't find us. Anna whimpered, and he put his arm around her and held her close.*

*He heard someone, a woman, talking in a language that wasn't English. It was very loud and even though he couldn't understand it he was sure she was swearing. He heard footsteps come down the hallway and pause, probably in the doorway to the kitchen, where their breakfast was cooling on the table. The words cut off abruptly. He heard another voice say something that sounded like a question. The swearing woman said more swear words. Mami would have made her put money in the peso jar.*

*The footsteps began again, two sets this time. He heard the door to the bathroom creak open and hoped the swearing woman wouldn't open the lid of the toilet to see where they'd used the toilet and how they hadn't been able to flush it afterward. After a moment the footsteps came nearer until they were there, right there in the bedroom. The woman said something. It sounded like a question, said too loud to be talking only to herself. He didn't answer, holding Anna tightly to him with one arm and with the other held desperately to the doorknob, keeping the door closed because there was no lock on the inside. He would not let her be hurt again.*

*The footsteps came closer to the closet, and the door was wrenched out of his hand, pulling him forward and Anna with him. They sprawled onto the floor and the woman, it was a woman, let loose with a bunch of words in the language he didn't know and he was sure this time she was swearing because she sounded like Señor Zelaya when David accidentally knocked him over with Pepito's bicycle. Behind her was the young woman who spoke Spanish.*

*He got to his feet shakily, and helped Anna to hers. She clutched his hand and they faced the woman together. She wasn't much taller than they were, with her hair cut short in front and on the top and a skinny braid down her back. If it had been dyed red she would have looked like she belonged to Hulespuma, one of the Latino punk bands Papi had loved to listen to. She was dressed in heavy pants and big white boots that looked like the boots astronauts wore, and the tip of her nose was bright red and ice was melting from the hood of her jacket.*

*He measured the distance to the door. If they could get around her, they could run.*

*He looked up and saw her watching him. She heaved a sigh and held up one finger and said something in English. Wait, he thought. She wanted them to wait here while she called the* policía.

*He tugged Anna closer to him and shook he head. No, he said as loud as he could. He knew it meant the same thing in both languages.*

"Ven con nosotros."

*He looked at the younger woman. She nodded.* "Ven con nosotros." *She spoke slowly and carefully.* "Esta bien. Venga con nosotros."

"No," *he said, without conviction.*

The swearing woman put her hands on her hips and glared at him. She heaved another sigh, tapped her foot impatiently, and said something to the younger woman. She turned and stomped to the door, pausing to glare at them over her shoulder.

We should go with her, Anna said.

Why?

I like her, Anna said, and she let go of his hand and walked forward to hold hers out to the younger woman, who smiled and took it.

Anna.

She looked over her shoulder. They won't hurt us, David. Come on.

# Twelve

T HEY LANDED A LITTLE BEFORE NOON.
Ahtna was the biggest town nearest to the Park which
made it the de facto market town for Park rats. It sprawled
between the Glenn Highway and the Kanuyaq River where
the two came nearest together at the river's northernmost
point. Both river and highway took opportunistic
advantage of an interruption of the 600-mile long arc
of the Alaska Range, with the Quilaks continuing on to
the Canadian border in the east and the rest of the range
building to a big finish with Denali and Foraker to the west.
The land was thickly forested and rich with fish and game,
and Ahtna made a good living off tourists, campers, and
sports fishermen in summer, hunters in the fall, and Park
rat shoppers year round. There was one big hotel north of
town that catered to cruise ship passengers brought by bus
from Valdez, an older and much more colorful one on the

river patronized by the locals, a campground that was wall to wall RVs from Memorial Day to Labor Day, and every Ahtnan rented out their spare rooms on Airbnb to all the college kids who spent their summers working at the hotels and restaurants and gift shops.

The architecture was a wide-spot-in-the-road blend of old log cabins and new prefab, with a district courthouse, a movie theater with three screens, and a Costco as its crown jewels. The bars outnumbered the churches and you could even get a lap dance if you knew where to go. South to Anchorage was almost three hundred miles, north to Fairbanks another two hundred and fifty miles, but why bother? In Ahtna if that nosy Kenny Hazen busted your meth cook it was only a little farther to the Canadian border. It was true that these days the Canadians were getting awfully pissy about letting you cross without a passport but there was a reason God had invented four-wheelers and snow machines and roads wasn't it.

Kenny Hazen met them at the side of the strip, which was five miles up the river from town. "Jim. Kate." Kenny was the size of Sasquatch and nearly as hirsute. His enormous hand engulfed hers in a dry, firm grip. "Looking good."

"How's the judge?" Kate said.

Kenny smiled. "Also looking good. Good and healthy."

Kate smiled back. "Good to know. Tell her I said hi."

"Tell her yourself. She's where we're going."

Where they were going was the Ahtna old folks' home, a newish construction of a one-floor, three-wing sprawl.

Independent living was in the left wing, assisted living in the right, with the common areas in the middle. It was lunch time and all the residents had turned out for deep-fried halibut and tater tots accompanied by remarks from their very own US Congressman, Pete Heiman. The son and grandson of stampeders, Pete had made a fortune in trucking during the oil boom and run his first campaign for the state legislature on the profits. He had since upgraded and was now Alaska's only voice in the US House of Representatives. Given Alaska's transient population he would only ever be one voice, but he was their voice and they loved him in spite of his being credibly accused of, in no particular order, selling his vote for a development on Forest Service land in Florida, inappropriate behavior with regard to the opposite sex (he'd sworn off marriage after his third and a good thing, too), and traveling to exotic lands on alleged fact-finding missions funded by corporations subject to Congressional oversight. In short, a standard of behavior one had been conditioned to expect from one's representatives to the federal government, and as a whole Alaskans could be thankful it was no worse. In exchange, he'd funneled every last federal dollar he had even minimal influence over into the state whether the state wanted the funding or not. And of course they did. Kate, Jim, and Kenny made it to their seats just in time for Pete's introduction and the following standing ovation. Pete beamed round the room, which only enhanced his resemblance to a toddler with a beard. He was short and plump and jolly and as one comedian had described the average eighteen-month-old, had a right-hand reach of eight feet. A reach with very sticky fingers, too.

When the applause died down Kate leaned over and said, "Hey, Judge. Looking good."

"Less gaunt, for sure," Judge Roberta Singh said, but the truth was she had more color in her face and flesh on her bones than she had the last time Kate had seen her. Kenny was sitting next to her and Kate was pretty sure they were holding hands under the table, and who could blame them? Mutt trotted around to pay her respects to the judiciary and was rewarded with a piece of halibut and an ear scratch, thereafter taking up station next between Kate and Jim, confident that all the eyes on the room not focused on Pete were on her and pleased about it.

Pete ran through his greatest hits. "Best economic recovery in history!" "More jobs created!" "Increased overseas markets for Alaskan oil and Alaska seafood!" "Opening the Tongass back up to the timber industry!" "Opening ANWR to oil exploration!" The follow-up Q&A was generally an opportunity for the residents to tell Pete how great he was. One little old lady stood up shakily on two crutches and asked about Medicare, and one old gent with pugnacious whiskers asked about kids in cages, but on the whole this was his crowd and he very nearly danced off the stage in a glow of self-satisfaction and began working the tables, shaking hands with both of his. When he came to their table he paused in mid-step but recovered at once. "Chief Hazen, Judge Singh, Jim, Kate, how the hell are you!" He gladhanded all of them and Kate didn't even feel like she had to wipe her palm down her jeans afterward. The true gift of the professional politician.

"Preaching to the choir here, Pete," Jim said, all smiles.

"They are my people," Pete said, all smiles back.

The building they were sitting in was the result of a massive grant from the Federal Housing Authority, and Pete so happened to sit on the congressional committee that oversaw the FHA. It was all about the bacon and who brung it home, and Alaskans, who received more federal funding per capita than Mississippi, knew that better than most, even if they did preach a lifestyle wholly independent of government interference. Great people did not have to think consistently from one moment to the next, Kate thought. And wasn't Emerson the guy who'd paid Thoreau's bail? "A word, Pete?" she said.

He made a show of consulting his watch, because he actually still wore one. "I don't know, Kate, they've got me on a pretty tight schedule—"

She stood up. "This won't take but a minute, Pete."

Kate knew where a lot of Pete's bodies were buried, of which he was well aware. Mutt woofed, and that did it. Pete followed Kate out of the dining room, Mutt ticky-tacking over the linoleum tiles behind them. Kate found an empty office and closed the door once they were inside, Mutt taking up station outside to discourage anyone so foolish as to try to interrupt them. Kate came straight to the point. "Erland Bannister named me his trustee."

Pete's jaw dropped. "What—what the—what?"

She regarded him with interest. "You didn't know."

"Not only no, but hell no," he said, looking, Kate had to admit, a little shell-shocked. "I would have said Erland was the last person to invite you of all people to get all up in his business."

"So would I," she said. "You're on the board of the Bannister Foundation."

"Well." Pete was thinking, never a good thing.

"Your photo's on the website, Pete, along with a lovely little bio."

"Well, yeah, okay. It was an honor, and hell, Kate—" out flashed Pete's electioneering grin "—so was everyone the hell else on the board. Even your own cousin, granddaughter to the great Ekaterina Shugak herself."

Kate tried not to grit her teeth. "And then there were those wonderful all-expenses paid quarterly vacations. Hard to turn down."

"Those are board meetings, Kate." Pete was trying for dignity and not quite making it. A thought occurred that did not appear at all welcome to him. "Are you investigating the Bannister Foundation, Kate?"

"Do you think I have cause to?"

"Not to my knowledge, and I'm a plankholder," Pete said. "I've been there since the beginning and I've never caught a whiff of improper behavior. We get donations, they go straight into the endowment, we're required by federal law to spend four to five percent of our income every year, and we meet four times a year to hear our executive director brief us on the applications. We vote on who gets how much and we're done, and in another three months we do it again." He pointed a finger at her. "And a condition of the application is that the person or the organization has to be Alaskan. That right there is why it's worth doing. And Jane—Jane Morgan, or Wardwell I think she is now, Erland's assistant—she's done excellent work in curating and vetting applications." He caught himself. "Morgan. Morgan? Any relation to Jack?"

"His ex."

Pete stared at her for a moment and then burst out laughing. It was the kind of laugh that suited his appearance, full-throated, rollicking, roisterous, infectious. Kate maintained her stone face, but then she'd been subjected to Pete's laugh before. Every time his laughter started to die down he'd glimpse her expression and go off into whoops again. After what felt like an inordinately long time he knuckled the tears from his eyes, blew his nose on a gigantic red handkerchief, and said, "Jesus. Erland really knew where and how to stick in the knife."

"You think that's why he did it? Named me trustee? Because I'd have to work with her?" Kate's voice was deceptively calm.

Pete gave her a curious glance, the last of his amusement fading. "Isn't it obvious? Erland might have hated your guts but he sure couldn't have named anyone to be his trustee who was better known to be less on the take. But it'd be like him to force you to hang out with Jack's ex while you do. He was a malicious old bastard."

Erland also might have thought I'd get to Jane Morgan, think the same thing, and stop there, Kate thought. Or run away screaming. "You're probably right," she said out loud. "Let's get you back to your adoring public."

"Kenny," Kate said as she sat down again, "do you know where the Ahtna Women's Shelter is?"

It was a rambling frame house set well back on a four-acre lot, around which a small forest of spruce and quaking aspen had been encouraged to grow. It was located off the highway and down a dirt road which led to another, smaller dirt road and then the route turned off on a third that was barely wide enough to allow Kenny's vehicle to pass. Motion detector lights were mounted on all four corners of the roof and there was a video doorbell. Kenny pressed it. "Marlena? It's Kenny. Got that person here I called you about."

A moment, and then the door opened on a heavy chain. "Hey, Kenny."

"Marlena, this is Kate Shugak."

One eye surveyed Kate through the crack. "Do you need shelter?"

"No," Kate said, stepping forward so the other woman could see her better. "I'd like to ask you some questions about your funding, if you wouldn't mind."

The eye travelled past Kate and landed on Mutt, standing at Kate's side with her ears way up. "What did you say your name was again?"

"Kate Shugak."

"From the Park?"

"Yes."

"And that would be Mutt."

Mutt ducked her head and tried to look modest.

"Jim and I'll wait in the car," Kenny said, and vacated the porch.

The door closed, there was the sound of the chain running back. The door opened again, revealing a short, dark, round woman in her fifties with a strong jaw and a resolute expression. She was dressed in sneakers, jeans and a UAF sweatshirt and her hair was cut in a Dutch boy with bangs. Tiny silver frog earrings dangled from her ears. "Frog Clan?" Kate said.

The woman nodded, looking surprised.

"I had a Frog Clan classmate at UAF. Again, I'm Kate Shugak." She held out her hand.

The other woman took it. "Marlena Peratrovich."

Kate smiled. "Any relation to Elizabeth?"

"A distant cousin." Marlena smiled back. "I expect you get that kind of thing a lot, too, being Ekaterina Shugak's granddaughter."

"You knew her?"

"Who didn't? I made an adverse remark about ANCSA on a panel at AFN one year and she eviscerated me in five words or less. She absolutely terrified me."

"Welcome to my world."

A young woman with a bruised face carrying a baby wearing a tiny splint on one arm crossed the hall, avoiding their gaze. A murmur of voices and a waft of frying hamburger came from the back of the house. Mutt looked up at Kate and twitched an inquiring ear. "Better not," Kate said. Marlena led them to an office just big enough for a desk, a filing cabinet, and two client chairs. Mutt lay down in the doorway and put her head on her paws. Through the single sash window on Marlena's office wall Kate could see Kenny and Jim sitting in Kenny's vehicle, puffing out exhaust as it idled. "You don't let men in here," Kate said.

"No," Marlena said. "We try to keep our location a secret, too, although of course Kenny and his guys know."

"Problems with exes?"

"Always. It takes an average seven times for a woman to leave an abusive partner. A lot of those partners never give up trying to make their women come back."

"Have they showed up here?"

"A few have. No matter how much we advise against it, our residents will get on Facebook to update their families on where they are and how they're doing."

"I saw the motion detector lights and the security cameras."

"We upgraded the windows and the doors, too," Marlena said. "We can probably keep anyone out long enough for the cops to get here. It's almost always a violation of a restraining order so they can arrest them and haul them off to jail for that, if for nothing else." She shrugged, her expression grave. "What was it you wanted to ask me, Kate?"

"You're a non-profit, correct?"

"Yes, IRS-certified. All of our funding comes from donors. We're a refuge, a way station for victims of domestic violence. We haven't figured out how to make that a money-making proposition yet."

Kate didn't take the sarcasm personally. "And one of your donors was the Bannister Foundation?"

Marlena's face brightened. "Yes. In fact all the security upgrades I just told you about were made possible by their grant."

"Good for them." Kate tried to say it with the requisite amount of enthusiasm but saw by Marlena's expression that she had fallen short.

"They were terrific, Kate," Marlena said, leaning forward. "They sent their representative out here personally to help us fill out the forms. After she went back to Anchorage she kept in touch with us every step of the way, and then she called me the day they met and told me they had decided to award our grant." Marlena leaned back again. "I have to say, I've worked a lot harder for a lot less than $25,000."

"Who was that? Their representative?"

"Jane Wardwell."

Kate's phone dinged with an incoming text. It was from Jim.

He need to get home NOW.

They spent the time in the air poring over a copy of the *Alaska Almanac* and entering various airport codes on the AOPA website's page on Alaska. Every hour they'd log onto the NOAA website to check the forecast.

"Doesn't look wonderful."

"But flyable."

"Barely."

"Who's the pilot here?"

"I've ridden right seat with you before. I know what you consider flyable."

An edged smile. "Think of the money."

Al grumbled. "When do we get the guns?"

"There's a guy who works at Cabela's. He says there are too many cameras inside and outside the store. He'll meet us at the tiedown."

"Glocks?"

"And the extra magazines, and boots, bibs, parkas, and gloves. Don't worry." Kev tapped the map. "We'll land here. We'll time our departure to arrive at sunset."

Al peered at the map. "We're not landing at the village?"

"Too many people."

"*But we have to go there anyway.*"

"*There'll be sleds at the other strip. I'm told it's basic transportation in the winter there. We won't stand out on a sled. That's where you take over the operation, by the way. I've never been on one.*"

A sigh. "*We're gonna freeze our asses off.*"

"*We were gonna do that anyway.*" Kev checked his phone. "*Time to call in.*" He entered a number and waited. "*Jared. Kev.*" He listened for a moment and then hung up. He leaned over the map and pointed. "*Someone called out on the phone again, still from here. He's sending a location. The GPS should take us right to it.*"

"*The back of fucking beyond, that is. Lucky for us they've got cell towers that far out in the boonies.*"

"*A recent acquisition, to service a mine development in that area. Timing is everything.*"

In Anchorage a Beaver on wheel-skis was waiting in the designated tiedown with the keys under the mat. It had not one but two GPS systems, one in the dash and one mounted on top of it. The pilot of the two of them checked the fuel and did the rest of the preflight.

Kev's phone dinged.

"*And we're good to go.*"

# Thirteen

SATURDAY, JANUARY 5
*Niniltna*

THEY ARRIVED AT NINILTNA MARGINALLY before sunset and taxied to George's hangar. They tied down and winterproofed the Cessna as much as they could before Matt showed up on his sled and loaded them onto his trailer and lurched off down the hill at his standard MPH of Indy 500. It was a brisk and brutal and mercifully abbreviated trip from strip to clinic, and they piled off and trooped gratefully into the warmth of the house. There they were greeted by a tear-stained Laurel and the other three Grosdidier brothers, who looked pissed off to a man. "What happened?" Kate said.

"We woke up Friday morning and they were gone," Luke said.

"Yesterday?" Mutt's ears went up at Kate's tone. "They have been gone since yesterday?"

"And you just called us today?" At Jim's words Mutt's ears achieved a hitherto unknown elevation. It was one thing for Kate to be mad, because she was mad a lot. Jim never raised his voice, he was always calm and in control. Mutt was a little confused as she knew she was among friends but in solidarity alone she was incapable of holding back a low, rumbly growl that made everyone in the room who wasn't named Shugak or Chopin cringe in unison. The aforesaid Shugak and Chopin didn't shush her, either.

"We've knocked on every door and looked behind every tree, Kate," Matt said, and when the red cleared from her vision she saw that he had bags under his eyes that stretched all the way to his knees. None of the rest of them looked as if they'd had any sleep for the last thirty-six hours, either. She could feel Jim relax a little next to her as he saw it, too.

"Did someone take them or did they leave?"

The five exchanged glances. "Left. We're pretty sure. The boy especially didn't trust us."

"You can understand why," Laurel said bitterly. "He probably doesn't trust any adult at this point, and we're all strangers to him."

"He wouldn't talk to you?"

"He only spoke Spanish, Kate," Matt said. "Vanessa managed to chisel some of their story out of him, as you know, but I don't expect for a moment that was all of it."

"And his sister never said a word," Laurel said.

"You've talked to everyone in town?"

"We went as far downriver as Ruthe Bauman's and all the way up to the Step. What with the government cuts to the Park Service Dan gave all his guys a month's unpaid leave and there's no one left up there except the poor sucker who drew the short straw and had to stay behind as caretaker. Dan's on vacation in Hawaii with Hilde Gundersen and Ruthe Bauman is Outside spending the holidays with relatives, but we looked in every room at Park HQ and we looked inside every outbuilding at Ruthe's and everywhere in between."

"Did you go out to Bernie's? They could have stowed away in the back of somebody's truck."

"We called. Bernie checked every room in the bar, all the cabins, and every room in his house. They aren't there."

"It's like they vanished," Peter said. His voice sounded hollow and his face was pale and strained. He was the youngest of the brothers and the one who felt things most.

"Well, they didn't," Kate said bracingly, determined to beat back the despair that emanated from the five of them in a miasma that threatened to subsume them all. Time to be blunt. "You may not have found them but you didn't find their bodies, either. They're alive, they're hiding out somewhere not very far away, and we'll find them. Did you check all the empty houses in Niniltna?"

Laurel and the Grosdidiers looked at each other. "We tried all the doors. They were locked."

"The windows, too?"

Mark nodded. "Locked and none broken."

"All those doors lock from the inside, too." Kate folded her arms and frowned at the floor. "Did you bring in a dog?"

Everyone looked at Mutt, who thumped the floor with her tail.

"A couple," Matt said. "But neither of them picked up a scent."

"Did they leave anything behind?"

"They put on every item of clothing they had before they left," Mark said.

"Show me," Kate said. They went into the clinic. "Have you changed the sheets on the bed?"

A general shaking of heads. Kate took hold of the blanket and yanked it and the top sheet back. She looked at Mutt and patted the bed. Mutt made a single graceful leap that resulted in a four-point landing. Kate held the top sheet to her nose. "Get a good whiff, girl."

Mutt sniffed the sheets from one end to the other, going so far as to nose the pillows over so she could smell both sides. When she was done, she looked at Kate. "Woof."

"Find," Kate said.

Mutt grand jetéd to the floor and snuffled corner to corner around the room. She spent some time at the single ʼf to the side—"The kids' clothes were there," Matt headed for the door. The humans followed in a ʼt led the way into the kitchen refrigerator— the rest of the pie went," Luke said, and

Mark said, "I told you I didn't eat it"—and back down the hallway to the front door. She looked up at Kate.

"Bundle up, guys," Kate said, zipping up her jacket and pulling her knit hat down around her eyebrows. The wind was still only a breeze but at that temperature it might as well have been a gale. Its sharp teeth sliced right through any outer clothing, laughed at layers, and got to work cooling the body temperature down to just above where they could be declared legally dead. Lips, fingertips, and toes went instantly numb.

"Goddamn," Matt said. There was a communal mutter of agreement but no one turned back.

Mutt, blissfully unaware, trotted up the street a little way, came back down again, passing the house they were standing in front of, and then crossed the street to Phil McKracken's cabin. The thick cloud cover that seemed to have assumed permanent station over central and southcentral Alaska had leeched the last of the light from the sky even before the sun set and since Niniltna didn't have street lights, only the lights of the houses themselves showed the way. Phil's two sash windows were set deep inside the logs that formed the walls and were lit from within, casting rectangular outlines of light on the snow. Smoke was puffing out of the chimney and they could hear Benny Goodman's "Stompin' at the Savoy" coming from inside. As with many who lived in the Park Phil hadn't bothered with curtains and as one they forgot the flash freezing of their extremities when Phil boogied the window with Elsa Kvasnikof. Phil leaned Elsa into a spectacular dip and laid a kiss on her that would have done Rhett Butler proud. It certainly seemed to have the same effect on Elsa it had had on Scarlett O'Hara. Before they could avert their eyes Phil was maneuvering Elsa toward the back of the cabin where in their collective nightmare they could plainly see the bed, as the music segued into Glenn Miller's "A String of Pearls."

"They have to be in their seventies!" Laurel said, revolted.

"Not bad for an old man," Peter said, impressed.

"My eyes, my eyes!" Luke said.

"So that's why he wanted the Viagra scrip," Mark said.

"Mark!"

"Sorry, Matt."

Next to her Kate could feel Jim shaking with suppressed laughter and gave him an admonitory nudge with her elbow. He retaliated with a pinch of her ass and she was hard put to it not to squeal like a teenage girl.

Mutt growled at them from around the corner. They were recalled to their duty and followed her as she shoved her way through a stand of alder to a small frame house with deteriorating T1-11 siding and a roof that was more moss than asphalt shingles. An ice dam hung off the back eave th reatened to pull down the rain gutter and part ng with it at the first sign of a thaw.

is this?"

Old Sam used to own it. He rented it out rs and then he sold it to—"

The door opened to reveal Martin Shugak, a distant cousin of Kate's and for a long time a fairly useless human being who walked a tightrope between good and feckless and more often than not fell off it on the wrong side. "Hey," he said, looking around the crowd. "What's going on?" His eyes lit on Kate. He swallowed. "Hey, Kate."

"Martin," she said. Martin looked... there was no other word for it, he looked good. He looked—and smelled—clean, a first, and his clothes looked as if they'd been laundered in memory of man, not a look Martin had been wont to cultivate. His eyes were clear, he'd shaved that day, and his hair was cut. A husky with golden fur and violet eyes poked her head out between his leg and the door. She saw Mutt, whined, and vanished.

"I—is that a dog?" Kate said.

Martin nodded. "One of Mandy's retirees. Her name's Diamond."

"You got a dog?"

He sighed. "Yes, I got a dog, Kate."

"And this house? Did you buy it?"

"I'm renting. Now, unless you're taking the census maybe you could get to the point, before I heat up the entire outdoors."

A reasonable observation, and Kate pulled herself together. "We're looking for a couple of kids. Real young, kindergarten or younger. They speak Spanish, no English. Have you seen them?" She looked over his shoulder. It was a typical one-room cabin with a sleeping loft, and empty but for Martin and Diamond.

"Not those kids from the plane wreck up at the hot springs?" he said. "No, I haven't seen them. They're missing?"

"Yes."

"Do you need help looking?" He reached for the parka hanging next to the door.

Kate suffered this third shock womanfully and said, "No, it's fine, plenty of help. If you do happen to see them, give Matt a call, okay?"

"Sure. Well, you know where I live if you decide I can help more."

He smiled at them all and Kate turned away, hearing the door close behind her as she tried to regain her equilibrium in this alternate universe she had stumbled into all unaware. "Who was that?" she said in a low voice.

"And what have they done with the real Martin?" Matt said.

"What is wrong with you guys?" Laurel said. "Maybe he just decided to grow up. People do."

"Generally before they're forty," Matt said, and was quelled by a look from his fiancée.

They followed Mutt all the way around Martin's house and on to the next house, where she went to the back door and stopped. She looked at Kate and sneezed.

"Auntie Edna's," Kate said.

Jim made the sign of the cross and she slapped his arm.

They tried the back door but it was locked. Someone had shoveled the doorstep recently, though.

"Come on, Mutt," Kate said, and led the way to the front of the house and had her sniff the front door. Mutt's tail went up again and began to wag.

"They went in the back and came out the front?" Jim said.

"It would seem so," Kate said. "Mutt." She had taken the bottom sheet from the bed the kids had slept in and brought it along. She let Mutt sniff it again, although the insides of her own nostrils felt frozen solid and she couldn't understand how Mutt could smell anything at all, let alone a two-day-old scent. But Mutt sneezed again and, nose to the path she trotted down to the street and turned right. The rest of the village passed in review, more homes, Emaa's old house and Auntie Joy's on the left, Laurel's Riverside Café and Bingley's store on the right. When they came to the Step Road turnoff Mutt didn't hesitate, taking it at a lope they had to hustle to match. She took the first right off the road, a snow-blower-cleared path that led right up to the front door of Auntie Vi's B&B. Mutt stood on the porch and looked at Kate over her shoulder, eyes bright, ears up and tail wagging furiously, clearly visible in the porch light. If she'd been a dog in a *Looney Tunes* cartoon it could not have been more obvious.

Kate let out a long, heartfelt sigh. "The kids are fine, guys. Go home."

They dispersed without argument, such was the power of Auntie Vi even in absentia.

"Van asked Auntie Vi if she had any copies of an old local newspaper," Kate said. "So Vi took Van over to Auntie Edna's house and they found the kids and brought them back here." She looked at Jim. "And she didn't tell anyone because the story is all over the Park now about their circumstances."

"Okay," he said, "but I'd like to actually see the kids. Just to be sure."

"Me, too."

A snow machine went by and someone shouted a greeting but they were going too fast to be identified. Kate and Jim walked up the path to the steps and up the steps to the door. Kate tried the handle and, no surprise, it was locked, possibly for the first time since Auntie Vi had built the house and opened the B&B. She knocked, waited, and then knocked again, louder this time. From inside there were the sounds of a frantic scramble of chairs scraping back and hasty footsteps. Silence again, until they heard footsteps come up to the other side of the door. "Who that?" Auntie Vi said.

"It's Kate, Auntie," Kate said. "And Jim."

The door opened a crack and Auntie Vi peered out suspiciously. "Only you here?"

"Only us, Auntie. And Mutt."

Auntie Vi opened the door a centimeter more and looked behind them. Satisfied, she opened it all the way. "Okay. You come in."

Auntie Vi waited until all three of them were inside before closing and locking the door behind them. Kate refrained from comment.

Van leaned out of the kitchen. "Who was it, Auntie? Oh. Hi, Kate. Jim. Hey, Mutt!"

"Van. Where's Johnny?"

"Back at the house."

"You come," Auntie Vi said.

They followed her into the kitchen. "You sit," she said, and filled mugs with coffee and thunked them down on the table, along with a plate with two lonely rounds of fry bread on it. "So," she said, pouring her own coffee and sitting across from them. "What is news?"

"Not much, Auntie," Jim said.

"You eat," she said, shoving the plate at them and got up for a moment to find the shaker with the powdered sugar in it. She applied it lavishly, as if it would cover up the fact that there were no seconds, a thing unheard of in Kate's memory. "You find those kids yet?"

"Not yet, Auntie," Jim said.

She snorted. "Not much use, you," she said. "Good you quit the troopers."

"I think so, too," he said, unperturbed.

Kate got up to get a drink of water and saw two mugs stained with cocoa sitting in the sink. She filled her glass and returned to the table, contriving to give Jim a wink as she sat down. Auntie Vi missed it but Van didn't, and looked apprehensive.

"Did you find those copies of the *Pick & Shovel* over at Auntie Edna's?" Kate said blandly.

"Er, yes," Van said uncomfortably, shooting a glance at Auntie Vi, who rose to her feet and began making a tremendous clatter and bang of pots and pans.

"You eat dinner," Auntie Vi said, her back to them. "I make secret ingredient."

Kate perked up at that, because secret ingredient was about her favorite dish in the whole wide world.

"You chop." Auntie shoved a package of pork ribs at her along with a large knife in a manner that made Kate grateful it wasn't point first. Auntie Vi slammed into the pantry and slammed back out with a bag of rice, unearthed the rice cooker, and filled it and switched it on.

Kate began separating the ribs between the bones. "This sure is a lot of ribs for four people, Auntie," she said. She looked up to see Auntie Vi glaring at her. A lesser person might have quailed. "But then, kids that age eat at least twice their own weight every twenty-four hours." She smiled. "Don't they."

A deathly silence fell over the kitchen, to the point Kate could hear Jim and Van breathing. A couple of snow machines went by outside. She went on finding the meat between the ribs and slicing through it.

Auntie Vi broke the silence finally, with some words of Aleut that sounded very choice and a couple of which Kate recognized as not repeatable in polite company. Auntie Vi slammed the pot she had been filling down on the stove, the water sloshing over the side and extinguishing the burner flame, and stamped out of the kitchen and down the hall.

Kate wiped up the water, relit the burner, and put the pot back on. She finished slicing the ribs as the water began to boil and dumped them in and put the lid on, looking up to see Auntie Vi walking back into the kitchen trailed by the two kids Kate had last seen sleeping in one of the Grosdidier Clinic's beds on New Year's Day. Auntie Vi yanked two more chairs out and yelled at the kids in what was most certainly not Spanish. The kids seemed to understand it anyway and climbed up on chairs on either side of Vanessa. The little girl looked calm but the boy looked angry. Kate welcomed his anger. It meant he wasn't beaten, that he was still fighting.

She washed her hands and wiped them and went to the living room to roust Mutt off the couch. David's eyes widened when Mutt came into the kitchen but Anna smiled. Kate sat down across the table from them and took out her phone. She tapped into the browser, loaded Google Translate, and turned on the voice input. "My name is Kate," she said, and tapped on the speaker icon and waited for the program to translate. "What is your name?"

The boy looked mutinous, glaring first at her and then at Auntie Vi, who swore at him some more in Aleut.

"I'm Anna," the girl said, so then he glared at her. The resemblance to Auntie Vi was uncanny.

Auntie Vi shook her finger at him. "David," he said sulkily.

"Where are your parents?"

Kate kept the questions short and simple. The story came out slowly and reluctantly, and what with the wait for the translator it took a while to be told and understood. David and Anna's *papi* had been killed by the gangs, their *mami* had been hurt, and she had brought them to *el norte* where they would be safe. At the border someone took Mami away and two big men in blue jackets with white letters on the back took David and Anna and brought them to the place where there was snow like the book with the boy in the strange orange suit with the pointy hood. They drove them to the house with the star on the mountain next door and the two big men sold them to the Bad Man.

Auntie Vi shoved her chair back and went over to the refrigerator to yank open the freezer and grab a package of snow peas. She slammed into the pantry and slammed back out again with a can of Campbell's Cream of Mushroom soup. She opened the can and dumped it into the pot with the ribs and stirred it vigorously enough that she burned herself on the hot liquid splashing out of the pot. This called for more Aleut. She ripped open the bag of snow peas and shook them violently into the pot and slammed the lid back on.

Neither of the kids turned a hair. They knew she wasn't mad at them.

They had been with the Bad Man not quite a month when he took them on the plane. And then the plane crashed and they woke up at the clinic in company with a bunch of adults they didn't know and David didn't trust not to hurt Anna. So they left to find somewhere to hide. Auntie Edna's was the first door they'd found that was unlocked.

The rice was done and Auntie Vi pulled the liner out of the cooker and slammed it down on the table, Jim getting his fingers out of the way just in time. Plates came next followed by forks, a red-enameled cast iron trivet in the shape of a heart and the pot of ribs on top of that. She ladled food onto the plates and dumped one in front of each of them. Van got up and went to the refrigerator and brought back a bottle of soy sauce and Auntie Vi sent her a fulminating look like she was going to stab Van with her own fork right then and there.

The kids ate with good appetite and asked for more. So did everyone else. Mutt waited, looking hopeful, until Anna gave her a bone. She accepted it delicately between her teeth and retired into the living room.

Anna had already survived a lot worse than a half-wolf half-husky begging at the dinner table.

The kids started yawning after dinner and Van took them to their room and put them to bed. Kate texted Matt that the kids were fine. There was the distant buzz of a snow machine coming down the Step road.

"We found them at Auntie Edna's," Vanessa said, coming back into the kitchen.

Kate nodded. "I figured. Mutt sniffed out their trail."

"They didn't want to go back to the clinic. Well, they didn't really want to come with us, either, or David didn't, but Auntie Vi made them."

"How?"

"She just yelled at them. But I don't think they're afraid of her."

Kate didn't think so, either. "They know their mom's name. That's something."

"ICE has probably already deported her back to Honduras," Jim said.

"We will find her," Kate said precisely, "wherever she is."

He had enough of a sense of self-preservation to shut up.

Van looked up. "Did you hear that?"

"What?"

A knock sounded at the door, louder this time, followed by a man's voice. "Hey, is this Viola Shugak's B&B? Our plane broke down and we need a bed for the night. Hello?"

"Whole place full!" Auntie Vi yelled. "Go away!"

"What? I'm sorry, I couldn't hear you, what did you say?" Another knock on the door. "Ma'am, it's freezing out here. Could you at least let us in while we talk?"

Auntie Vi, swearing again, stormed out of the kitchen and they heard the door open. "We're full up! No beds! What—what are you—"

The next moment the door to the kitchen was remarkably full of two very large men, Auntie Vi buzzing around like a hornet in back of them. One was tall and blond, the other shorter and stocky. They had similar buzz cuts and a similar look, disciplined, businesslike, and utterly lacking in warmth. They were dressed in identical blue jackets and Jim saw the bulge under the heavy fabric under both their left arms.

They assessed the room: three women of three different generations and one man. Their eyes lingered longer on Jim and he took care to leave his hands motionless on the table. "Who are you and what do you want?" he said.

"We're ICE agents," the tall one said. He produced a badge and flashed it briefly.

"Immigration and Customs Enforcement," the stocky one said, producing his own even more briefly. "I'm Agent Gaunt. This is Agent O'Hanlon. We understand you're illegally harboring two undocumented aliens."

Auntie Vi shoved in between the two of them and marched around the table to the kitchen sink. One of the men almost reached for his weapon and then let his hand drop when she began furiously crashing the dirty dishes around, muttering in Aleut what Kate was certain were highly uncomplimentary comments about their uninvited guests' ancestry and character.

"Understand from whom?" Kate said. Vanessa looked at her with frightened eyes and Kate could tell by her body language that she was seconds away from bolting to the kids' side. She gave a tiny shake of her head.

"An anonymous tip," Gaunt said.

"Someone in the Park called you and alerted you to their presence?"

"Yes."

She folded her arms loosely and leaned her chair back on its rear legs. "And you came all this way into the Alaskan Bush in the dead of winter to retrieve two illegal aliens. As reported by an anonymous source."

"It's a serious matter, Ms.—"

"Shugak. Kate Shugak." The two men exchanged a glance. Jim looked at her and she knew what he knew, that these two men recognized her name. She had never seen either of them before.

"As I said, it's a serious matter, Ms. Shugak," Gaunt said smoothly. "Harboring an illegal alien is a felony, punishable by up to twenty years in prison. Much better to hand them over to the proper authorities, don't you think?"

Kate smiled. "Well," she said, her voice dropping to a dangerous purr, "yes, but I don't think you are the proper authorities. Are you?" She saw Jim's hands slide back to the edge of the table. She saw Van see him do it, too. She let her hands fall to her lap and pulled her feet back to plant them directly beneath her.

"What makes you say that?"

"You wouldn't have come all this way without contacting the local authorities. Since I know all the local authorities and I haven't heard from any of them, I don't think you're legit."

She cocked her head. "My guess is you work for the people Gary Curley worked for. Gary Curley being the pedophile whose plane your two illegal aliens were on. Your two very, very underage illegal aliens."

Gaunt and O'Hanlon exchanged a glance. O'Hanlon shrugged. "We just want the phone," Gaunt said. "Hand it over. There's no reason for anyone to get hurt."

"What phone?" Kate said.

"Don't play coy, Shugak." O'Hanlon reached for the gun under his arm at the same time Gaunt did.

From the corner of her eye Kate saw Auntie Vi reach down to open a tall, narrow cupboard next to the oven where any reasonable person would have kept their baking sheets, from which she pulled out a single-barreled pump-action shotgun. She brought it up and racked it. "You will leave this house. You can walk out or you can be carried, but you will leave."

As children the aunties had all been forced into boarding schools and taught to speak, read and write English so as to forget their Aleut. Once home, as a matter of everyday conversation they spoke Aleut to each other and a sort of pidgin English to everyone else, mostly, Kate thought, in rebellion against the attempt to strip them of language and culture by gussuks. When so moved, however, they could all sound like they graduated from Vassar.

It startled the fake agents, though, for just a moment as they were going for their weapons, just long enough for Jim to lean forward, plant a hand on Vanessa's chest and shove her over backward in her chair. It hit the floor and she slid off the chair and across the kitchen floor right under the swinging doors into the pantry, disappearing from sight and thankfully out of range. O'Hanlon's gun had cleared its holster and he was bringing it up when Auntie Vi's shotgun boomed. It sounded a lot louder in an enclosed space than it did when duck hunting from a skiff on a lake. It was one hell of a starting pistol and many things happened at once.

Auntie Vi had fired wide and mostly missed but blood bloomed on O'Hanlon's left shoulder and he cursed and fired at the same time the recoil of the shotgun slammed Auntie Vi back up against the sink. She slid to the floor and out of Kate's view.

"Mutt!" Kate yelled. "Take!" She shoved off with her feet and somersaulted backwards out of her chair to land on two hands, one foot, and one knee just like a superhero.

There was a terrifying growl and the sound of fabric tearing and flesh ripping. Gaunt screamed. "Al! Get it off me! Shoot it! Shoot it!"

Jim slid beneath the table and came up again with it on, top of him. He shoved it up on one end and pushed the surface towards the two men. Kate scuttled forward to help, cringing when she heard more shots. One of the bullets hit spang in the middle of a Royal Tara tea set, the Irish Treasure pattern that was Auntie Vi's pride and joy and that she never took down from on top of the cupboard except to wash. The bullet broke three cups, two saucers, the creamer and the serving plate and Kate heard a choked cry of protest from Auntie Vi but then there was another terrible sound of rending flesh and Gaunt screamed again.

"Al! Shoot it, Al, shoot it, get it offa me!" More shots were fired and holes appeared in the ceiling and one clanged into the chimney of the big black oil stove, knocking it apart and spilling a cloud of soot into the room.

Kate put her shoulder next to Jim's, Vanessa was suddenly on his other side, and together the three of them shoved the heavy wooden table forward. It banged into Jim's chair and shoved it into O'Hanlon, who fired again. The bullet hit the surface of the table and didn't quite go through although Kate had an uncomfortably close look at the outline of the round. They shoved hard again, catching one of the men between the door frame and the table. Mutt growled and Gaunt screamed again, more faintly this time.

Kate looked at Jim and pointed to herself and to the right. He pointed to himself and to the left. "Van, get Auntie Vi's shotgun. Go, now!"

Kate went low and came around the other side to see O'Hanlon shoving at the table. He saw her and raised his weapon, and then Jim hit him from the other side, grabbed his gun hand, put his other hand flat against O'Hanlon's elbow, and pulled back. A bone cracked and O'Hanlon screamed.

Another gun fired from in back of O'Hanlon.

"Mutt!" Kate yelled. "Off! Off! Off!"

There was another growl, more tearing of fabric and flesh, another scream, another gunshot. Kate shoved between the table and the frame of the door and dove over

O'Hanlon into the hallway beyond. David and Anna were peering around the corner, Anna frightened, David, bless him, angry, Mutt, on her toes, her hackles full on up, and looking all wolf, stood next to them, was growling at full volume. Gaunt was on his knees, bleeding from arm, thigh, and shoulder with his left arm dangling uselessly, but with his right he was bringing his weapon to bear. She stepped up behind him and kicked him in the lower back as hard as she could. He went down and she stepped on the wrist of his gun hand and put her full weight on it. His grip loosened and she picked up his weapon and put on the safety. "Mutt! On guard!" Mutt took a single leap forward to thrust her blood-stained muzzle into Gaunt's face and ratcheted up the growl. Gaunt quailed.

"Stay there!" Kate said to the kids, and felt for her phone to call for reinforcements.

"Kate." It was Vanessa, calling from the kitchen.

She must have dropped it in the fight. She looked around, feeling a little light-headed like she always did after hand-to-hand combat.

"Kate?" It was Vanessa again.

She saw that Jim had pulled O'Hanlon's coat down his arms and was pulling his belt off, probably to tie his feet. Kate bent over Gaunt and unbuckled his belt and pulled it free. She unzipped his pants and pulled them down around his ankles where they caught on his boots. He made a faint protest which she ignored. She restrained his hands at the wrist with the belt.

He was staring at her in pain mixed with disbelief.

"You don't fuck with the aunties," she said.

"Kate!"

"All right, all right, I'm coming." She looked at the kids and held her palm out. "It's okay. Go back to bed. *Dormez-vous*." And then she remembered that that was French.

"Kate!"

She heard Jim swear and turned to slide between the table and the doorway. Vanessa was on the floor in front of the sink, holding a blood-soaked dishcloth to Auntie Vi's shoulder. "I can't stop it! I can't stop it, Kate!"

Kate found herself on her knees next to Auntie Vi, who had her chin tucked in so she could squint down at her wound. She looked alarmingly calm.

"Goddamn it, goddamn it, goddamn it," Jim said. "I didn't think he hit her. I didn't think he hit anywhere close."

"Your arm is bleeding," Van said, looking at Jim.

He gave it a cursory glance. "I caught a couple of pellets. It's nothing serious." He looked back down at Auntie Vi. "Nothing like this."

"Jim," Kate said, "call Matt. Tell him to get here as fast as he can and bring everything with him." Without looking Kate reached for the drawer that held the kitchen towels and pulled it all the way out, grabbing a handful and shoving them over the one Van was already holding to Auntie Vi's shoulder. They were quickly soaked. Van was sobbing quietly, her hand smoothing back Auntie Vi's hair where it had come loose from its braid.

Jim stood up and in a moment she heard him talking urgently into his phone but all her attention was on Auntie Vi. "The boys'll be here soon, Auntie, and they'll get you all fixed up. Five minutes, just hold on till they get here and patch you up and you'll be fine."

Auntie Vi leaned her head back on the floor. She looked past Kate and smiled, and Kate turned to see David kneel down next to her. He leaned over so he could look directly into Auntie Vi's eyes. "*No mueras. No mueras, abuelita!*"

The words seemed to get Auntie Vi's attention in a way that nothing else in that moment could. She met David's eyes and an actual smile spread across her face. "Okay," she said, although she could have had no clue as to what he was saying, and then she winked at him.

And then all four Grosdidiers crashed into the room carrying all their emergency gear and Kate had never been so glad to see anyone in her life.

# Fourteen

## MONDAY, JANUARY 7
### *Niniltna*

"THEY FLEW UP TO THE STEP," AGENT Mason said. "It's in mothballs for the winter as you, ah, know, with just a single caretaker on site."

"Did they kill him?" Kate said. She felt bruised all over and was moving slowly but at least she was moving. Jim, a bandage on his upper left arm where Peter had dug out several shotgun pellets, was in the kitchen making coffee and fried egg sandwiches. She and Mason were sitting at the dining room table. Johnny and Vanessa were trying to disappear into the living room couch so no one would notice them and tell them they had to leave so the grownups could talk.

"They did, I'm sorry to say. But since you and, ah—" He looked over at the half-wolf, half-husky sprawled in front of the fireplace.

"Mutt. Her name is Mutt."

"Ah, Mutt and the rest of the cavalry apprehended them

in such efficient fashion, we have the, ah, smoking guns in evidence." He didn't smile. "Literally."

"Will they roll?"

"I don't know. I hope so, but..."

"Will you offer them a deal?"

He gave her a wary look. "That would, ah, depend on if they roll."

Across the room Mutt raised her head. Kate said, very gently, "They shot my aunt in her own home. The only reason she's not dead is that we had competent emergency medical aid five minutes away. I would not take kindly to hearing that the perps skated on a charge of attempted murder because they helped the FBI make a drug trafficking case."

"Noted." Mason decided it would be politic to change the subject. "What was your aunt doing with a shotgun in the kitchen, anyway?"

Kate pointed at the gun rack over the door, which held a double-barreled pump action shotgun and a .30-06.

"Yes, but your weapons are, ah, in a gun rack. A much more traditional method of storage."

She smiled. "I might have a backup not in plain sight in any number of places."

"Or two," Jim said from the kitchen.

"Or three," Johnny said from the couch.

"Or four," Van said from next to him.

"What about that hot pink Beretta I won for you at the NRA dinner?" Johnny said.

"Do you really think I'm ever going to shoot that thing? I'd be laughed off the range."

"Okay, four," Johnny said.

"You went to an NRA dinner?" Jim said.

Johnny spread his hands. "Some old fart Fairbanksan bought a bunch of tickets and gave them away to UAF students. It was a free meal."

"You should have seen it," Val said. "It was like Borderlands 3, only with real guns and no aliens."

"And nobody got shot."

"Good to know," Jim said.

Mason cleared his throat and looked at Kate. "I, ah, quite see your point."

"You were saying about Gaunt and O'Hanlon?"

"They're known to us and they're pretty tough nuts with very little leverage. Kevin Gaunt has several ex-wives, no children, and Allan O'Hanlon has one daughter, ah, estranged." Mason leaned back in his chair with his hands linked behind his head, speaking from memory. He'd flown into Niniltna the afternoon before. Nick, the trooper from Tok, had flown in at sunrise that morning and was thoroughly pissed off when Mason showed up to take control of a crime scene that would have been a slam-dunk case to his, Nick's, credit. "They both worked for ICE until four years ago, when they took early retirement and started a consulting firm, Gaunt, O'Hanlon Ltd."

"What does Gaunt, O'Hanlon Ltd. consult on?"

"Security procedures and installations."

"And you said that with such a straight face," Kate said, admiring. "Are they making a living at it?"

"They were operating at a healthy profit from their first year."

"Pretty good for a startup."

He inclined his head. "We haven't been following them, per se, but they have appeared in proximity to enough hard characters and near enough to some fairly hinky events that they have become persons of interest. I've got someone tracking their passport activity. They travel a lot, most frequently to New York, Seattle, and Mexico, but there are some trips to Central and South America, too. We noticed that over the past two to three years, their passports started showing up at the US–Canadian border."

"Which checkpoint?"

"Lynden, Washington."

"On the way to Vancouver, then."

"Possibly."

"New York, Seattle, Vancouver," Kate said. "And then Mexico, Central and South America. I don't suppose they've made any recent trips to China, Japan, or South Korea."

Mason shook his head. "Impossible for them to pass unnoticed through those countries."

"Where was their point of origin?"

"Most often? Chicago." He sighed, and brought his chair back down on all four legs and scrubbed his hands through his hair. He looked tired. "I'm sure they're working for whoever it was who put the pills on Curley's plane, which is the same whoever Curley was working for. Even without a successful interrogation it's pretty clear from what you report them saying that they were sent here to recover Curley's phone."

And kill any witnesses, Kate thought. "You cracked it yet?"

He snorted. "My guys are afraid it has some kind of failsafe that will make the phone explode if the wrong password is entered. They're working on it."

"What kind of money are we talking here?"

"You can buy a kilogram of fentanyl for $80,000 and turn it around for a $1.6 million profit. That Ziploc bag you found?" He nodded at Jim. "Just under two kilos. And you know there has to be more up there under all that snow." They all looked out the window. It was snowing again, big fat flakes that melted as soon as they landed. At the elevation of the wreck it would be sticking around until April or May, if not June.

"The kids identified Gaunt and O'Hanlon as the two men who sold them to Curley. They flew commercial, David thinks from Texas. At any rate he saw people wearing cowboy boots and big cowboy hats and bolo ties, just like in the movies."

"Can they remember what day?"

"It was after Thanksgiving, because they saw the star from the windows of Curley's house." She saw his look of confusion and said, "That big star on the mountains in

Anchorage. You could practically touch it from Curley's front window."

"Yes, I, ah, remember."

Jim came out with mugs hooked around the fingers of one hand and a plate of sandwiches cut in half. He sat down at the table. "Why'd they pick Niniltna to transfer the drugs?"

"Just guessing, but—" Mason shrugged. "It's the perfect spot. Forty-eight hundred feet long, newly paved, maintained by the Suulutaq so it's always plowed, no tower so nobody keeping track of flights in and out, enough traffic to hide in plain sight."

"I had a friend who works at Ted's tower. He says they don't have to file a flight plan at all, and even if they did they could say they were going to Fairbanks. Anywhere, other than where they were really going."

Mason nodded.

"About that Niniltna traffic," Jim said. "I was talking to Mrs. Doogan, the high school principal, last week. Her office window looks right out on the airstrip. She says she's seen a lot of small jets in and out over the past couple of years. She put it down to the Suulutaq mine, owners, investors, like that, coming in to take a look at where their money's going."

"She notice any, ah, identifying marks?"

Jim shook his head. "She recognized Erland's G II like we all do, he'd been in and out so often. But the rest of them rarely have even tail numbers, or not ones you can read from a distance anyway. Also, George Perry? Chugach Air Taxi? He says he might have heard two jets on New Year's Eve, not one. He can't swear to it because he couldn't see anything when he looked out the window because of the blizzard. But anecdotally at least it backs up your reconstruction of events."

"So," Kate said, "they make the pills in Canada and fly them into Niniltna, where they transfer the load to Curley's jet and he brings them back to Anchorage, where he repackages them and sees that they are distributed. From there they're sold to Alaskans or mailed or carried overseas. Right so far?"

Mason nodded and took a half a sandwich. The yolk was still a little runny and some dripped down his wrist. He licked it off and washed it down with coffee. "If we could get a line on the money, we could blow the whole thing." He was looking at Kate.

"I might have an idea about that."

Mason sat back in his chair, looking pleased. "I hoped you might."

I bet you did, you little sidewinder, she thought. She held up her phone. "Let me make a call." She grabbed her parka. Mutt leapt to her feet and followed her out on the deck. Kate closed the door behind them both and raised her face to the sky, eyes closed, and let the snowflakes melt on her skin, clean and cold. Mutt took the stairs in a graceful leap and disappeared into the underbrush, startling a willow ptarmigan into the sky with an indignant squawk. "Yeah, if she'd wanted to catch you, she would have," Kate told it as it beat air going away. She got out her phone and called Stephanie.

"Two calls in one week! Are you dying?"

It was meant as a joke but Kate was still too close to having nearly lost Auntie Vi not to flinch. "Not so far as I know. I need a favor."

"Name it."

Next she called Kurt. "How's it going?"

"On the hacking into the Bannister Foundation's records? Very slowly. I hate to say it, Kate, but so far as I can tell from these accounts, it looks squeaky clean. But Tyler had a thought last night and we're going to run with it today. I'll let you know."

"Any breadcrumbs you can find on the donors. The big ones, Kurt."

"Yeah, I was going to track back every $25 Erland got from that grandma in Tuntutuliak and report faithfully back to you."

"Smart ass."

"Is it true about Auntie Vi?"

"Yes. She's alive, Kurt."

Kurt took a long breath. "Auntie Joy's the one you can't help loving. Auntie Balasha never says much but she is always there to talk to, and sometimes that's all you need, and sometimes it's what you need most. Auntie Edna scared the bejesus out of me."

"She scared the bejesus out of everyone."

Kurt laughed. "True dat. But Auntie Vi? She always has your back, no matter what. Right or wrong, good or bad, she'll go to the mattresses for you."

"She did this time, too."

"Those two guys involved somehow in this Bannister Foundation thing?"

"I think so."

Kurt's voice hardened. "We'll get it done, Kate."

He hung up and Kate's phone rang immediately. It was Stephanie. "How'd you find out so fast?"

"It only took one phone call, Kate."

She went back inside and laid it out for Mason. "Is that enough for a warrant, do you think?"

"Do you think the people in Anchorage are in on it?"

Kate really, really wanted to see Jane doing the perp walk on the ten o'clock news. "I don't know," she said reluctantly. "I don't have any proof one way or the other, not yet."

Mason shook his head. "I don't know that I can get a warrant for his entire office based on evidence so wholly, ah, circumstantial."

"Somebody shot his lawyer. Two to the chest, one to the head."

"Gaunt and O'Hanlon weren't yet in the state. We believe Curley's employer may have employed local, ah, talent in that instance, and called in Gaunt and O'Hanlon when it failed. Fun fact: We have no record of them arriving via commercial carrier. A private jet did land that afternoon in Anchorage. Its flight plan said it originated in Chicago. It took off again yesterday afternoon at one p.m. It did not land back in Chicago."

"Got an owner?"

"It belongs to a consortium called Executive Air Charters. Private jet rentals for corporate executives. We've been in, ah, contact, and they're having some difficulty sorting out their records."

"They're saying they don't know who rented a piece of equipment that cost them $50 million?"

"More like sixty, but I get your point." Mason's smile was thin. "We're, ah, encouraging the recovery of their memory."

Kate thought for a few moments. "Gaunt and O'Hanlon wanted Curley's phone. Whoever they're working for was monitoring the number and when David tried to call his mom it let their bosses know where it was, and they went to a lot of expense to get it back. If Erland was in the same business with the same people, they might have given him the same kind of phone." She looked up. "If you could crack both phones, there would be all the evidence you'd need."

"We haven't cracked Curley's yet."

Cyber security was the overriding concern for businesses everywhere now. It was entirely possible that the elevated encryption was merely a symptom of that. It was also entirely possible that it was evidence of the paranoia of every criminal organization on the planet.

Or not. "I wonder who has Erland's personal effects," she said.

Jim smiled at her from across the table. "After all," he said, "you're his trustee."

"Which you knew," Kate said, looking at Mason.

Agent Mason didn't even try to look innocent. "You were a way in."

"You do push your luck, Agent Mason."

He smiled. "It's Gerry, Kate."

# Fifteen

## TUESDAY, JANUARY 8
### *Anchorage*

"E RLAND'S PERSONAL EFFECTS?" JANE frowned and then remembered that it caused frown lines. "The smaller valuables I put in his safety deposit box. The rest I expect are at his home."

"His phone?"

"In the safety deposit box."

"Where's the safety deposit box?" Kate said, and was sorry when Jane didn't even try to argue with her. Probably had something to do with walking into Jane's office with an FBI Special Agent at her heels.

The phone was in the box. It was the exact same make and model as Curley's phone. Kate turned it on. It was password protected. Jane denied all knowledge of passwords but Kate noted a sheen of sweet on her forehead.

Kate handed the phone over to Mason. "Now you have twins," she said. "Will it help?"

"Was there anything else in the box that might have been of use?"

She shook her head. "Some jewelry, a photograph album of family pictures going back to the Stampede."

In the bank's parking lot she said, "Something you should know. In my capacity as trustee of Erland Bannister's estate, and given that he had reduced his holdings to the Bannister Foundation, I, ah—" he grinned "—copied the Bannister Foundation work product files from Jane Morgan's laptop. At present, my people are working on tracing all of the donations back to the people who actually wrote the checks."

He looked at her sideways. "We could look at that, too."

"You could but until you crack those phone—" she nodded at it in his hand "—and find evidence that Erland was in fact involved in this mess, you have no standing."

"Whereas you as his trustee—"

She nodded. "I can legally volunteer any and all access." Jim got out of the Forester and opened the back door for Mutt, who bounced over exuberantly and banged into Kate's thigh, knocking her back a step. A sound like a bee whizzed by her cheek and there was a crackle of broken safety glass behind her.

"Gun! Gun! Gun!" Mason screamed, and the next thing Kate knew she was on the ground with Jim on top of her. Mutt barked, the deep, menacing sound rolling across the parking lot. Jim had his arms around Kate and they were rolling over the ice-encrusted pavement until they came to rest beneath some heavy vehicle with high clearance.

Mason was yelling at the other people coming and going from the bank. "Get down! Shooter on the roof! Get down, get down, get down!" The security guard inside the bank opened the door. "FBI! Call 911! Active shooter this location!" The security guard earned his paycheck that day by doing what he was told, ducking back inside and barring the door against a flood of customers stampeding outside.

"Are you okay?" Jim's voice sounded distantly in Kate's ears. He was running his hands over her body. "Are you shot? Are you hurt? Kate?" Another shot hit the vehicle above them with a crunch of metal and he flinched. "Mason! Where's the shooter?"

"I'm a little busy here!" Another shot hit a different vehicle nearby and a tire went suddenly flat.

Mutt shoved in next to them and hunkered down, a long, low, steady growl issuing forth with enough menace in it to shrivel any shooter's balls. "Good girl. Stay here." Jim looked back down at Kate. "Kate," he said with an obvious effort at some measure of calm. "Are you hurt?"

Kate tried to think past the adrenaline. "I don't think so," she said. She clenched her hands and flexed her feet. "I can feel everything, and everything seems to be working." Her heart especially, it was working really well, peak efficiency.

"Good." He slid off her to her free side and peered out. "Mason! What's happening?" They heard a siren approaching.

"Stay where you are!"

"Where is he?"

"I think on top of the Century 21 building across the street!"

Jim scrabbled around until he could look in that direction.

"Be careful!" Kate said. The siren grew louder and tires crunched over the ice into the parking lot from both Ingra and Gambell.

Jim pulled the ball cap from his head and held it out. Nothing. "He heard the sirens. He probably heard them before we did."

"APD responding to shots fired! Identify yourselves!"

"Special Agent Mason with the FBI!" Mason shouted.

"Come out with your hands up!"

It took ten minutes for everything to sort itself out, and another five minutes before Mason convinced APD to check the roof of the Century 21 building. By then the shooter was long gone, but there were security cameras on every single corner of every single one of the nearby buildings and Mason was busy confiscating all the footage he could before APD got it together enough to realize this was their crime scene.

Kate, trembling a little, stood leaning against the Forester with Mutt on one side and Jim on the other. They knew a couple of the responding APD officers, which helped when it came time to give their statements.

They were just finishing up when Mason approached. Kate's look literally stopped him in his tracks. "On New

Year's Eve a small jet crashed in the Quilak Mountains above Niniltna. Two children were recovered from the wreck alive, along with a wholesale quantity of fentanyl and, as it happens, a phone belonging to the owner of the aircraft. The phone was used to make a call, and evidently alerted someone to its location.

"On Wednesday night someone tried to break into our house in Anchorage while Jim and I were in residence. That same night possibly the same someone shot and killed Erland Bannister's attorney.

"On Saturday night my aunt, Viola Shugak, was shot by two men who invaded her home looking for the two kids and Gary Curley's phone.

"Half an hour ago someone took a shot at me from the top of that building—" Kate pointed "—as I was exiting this building—" she pointed again "—after having accessed Erland Bannister's safety deposit box."

Mason was smart enough to restrict himself to a nod.

"The only people other than Kurt Pletnikof, my partner in Pletnikof Investigations, and Brendan McCord of the Anchorage District Attorney's office, who knew I was in town either time was the FBI and Erland Bannister's executive assistant." She stepped forward nose to nose with Mason and said, "That feels an awful lot like probable cause to me, Gerry."

"She did give us his phone," Jim said in a voice barely above a murmur.

"It doesn't have to be her," Kate said without looking

away from Mason, "but it does have to be someone in that office." She leaned in. "Or yours."

"I believe I can make that case," Agent Mason said, eschewing ahs entirely.

"Please do." Kate turned to Jim. "I'm starving. Let's go to the Bone."

So they went to the Bone, a diner frequented by city employees from the mayor on down including a vastly comforting number of cops.

"Man, you've really got it in for Jane Morgan," Jim said, shaking malt vinegar on his fries with a free hand.

"She never once asked about Johnny," Kate said flatly. "He's her son. So far as I know her only child, and a seriously good kid who is going to grow up into a seriously good, productive man. She used him as a weapon against his father so long as his father was alive, and now likes to pretend he doesn't exist. I don't have it in for her, Jim. I despise her."

"All righty then."

They called Kurt from the car. "Kate, it's too soon to—"

"Kurt, how many grants did the Bannister Foundation give out last quarter?"

"Uh, twenty-seven? Lemme count." A moment's silence. "Sorry, thirty-two."

"All for six figures or more?"

"They ranged from $100,000 to $1.5 million."

"That $1.5 million to Bering VoTech?"

"Yes."

"Give me three names no more than an hour's flight time in a Cessna 206 from Anchorage, preferably not on the road system."

"Hang on."

Kate held the phone against her leg so Kurt couldn't hear and said, "Pletnikof Investigations would like to hire you and your Cessna to fly me around tomorrow. Probably the next day, too."

"Where we going?"

"Since people are shooting at us both at home and in Anchorage, I thought we should go somewhere else for a bit."

"I'll do it for fuel."

She shook her head. "You, sir, are a lousy businessman. Done."

Kurt's voice came back on the phone. "It turns out that very few Bannister Foundation grants go to communities that are on the road system. You ready? The Bannister Foundation gave the Seldovia Public Library $100,000. Alaskans for a Sustainable Future got $300,000." Kurt snickered.

"What?"

Kurt snorted. "'Sustainable' is a trigger word for progressives. Reeks of all the causes—climate change, food independence, alternative energy, all that shit. Be a long time before anyone audits their books. It'd be politically incorrect."

"Okay," Kate said, rolling her eyes. "Where is Alaskans for a Sustainable Future?"

"King Salmon."

"Gimme another."

"Let's see, let's see. Okay, here. Kichatna Academy got a whopping $400,000."

"Where the hell is Kichatna?"

"About a hundred miles south of Denali."

"Text me the correct spelling of Kichatna so Jim can look it up on AOPA. And call me when you track down the donors."

"If."

"When. I have faith. But no pressure." Kate hung up. Jim was looking up forecasts on his phone. "How's the weather?"

"Holding, but I'll bet there is one hell of a blow building up in back of this high."

He'd clicked over to the AOPA app. "Do they all have fuel?"

"Not Kichatna but if we're running low Talkeetna's not even an hour away."

"Which one first?"

"Weather comes out of the Gulf of Alaska, so Seldovia first, King Salmon second, Kichatna last so we can run before the storm if and when it hits. If we hop quick we might maybe beat it back to Niniltna."

"How long to hit all three?"

"We can be in and out of Seldovia before noon tomorrow, but we might have to overnight in King Salmon."

"Got sleeping bags in the back of the plane?" He nodded. "So we can always sleep in the gym if we have to."

"Wouldn't be the first time. Better bring food, too."

"That's what I love about you, Chopin, always thinking with your stomach."

# Sixteen

THEY SPENT THE NIGHT IN THE TOWNHOUSE and were in the air by sunrise. Mutt stretched out on the sleeping bags and mats in the back. "Bee-yatch," Kate said. Mutt yawned and snuggled down.

Once in the air there was nothing to do but think as the Cessna ate up the miles. "I wonder if they'll really pay me."

"Who, the FBI?" He looked at her. "Do you really care if they do?"

She knew what he meant. Mason had helped her find the poisoned worm in the apple Erland had tempted her with. She didn't know that she would ever have bit freely into that apple on her own, but the expression on Marlena's face when she talked about how Jane had come to Ahtna to help them and the tiny splint on the baby's arm would live long in her memory. The temptation to do good was almost universally irresistible, as was the ability to justify means to an end, especially once one was well into the doing good business. Philanthropy could be every bit as addictive as, well, fentanyl.

Of course Erland would have known that, too.

But Jim was right. Mason's arrival on the scene had been timely. No plane crash was a happy event in a state where one in thirty-seven citizens was a pilot and nearly everyone had at least one pilot in the family, but any plane crash that took out Gary Curley couldn't be judged all bad, and that it precipitated the FBI's involvement was only a bonus. No, she had cause to be very grateful to Special Agent James G. Mason, because working with him beginning three days after she'd met with Erland's attorney meant she would be well suited up in good citizenship armor when the indictments started coming down. She'd fingered the Bannister Foundation—although she was certain that Mason, the twisty little weasel, had already been looking at it—and she'd not only cooperated with the FBI, she was very nearly leading the investigation. Probably didn't hurt that she'd been shot at in the process, either, although she wasn't feeling quite as grateful to either shooter.

The gray skies were continuing to glower with a threat as yet unrealized, so Jim flew a diagonal course over the Kenai Peninsula that debouched into the head of Kachemak Bay. From there it was twenty minutes until they touched down on the dirt strip on the mountain-lined, thickly forested fjord that managed to look spectacular even on this grim day. Seldovia was a village of three hundred people and at this time of year they were happy to see anyone new. An attractive older woman named Darlene, who had a twinkle in her eyes and a bubbly manner, gave them a ride to the library. The library was one room in the municipal building and it was closed but they found the librarian at home. Her name was Shirley and she had red hair and freckles and a hardcover copy of *To The Hilt* in one hand. Naturally this created an instantaneous bond between Shirley and Kate and promoted a fifteen-minute dive down the rabbit hole of crime fiction, which included the relative merits of Dick Francis and Ellis Peters and the need for decency in crime fiction heroes which of course created a natural digression into Damien Boyd's Nick Dixon series, with a brief animadversion to Adrian McKinty and John Sandford and just how bad a good detective could be. People who read are never strangers.

Jim, more of a nonfiction man, managed to keep himself out of the line of fire, communing silently with Shirley's husband, Les, over a mug of coffee mutely offered. When the cataract of learned criticism began to abate, he caught Kate's eye and she looked a little conscious but not at all guilty. "I'm Kate Shugak," she said, "and this is my friend Jim Chopin. I'm a private investigator—"

"No way! For real?"

"For real," Kate said gravely, avoiding Jim's eye. "I've recently been, ah, retained by the Bannister Foundation to follow up on a few of their grants. Purely as a matter of quality control." She didn't know what that meant but

Shirley didn't, either, and Kate made a pretense of consulting the Notes app on her phone. "As I understand it, last year you applied for and received a grant from the Bannister Foundation."

Shirley was more than happy to talk about the grant, extolling the Bannister Foundation's generosity and echoing Marlena's glowing reference of Jane Morgan. Fifteen minutes later Darlene, who had evidently constituted herself as their personal taxi, pulled up outside and returned them to the airstrip by way of the Seldovia Native Tribe's office. The president, a willowy woman named Crystal who would have looked at home showcasing Givenchy's latest on a fashion runway, fed them on salmon and rice and her grandmother's famous donuts for dessert (with dried salmon for Mutt) and showed them photos of Seldovia's glory days before the 1964 earthquake, when there were five canneries and king crab and shrimp could still be taken commercially from Kachemak Bay. They barely made it into King Salmon before dark.

# Seventeen

K ING SALMON SAT ON A BEND OF THE
Naknek River, which wound between Naknek Lake
and Kvichak Bay. It was built on sand dunes thrown up
by thousands of years of glacial erosion and changing
river courses, overgrown with coarse grass and a few trees.
Anything less like Seldovia could not be imagined, and the
view as they came into land reminded Kate yet again of
how rich Alaska was in its geographical diversity. It was a
company town, the company in this case being the federal
government. It had begun life as an air force base, which
explained the two runways (the north/south the same
length as Niniltna's and the east/west twice as long). After
World War II it had morphed into a home for the National
Park Service and NOAA. The Alaska Department of Fish
and Game and a Japanese aurora research radar station
also contributed to the local economy, and in summertime

proximity to the Bristol Bay salmon fishery would triple the population, which explained the multiple docks extending into the river from large buildings housing salmon processors on the shore.

King Salmon Alternative Energy Resources was traced to a guy named Ralph who had seven bent props nailed to the outside of his house. He was of an age roughly somewhere between fifty and a hundred, short, bald, wiry, and irascible, and inclined to take his and Jim's sixteen-inch difference in height in bad part. However, once he and Jim had compared logbooks, proving to Ralph's own satisfaction that he had ten times the hours Jim had, and once Jim had perforce accepted his lower-tier pilot status (so long as one ignored those seven bent props and Jim studiously did), Ralph became quite human. He was perfectly willing to tell them all about the Bannister Foundation grant, which was going to help fund a wind farm he was building on the side of the river west of town. The turbines would be networked with furnaces in each individual home and business in the area. Given that the single biggest expense in the Alaska Bush was heating oil and that it had to be brought in by barge after the ice had thawed, this seemed like a worthwhile and potentially very lucrative endeavor.

Ralph drove them out to the wind farm the next morning. The turbines were massive, two hundred and twelve feet high with nacelles the size of the 206's fuselage and blades a hundred sixteen feet long. When they lifted off later Jim made a slow circle around the wind farm, which looked oddly even more impressive than it had from the ground.

"Admit it," Jim said over the headset. "You're already thinking about building a wind farm in the Park."

"If it didn't cost so much to live in the Bush, maybe the kids would decide to stay home," she said. "Some of them, anyway. Enough to keep the town alive, maybe."

"Johnny's already figuring out a way." He told her about the conversation they'd had.

"Legal Eagle, huh?" Kate smiled, and thought about her conversation with Van. On her 160-acre homestead there were five acres on the road midway between her homestead and Mandy's from which the ground on the other side of the road fell away into a stunning view of the Kanuyaq River valley. She made a mental note to contact a surveyor in Ahtna to see how much it would cost to carve those acres out from her own. If it seemed like a good idea. At some future date. If someone she knew wanted to build their own home in the Park.

The Mother of Storms brooded on the horizon but held her fire and a little over two hours later they touched down on a dirt strip packed hard with snow. The overcast scraped the tops of the Alaska Range and Denali and Foraker floated on the northern horizon like ghosts of themselves haunting the landscape. The nearer view was a geologic tumble of rolling foothills and abrupt buttes and narrow canyons and wide valleys, well-watered by the meltoff from the Alaska Range in the north, thickly forested with spruce and aspen, and rich with wildlife furred, finned, and flying, an all-you-could-eat buffet for the taking for people willing to settle down, shoulder in, and do the hard work of forcing it to feed them.

The village of Kichatna was built at the confluence of two rivers on the remains of an old gold mine that had gone out of business after the Gold Rush. It had been revived again when Nixon took the US off the gold standard and the price per ounce went stratospheric, hunkered down through the whiplash of rising and falling prices over the next eleven years, and then closed again when the inevitable hangover set in and the price dropped almost thirty-one percent. Most of the whites had moved on to the next mine just in time for the original Dena'ina to take title of their ancestral land under the auspices of the Alaska Native Claims Settlement Act.

One result was that, unlike the Kanuyaq Mine, the Kichatna Mine infrastructure was more modern and in much better condition. The village chief was a dynamic woman in her thirties with a lot of ideas. One of them was adapting the mine buildings into a voc ed school. Kate was—barely—allowed to say her piece and receive final confirmation of her suspicions before Jim elbowed her to one side and took over. Chief Nadya took them on a forced march through the entirety of the has-been mining operation and expounded at length on her plans, which included a course curriculum aspirational of universal accreditation in engineering. Jim listened, rapt, until Kate shoved her phone under his face with the clock app up. He surfaced as one does from a dream and bade Chief Nadya farewell with genuine sorrow. The new besties vowed to keep in touch.

The sky was a bubble of gray that seemed to surround the aircraft and move with them as they flew into the southeast. The Alaska Range sank behind as the Quilaks rose up before. Kate thought of the various landscapes they'd seen over the past two days. Seldovia's 84-fathom fjord that looked like something out of a Norwegian travel brochure. The sandy river delta of King Salmon that might have looked familiar to Mark Twain from his days as a pilot on the Mississippi River. Kichatna, Triassic gold on a Mesozoic lily. Ahtna, the head of an immense river valley that depended into the Gulf of Alaska and the vast north Pacific Ocean, a stretch of water that rolled south with only intermittent island interruptions all the way to Antarctica.

Viewing Alaska from the air was a sobering exercise in perspective, capable of making one small insignificant human being feel that much smaller and even less significant. "What was all that about back there?" Kate said.

He leveled out and watched the gauges for a few moments. "I was twenty-two years in the troopers, Kate." He sounded somber over the headset and she leaned back in her seat so she could watch his profile as he spoke. It was a good profile, broad forehead, strong nose, a well-cut mouth bracketed by laugh lines, all of it held up by a firm chin. Kate had never trusted good looks as the outer man so seldom matched the inner man but in Jim's case it did. Authority without arrogance, commitment without fanaticism, firm but not inflexible, and always approachable. It was a rare combination and one of the reasons she loved him.

Wait, what?

"All those years I always got there after. After the wreck, after the overdose, after the abuse, after the murder." He was silent for a moment. "After the suicides. The teen ones were always the hardest to take." He glanced at her and smiled to see her watching him. Well, wow. That thick blond hair, those intense blue eyes, that white shark's grin. Sometimes he did take her breath away, and sometimes she let it happen.

"Money's weird, Kate. You have enough of it, it just goes off into a dark corner and breeds."

She blinked at the change of subject.

"I told you my father left me a lot of money," he said, misreading her expression.

"No, not really." She laughed a little. "But the strip and the hangar and the Cessna were kind of a clue. What, did you spend it all already?"

"Far from it." He hesitated and gave her the side eye.

"What?"

"You should know."

"Why? It's none of my business."

"It kind of is." He hesitated again.

"Just spit it out."

He blew out a breath and started laughing.

"Okay, you're starting to scare me."

Still laughing, he said, "You're my trustee."

"I'm your what!"

"You're the trustee of my will. The boss lady. The gal who writes the checks when I pass on to that Big Waypoint in the Sky."

For a moment she forgot how to say words. He was still laughing beside her, to the point that Mutt sat up and pushed her head in between the two of them, wanting in on the joke. To occupy herself Kate fished out a strip of salmon jerky, a parting gift from the kind folks in Seldovia, and passed it over. She wiped the grease from her fingers and said finally, feeling aggrieved, "What, were you and Erland Bannister communing telepathically or something?"

"We must have been," Jim said, chuckling. "Don't worry, there are step-by-step instructions." A pause. "Although I think I'm about to change all that."

"Why?"

"What I said before, about always getting there after?"

"Yeah?"

"I'd like a shot at getting there before."

"Okay...?"

He needlessly adjusted the prop pitch and gave her the side eye again. "I think I want to start a school."

She stared at him, realized her mouth was hanging open and shut it again with a snap. "A school."

"A voc ed school like the one Chief Nadya is talking about in Kichatna. But in Niniltna."

"In Niniltna."

"Yes. You heard about the Topkoks."

"Of course," Kate said, faint but pursuing.

"I talked to Auntie Vi." He looked at her but she was speechless. Seemed to be a lot of that going around lately. "She said none of the Topkok kids were interested in moving back to the Park and that she figured they would slap a for sale sign on the shop first thing. I took a look at it, and it's in good shape. Their house is right next door, and it looks good, too." He was gathering steam as he went, the accumulation of ideas over days having built by now to critical mass. "The shop can be the classrooms and the house can be the dormitory."

"Dormitory?"

"We'll need one if we want students from all over the Park. Luckily, Herbie and June had a lot of kids so it's a big house. I'll need help with the curriculum. A lot's going to depend on Herbie's inventory, at least to begin with."

"Curriculum?"

He drummed his fingers on the yoke. "I'd like to focus on teaching students to provide services the Park most needs. R&M for sleds and ATVs, marine engineering, A&P, like that."

"What about faculty?"

He made a face. "Well, my number one pick for superintendent would have been Herbie. There was nothing with moving parts that guy couldn't fix."

"I don't think Herbie Topkoks are that thick on the ground."

He tsked impatiently. "No, but we've got two thousand plus people scattered over twenty million acres, who because of their isolated living conditions have to make and mend themselves. There have to be a couple of go-to guys who are at least budding Herbies who might like full-time jobs that would keep them in the Park year round. Those aren't very thick on the ground, either."

"True enough." In spite of herself, Kate was getting into this. "And you never know, there might be some misguided soul with the exact CV you need who actually wants to move to the Bush."

There was a smile in his voice when he said, "I can see that happening." He became serious again. "Whoever we hire, Kurt does the full background check."

"We can trade. Hours for background checks for hours in the air. Pletnikof Investigations could use an on-call pilot." They flew on in silence for a few moments. "What do you see as your role in this new educational facility?"

"I'm not going to run it, that's for sure. I went to school. Doesn't mean I know a thing about running them. I thought I'd talk to Valerie Doogan about it. See if she could help with the, you know, structure."

"Good idea. You might want to talk to Annie Mike. Seems like anything that had a shot at keeping the kids home would be something the NNA would be interested in."

He looked at her, hands in his lap. There was very little turbulence and in January very little traffic. "So what do you think?"

"It won't be easy."

"Nothing worthwhile ever is."

"There is bound to be a shit ton of government rules and regulations to wade through."

"I'll hire a lawyer."

"State and federal."

"I'll hire two."

"You really do have a lot of money, don't you?"

He laughed. "So, you with me?"

She thought about what he'd said, about law enforcement always arriving after, and about wanting to get there before. "Yeah. I'm with you. However I can help, I will."

He put his hand on the back of her neck and pulled her into a kiss, the mikes on their headsets clashing but not letting that stop him. He sat back, grinning all over his face. He looked happy, she thought. Been a while since he looked happy. It suited him.

They overflew Ahtna. "Home or town?" he said.

"Town. I want to ask Mrs. Doogan about her Bannister Foundation application."

"Promise you won't scare her."

She made with the wounded eyes. He snorted.

They landed in Niniltna an hour before twilight, tied down in front of George's, said hi, and hotfooted it over to the school, where they found Doogan in her office. "It was the simplest grant application process I've ever gone through," she said. "Basically all they wanted to know was how much I wanted and when." She reflected. "Now that I think about it, I had to kind of force her to listen to what I wanted to do with their money."

"Force her?"

"The Bannister Foundation representative. The one who flew here to help me fill out the application. Jane Wardwell." Doogan's eyes sharpened. "Why do you want to know? Is there something wrong with the Bannister Foundation?"

Valerie Doogan always had been better than average bright. "I've got a little project of my own going on that I want to talk to you about," Jim said. "Buy you a cup of coffee down at the Riverside sometime?"

"Sure," Mrs. Doogan said, still suspicious, but after a quarter century in the teaching trenches recognizing a stonewall when she saw one.

Outside, the sun was a dim memory behind the cloud cover and a faint breeze chilled the skin exposed between hat brim and scarf down to icicle levels. Jim said, "Where to?"

"I can't face Auntie Vi's," Kate said. "Let's go to Bobby's."

The sled had not frozen quite solid, a good thing, and they drove to the A-frame two miles downriver and off the road. The windows shone with a warm glow that invited everyone in, and they accepted, kicking the snow from their feet, opening the door and stepping inside. Dinah looked up from the kitchen counter and greeted them with a broad smile. "Perfect timing," she said, "the pot roast is about to come out of the oven."

Katya exploded out of her bedroom. "Mutt!" Mutt met her halfway and the two of them went down in a rolling tumble of fur and pigtails, Katya's deep, chuckling laugh competing with Mutt's fake growls as they wrestled for dominance. It was hard for both of them not to compare Katya to David and Anna. Katya, secure in a safe home with loving parents. David and Anna with neither.

Bobby had a fistful of scribbled notes and was talking into a microphone. "Save the date, January thirtieth, the next meeting of the Tet Offensive Book Club, at which we'll be discussing William Manchester's *Goodbye, Darkness*. Yes, Sergei, you do have to read the book, and no, it doesn't have any pictures in it. This is your very own home-grown pirate radio station, Park Air, live with the latest episode of *Park Palaver*. So far we have five people looking for someone to fix their sleds, one to change out an impeller on a bow picker, and three, count 'em, three different love letters for Demetri Totemoff. Here's a good one to go out on." He sorted through the slips. "'To Demetri at the Lodge. Your side of the bed is awfully cold. Please come home soon and help me warm it up. Love, Hot to Trot.' Demetri, buddy. Call George for a ride into town now. Or, you know. A friend could step up. It's what friends do." He ducked just in time and the ladle shaped like a purple brontosaurus smacked into the mike instead of the side of his head. It was almost like he'd known it was coming. "Incoming! I believe that was the signal for soup's on. Okay, folks, we'll be back to talk with your very own congresscritter, the Honorable Pete Heiman, visiting from that place where they deal from the bottom of the deck better than anywhere else in the world, the one and thank god the only Washington, DC!"

He punched a button and turned a knob and Lil Nas X and Billy Ray Cyrus galloped out of the speakers. Speaking of unlikely combinations, Pete Heiman was sitting at the kitchen table and laughing. He stopped, momentarily, when he saw Kate and Jim walk in. Jim nodded at Pete and went to get a beer out of the refrigerator. Kate walked into the kitchen and said to Dinah in a low voice, "Who's got the kids?"

"They're back with Laurel and the bros," Dinah said. "Van told them it was okay and they seem to have settled in for the duration. At any rate they haven't run away again."

"Van?"

"With Johnny at your place. She's still a little shook."

"Have you seen the aunties?"

"Joy's at the hospital in Ahtna with Vi. Balasha is leading the charge at Vi's house. She rounded up any Park rat Auntie Vi ever made fry bread for."

"So, all of them."

Dinah smiled. "She sent Bobby on a supply run to Ahtna for materials this morning. The idea is to have it cleaned up, repaired, patched, and painted before Vi gets home."

"A good thought." Although Auntie Vi, being Auntie Vi, might have liked to have been able to point to the scars of bullet holes during what was sure to become the oft-told tale of The Battle of the B&B.

Dinah opened the oven and pulled out a massive casserole dish heaped with moose roast and crisp squares of beef fat and mushrooms and onions and celery and potatoes and carrots. It smelled like garlic and heaven. Kate pulled more plates from the cupboard and more silverware from the drawer and filled out the place settings on the table. Dinah filled a pitcher with a rich brown gravy. "Come and get it!"

They settled in and other than a few moans of ecstasy conversation ceased for the near future. Katya sat across from Kate and Kate could see the two points of Mutt's ears sticking up over the edge of the table next to her. Katya had always been a messy eater. And then she forgot about them and just ate.

Dinah said, "Don't forget about dessert. It's rhubarb tart with whipped cream." Pete groaned and Jim swore and Bobby said, "Did I marry up or what?" and Dinah smiled a very self-satisfied smile. Afterward they sat around in a collective state of food coma, from which Pete managed to rouse himself enough to say, "I heard about Viola. I hope she's doing well?"

"As well as can be expected after being shot in her own home."

Kate continued to look at Pete with what she hoped was a thoughtful, considering gaze. Bobby, who had known her longer than anyone else around the table except for Pete, looked from her to Jim and seemed to telepathically divine some message from Jim's poker face. He sat back and folded his arms and prepared to enjoyed the show. Dinah looked as if she wished she had her video camera in hand.

"You may have missed some other news in all the, ah, kerfuffle, Pete." Good lord, she was even starting to sound like a Special Agent.

"What other news? Why are you looking at me like that?" Pete said. "It makes me nervous."

Kate smiled at him. "It should."

Pete laughed but it wasn't his best effort. Practicing politicians were generally comfortable as the focus of attention but something in the atmosphere had changed and his eyes darted around the table as if seeking a way out, from this conversation, from this house, from the Park itself.

"There are lines even politicians don't cross, Pete," Kate said, her voice mild, "and operating a money laundry for a drug cartel is one of them."

He gaped at her.

"I don't know what lure Erland Bannister cast your way but I thought you were smarter than to swallow it. I'm guessing it was a campaign contribution, and probably more than one. Am I right?"

Kate had read about people going white but she had never seen anyone actually do it before. Pete couldn't produce an articulate word for a full minute, which had to be a record for him or any other politician. When he did speak, he was trying hard to be offended but all Kate could see on his face was fear and all she could hear was sputtering. You knew, you son of a bitch, she thought. You at least suspected.

Pete swallowed. "I don't know what you're talking about, Kate, but I resent the implication that I would ever have anything to do with something so heinous as profiting from a scourge that has been decimating Alaska communities for decades. How dare you say such a thing? I could sue you for slander."

"Sure you could," Kate said. "If it weren't true."

Pete surged to his feet. "It isn't!"

She held his gaze with her own and said nothing.

The lengthening silence was broken when Bobby smacked his hands together. "Okay! Let's hit the air!"

But Pete found that he had an urgent appointment somewhere else for which he was disgracefully late. Apologies, but… "Thanks so much for the terrific dinner, Dinah." He was trying to shove his arm into the sleeve of his parka. Dinah got up and untangled it for him. "Thanks, again!" He summoned a simulacrum of his standard Jolly Old St. Nick grin, waved as if he were saying his farewell to a much larger crowd, and disappeared. Dinah closed the door behind him.

Bobby looked at Kate. "If I'd known you were gonna fuck with my programming I wouldn't have fed you dinner."

"Play some funky music, black boy," Kate said.

"Just for that you get Toby Keith back to back."

"Maybe Patsy Cline?"

He reconsidered.

Later, when Jim and Kate were bedded down on the couch, the fire crackling and popping in the fireplace, Jim said, "Why here and now?"

"I wanted him to know that I know," she said.

"Why?"

"Because I'm going to need a pretty big favor shortly, and I need Pete to think I'll keep my mouth shut if he gives it to me."

"Ah." Jim had a pretty fair idea of what that favor was, and he couldn't say he disapproved.

"Hey." She raised up on her elbow to look down at him. "I didn't tell Mason I'd connected all the dots."

"True enough." He pulled her back down and tucked her head under his chin. "No judging going on here."

"But?"

"But nothing. Get it done, Kate. It's what you do best."

# Eighteen

## MONDAY, JANUARY 14
### *Anchorage*

"I DID WHAT YOU WANTED," KATE SAID. "Specifically, I did your job for you."

"You hacked the encryption?"

"No," she said. "My people couldn't manage that. So they came at it from another direction. The Bannister Foundation backed their books up into the cloud. My guys found the second set of books."

"Where were they?" Mason said. "We couldn't find them."

Kate looked irritatingly tolerant of the Federal Bureau of Investigation's ineptitude. She also looked as if she were enjoying herself immensely. What Jim, leaning up against the wall with his arms folded, thought was even more interesting was that Special Agent James G. Mason was letting her enjoy herself at his agency's expense. It made Jim think more highly of him.

They were back in Mason's office in Anchorage. "There is a second set of books." It wasn't quite a question.

She gave him a very old-fashioned look. "As we all knew there would be."

"Where are they?"

"I'll have them emailed to you as a digital file," she said. "But I want something first."

His eyes narrowed. "I told you we'd pay you."

"Indeed you will," she said. "This is something else. I want the FBI to find someone for me."

"Who?" She handed him a piece of paper. He read it out loud. "Maria Jose Trevioso." He looked up. "Who's this?"

"It doesn't matter, it only matters that you find her."

"US citizen?"

"No." Kate nodded at the note. "Read the rest."

He did. "Tegucigalpa? She's Honduran?" He tossed the note down on his desk. "She's an illegal." He squinted at her. "She's those kids' mom, isn't she?" Kate did not reply. "You'll notice, Kate, that I haven't said much about those two kids."

"No, you haven't and I can't tell you how much I appreciate your restraint." Jim had to bite back a grin. "Ms. Trevioso is their mother. They were separated from her at the border and held in cages, before Gaunt and O'Hanlon, representing themselves as federal agents, kidnapped them and sold them to a known pedophile. They transported two minors across state lines for the purposes of sex trafficking. They are ex-federal agents. You'll notice I haven't said much about them. It's not a good look for any of you, especially in the current political climate. With an election coming on fast."

Mason, wisely, Jim thought, remained silent.

"Find her, Gerry. I want her reunited with her children in twenty-four hours, and then I'll give you all the information I have uncovered in my investigation." It was her turn to lean forward. She even let her voice drop to its lowest register, the one she hardly ever bothered to use, except in bed. "It'll be worth it. I promise."

I can vouch for that, Jim thought.

Mason started at Kate like she was a cobra with its hood spread. "You'll have to give me the kids so I can send them to wherever she is."

"Oh, no, Gerry. Those kids aren't leaving the Park. You're finding her and having her brought here on the first flight heading north from wherever she is. I don't care if she's already back in Honduras. I expect to be picking her up at Ted Stevens International Airport tomorrow or I will tell my guys to erase what they've found from existence. They'll do it, too. They're my guys."

There might have been a little sputtering. "But that's conspiring to conceal evidence in a federal investigation! Besides, there are procedures, and custodial issues! All those things take time!"

Kate's lip curled. "No, there aren't, and no, they won't. No federal agent is putting their hands on those kids ever again. In fact, they and their mother are going to be put on a fast track to become fully enfranchised citizens of the United States of America."

Mason said, still faintly protesting, "They'll need sponsors."

"They'll have them. One very highly placed one, too."

"You can't save them all, Kate."

"No, I can't, more's the pity, but I can save the two right in front of me. Go find their mother. We'll take it from there."

Jim didn't know which Mason found more scarifying, that Kate Shugak, essentially a civilian in the war on crime, knew more about a case than he, Mason, a soldier sworn to that duty, or that she was holding said information hostage to her own terms.

He, Jim, had never been more proud.

That night Kate called Johnny. "Hey, kid."

"Kate, hey. How's it going with Hoover's Finest? Do you have them over that barrel?"

"Did you expect anything less?"

He laughed.

"Where are you?"

"At the homestead, me and Van both. Did you know she's writing up the story of the attack on Auntie Vi's house? She's thinking it's just the thing to ace her English Comp class."

"I'll say," Kate said drily. "What I Did on My Christmas Vacation."

He laughed again. "I know, right? Anyway, what's up? Just checking in? All good here."

"No. There's something I need to ask you." And then for a moment Kate found herself uncharacteristically struck dumb. There was no easy way into this conversation.

"Kate?" Johnny wasn't laughing now. "Is this something I need to sit down for?"

"I don't know," she said heavily. "It's about your mother."

A brief silence. "Is she dead?"

"What? No. Nothing like that."

"Don't worry," he said comfortingly. "It wouldn't have mattered if she was. What then? Hold on a minute, I'm putting you on speaker so Van can hear. Okay, go."

Well, what had she expected? In her observation, the younger generation of Park rats coming up was truly different than her own. They formed romantic attachments early—see Johnny and Van—and defying all the actuarial tables they stuck together. Their possessions were only valuable insofar as they were useful and economical— Johnny and Van shared a lime green Volkswagen Bug (or New Beetle, as the manufacturer put it more loftily) that was nineteen years old. They'd bought it online for $2000 in Anchorage and driven it up the Parks Highway when the semester started at UAA the previous fall. It showed its age, but as Johnny said, "It starts and the heater works." Kate was old enough to remember when what car a man drove defined him not only to himself but to the women who condescended to sit in the seat next to him. They weren't buying houses, preferring to share or rent. If they did own they bought land and built when they could afford it and not before. They believed in climate change, Medicare for All, dumping the Electoral College, and, most unbelievably, in voting. Both Johnny and Van had registered the day they turned eighteen. Kate was hoping to live long enough to see how all that worked out for them, the park, the nation, and the world.

There were some rustling movements. "Kate? You there?"

"Sorry. Here's the thing. Jane has been caught up to her ears in a criminal enterprise. I can explain if you want me to, but short story is, she's going to be arrested, Johnny. It's federal, not state, so unless she cuts a deal she's going to prison, likely for a long time."

There was a long silence. "Johnny?"

"Yeah, I'm still here, Kate."

"I don't know that I can stop this, because it's kind of taken on a life of its own, but if you want me to, I can try."

Another long silence. "She made her own choices," Johnny said finally. "She can live with them."

"You want to be sure about this, Johnny. You could very well never see her again."

"She never gave a shit about me," he said, his voice cold and flat. "Except how she could use me to stick it to Dad or you. After Dad died she dumped me on my grandparents in Arizona when they lived in a place that didn't even allow kids. She's never once bothered to ask me how I got home. I don't owe her a goddamn thing."

Another thing Kate didn't hear his generation do a lot of was swear. "Okay then."

"Tell Jim that furnace he bought for the hangar is throwing out the BTUs like there's no tomorrow. It feels like Panama in there."

"And you would know this how?"

"Just tell him everything's fine. When will you be back?"

"Tomorrow, I hope. Love you both."

"Love you, too. See you soon."

Their generation wasn't afraid to say "I love you," either. Altogether a vast improvement over her own.

# Nineteen

T HE NEXT DAY JIM WAS WAITING AT TED
International when Alaska Airlines Flight 83 arrived
five minutes ahead of schedule. He stood just outside
security, holding up his phone. On the screen was a photo
of the kids that Laurel had texted him that morning. She
came through ten minutes later, a thin, exhausted woman
with dark, unkempt hair and sunken dark eyes. He thought
she looked much older than she probably was. She was
wearing a thin windbreaker over a white tee, baggy khakis
and worn leather sandals through which her feet showed,
encrusted with dirt. A plastic grocery bag dangled from one
hand. A woman dressed in a business suit walked around
her with a look of disgust, and made an inaudible remark
to the man next to her, and they both laughed.

The woman looked around and saw him. Her eyes went
to the photo on his phone and she came toward him in a

stumbling run. She clutched at the arm holding the phone and unleashed a flood of Spanish.

"I'm so sorry, I don't speak Spanish," he said, and guided her away from the gate and toward the chairs that lined the windows. He sat her down gently and let her have the phone. "Ma'am, do you speak any English? *Habla* English?"

A voice spoke from over his shoulder. "She speaks English just fine."

She shuddered and fell silent, clutching the phone, staring at the photo of David and Anna as tears slid down her cheeks.

Jim stood up slowly and turned to see a young man of maybe legal age in an ICE jacket too big for him. He had thin features and small eyes and greasy hair cut short on the sides with a floppy top. It appeared that contempt was his factory setting because there was plenty of it on display and it was all directed at the weeping woman sitting in front of them. "Here," he said, shoving a piece of paper at Jim. "You're supposed to sign this."

Twenty-two years on the job you learned something about taking command of the scene, about never losing your cool, about never raising your voice, about maintaining your authority in any and every situation no matter how far south it was headed. Jim backhanded the paper out of the little snot's hand and grabbed him by the front of his jacket and hauled him up on his toes. Even then he had to bend over to get into his face and Jim was meanly glad this was so. "Who do you really work for?

Blackrock? GEO?" He shook the kid hard enough for the greasy hair to flop back and forth and might have done more if he hadn't seen Mason's man approaching at a near run. He'd met him coming up the escalator. "Get this piece of trash on a plane south," he said. "Do it now." He pushed the young man hard so that he stumbled backwards into the agent's arms.

He hunkered back down in front of Ms. Trevioso. "Could I have the phone for a minute?"

She had shrunk away from the altercation, her face turned aside. She handed him the phone without speaking. He called Laurel. "Put the kids on. Right now." He handed the phone back. "Look. See. Your son and daughter." She stared at him, unbelieving. He pointed at the screen. "Look. There they are. You can talk to them."

A girl's voice said, "Mami? Mami!"

Ms. Trevioso crumpled over the phone again. "Anna! David!"

Jim stood up and turned his back, sheltering her from curious stares to give her as much privacy as he could.

Jim called to let Kate know he had Ms. Trevioso and they were on the way to Merrill. "She doesn't want to stay overnight in Anchorage, Kate, she wants to go straight to her kids. I'll come back in tomorrow to pick you up."

"Okay."

"Have fun with the Feebs."

"You'll pay for that." Kate hung up and put away her phone and looked at Mason across his desk. There was a stenographer present this time, taking down Kate's statement. There were half a dozen other agents there as well, not to mention Mutt. The small office was very crowded.

"You have the digital file, but I'll run down the timeline for you," she said. "On New Year's Eve, a small jet crashed in the Quilak Mountains at the edge of property I own. There's a cabin there and two friends were staying in it who responded to the scene, where they found the aft fuselage of the aircraft largely intact. There were two survivors inside, two minor children. The next day, New Year's Day, they were brought to the clinic in the village of Niniltna. Unknown to their rescuers or anyone else at the time, they carried a mobile phone with them.

"Local pilots Jim Chopin and George Perry returned to the scene the following day where they found the body of Gary Curley, presumed to be the owner of the wrecked airplane."

"I spoke with the director of, ah, Aurora Flight Services this morning, and she said that he and his pilot and two small children whom Curley referred to as his niece and nephew—" Mason looked as nauseous as Kate felt "—departed in his aircraft at ten p.m., destination Fairbanks. Fairbanks has no record of their arrival, and we believe that the aircraft flew instead to Niniltna. There was a massive storm ongoing at the time and witnesses on the ground in Niniltna recall hearing the sound of one jet aircraft landing and taking off, and possibly two, although the wind was howling so hard they couldn't be sure, and with the snow coming down like it was they didn't see anything out the window, either.

"Found with Curley's body was a gallon Ziploc bag filled with white tablets with no maker's mark."

"Subsequently determined to be fentanyl," Mason said.

"In the meantime, I received the news that I had been named trustee for the estate of Erland Bannister," Kate said. "For those of you who haven't heard of him, he was a long-time Alaskan mover and shaker who died last November. His record makes for entertaining reading, you should take a look at it sometime, but for now understand that about four years ago he started a nonprofit foundation whose stated purpose was to raise and distribute money to worthy causes in Alaska. It came together very quickly and was funded to where it could begin soliciting grant applications almost immediately. It gave out grants its second year in business, to the tune of over $10 million. The grants have subsequently increased in number and amount every year."

She paused. Mason handed her a bottle of water. She cracked it and took a welcome swallow. She preferred doing to talking. Talking was dry work and no one ever believed half of what you said or did any of what you recommended. Dry and disheartening.

"Erland had a lot of money. Maybe even that much money. But..." Kate shook her head. "During his lifetime, he might have given ten bucks to the Red Cross when no one was looking, but Andrew Carnegie he was not.

"And we didn't have the friendliest relationship, to put it mildly. He tried to kill me at least twice that I know of and I was a proximate cause of him going to jail for it. The only reason I could think of that Erland would name me his trustee was that there was something hinky enough about his estate that it would destroy everyone it came in contact with. To that end, or so I believe, he convinced my cousin Axenia Shugak, to be on his board. Even if I refused the job of trustee, she would still be at risk. Erland knew me well enough to know that I couldn't let that happen."

She didn't mention Pete Heiman, but she'd had Kurt check with the FEC. Erland had donated half a million dollars to both of Pete's campaigns for Congress. Up till then Erland hadn't been a big political donor. He'd wanted Pete's name on the organization and he'd paid for it. The evidence was there for Mason to find, if he wanted to look for it. Kate hoped he would and that he would make a meal out of it, but she owed Pete for the Treviosos and she wouldn't help Mason get there.

"None of it felt right, I don't care how reformed Erland claimed to be when he got out of prison. So, acting in my authority as Erland's trustee, on January second I copied the Bannister Foundation's records from Erland's assistant's laptop and had my people go over the numbers. Everything on the face of it seemed legit, money coming in from big donors, money going out in the form of grants to various organizations and causes in the state.

"A few other odd things, though. Erland's assistant, Jane Wardwell, is someone with whom I have an unpleasant history. Why hire her as the point person to an organization I, as his trustee, was supposed to be overseeing? My best guess is that Erland hoped that our contentious relationship would divert my attention from what business the Bannister Foundation was really in.

"Then, when I visited the Bannister Foundation offices, there wasn't even a receptionist. I was met by Jane Wardwell and asked her where everyone else was. She said the other employees were on holiday. This was the first week of January.

"On my way out, I fell into conversation with one of the construction workers who was doing finish work on the business park the foundation headquarters is in. He was puzzled, he said, because the building was ready for occupancy and while the signs indicated that it was fully occupied and staffed, he saw very few people working there."

She shook her head. "According to their website, the Bannister Foundation was giving away millions of dollars in grants four times a year. The level of largesse indicated the necessity of grants managers, program managers, an events manager, an office manager."

She nodded at Mason. "Then you contracted me to find out how Curley's people were handling the money end of his drug operation. I guessed you knew I'd been named Erland's trustee, and that's when it all started to come together. You had already been looking at the Bannister Foundation, hadn't you?"

He bounced back against the springs of his desk chair and smiled.

"It was pretty obvious that either you were trying to figure out if I was complicit, or you wanted someone on the inside."

She took a long, hard pull at the bottle of water. "It happens that I know one of the students enrolled at Bering VoTech, one of the Bannister Foundation's grant recipients last year. I had her check on the amount of the grant. She said it was half a million. The teachers have the students write thank-you letters to donors and foundations who give them money, so the number came easily to mind. But here's the thing. The amount given to Bering VoTech as listed in the Bannister Foundation accounts is $1.5 million."

Someone in the room drew in a sharp breath.

She met Mason's eyes. "Bannister doesn't put the amounts of the grants on their website. They don't issue press releases, they don't host fundraisers or donor appreciation events, and, as I later discovered, they seem to have no mechanism in place for grant recipients to report how they, the receiving organizations, had spent Bannister's grants. All that seemed unusual, not to say bizarre. Week before last I happened to be in Ahtna, so I went to talk to the people at the Ahtna Women's Shelter, another grant recipient of the Bannister Foundation. The foundation's records showed a grant going out for $250,000. When I asked Marlena Peratrovich, their executive director, about it, not naming the sum, she told me, and I'm quoting her verbatim here, 'I've worked a lot harder for a lot less than $25,000.' She expressed her gratitude to Jane Wardwell for the personal care she had taken in guiding her through the application process. Another applicant told me it was the simplest grant application she'd ever gone through and, again I'm quoting here, 'I had to kind of force them to listen to what I wanted to do with their money.' 'Them' in this case being, again, Jane Wardwell.

"Last week I flew to Seldovia, King Salmon, and Kichatna, home to organizations who had received Bannister Foundation grants. The story was similar in all respects. Jane Wardwell was the only person they talked to at the foundation, and that the grant application process was basically ask and ye shall receive. And they did, but again, the amounts they said they received were markedly different than the amounts the Bannister Foundation had listed in their accounts. Seldovia received $10,000 for their library, Bannister's accounts showed $100,000. A wind energy company in King Salmon got $300,000 but the books showed $1 million. Kichatna Academy got $400,000, whereas the books showed $1.4 million."

She shrugged. "The Bannister Foundation has a lot of money coming in and on the face of it comparatively little going out. Whatever could be going on here, do you think?"

Mason sat back in his chair. "Why don't you tell us."

"Mr. Chopin spoke to Valerie Doogan, the principal of the Niniltna School. Her office has a front row seat to the airstrip. Ever since they started doing the prep for the Suulutaq Mine she says air traffic has exponentially increased, including a lot of small anonymous private jets. She thought it was muckety-mucks flying in to check on their investment. Oh, and—although you'll have to dig into this yourselves to find out the specific details—it is anecdotally known in the Park that Erland Bannister had a substantial financial stake in the Suulutaq Mine. It provided all the cover he needed for frequent flights to Niniltna."

"Jesus," somebody said. "Fucker really lined this out."

"He had some time to think about it," Kate said. And how he would have loved incorporating the Park into his plans. Making her complicit in her ignorance. "What I think is that Erland set up the Bannister Foundation from the get-go to launder money from drug trafficking. The drugs were smuggled into Alaska by way of transfers on the Niniltna airstrip, easily camouflaged as business trips to the mine. Maybe even sometimes by Erland himself, he was in and out of there often enough. The drugs went to Gary Curley for breaking down into retail quantities, some sold in Alaska and the rest sent on for sale out of the country. You'll know more about that than I do. The money went to the Bannister Foundation in the persons of Erland Bannister—who was his own executive director, a direct conflict of interest—and Jane Wardwell, and subsequently appeared as donations by multiple conveniently anonymous donors to the Bannister Foundation, who then gave a small fraction of it away as a cover story. The rest of it was forwarded on to the illegal drug manufacturers, whose operation this was."

"Any ideas on that front?"

Kate shook her head. "That's your bailiwick. Although I'd appreciate it if you'd figure that out so they'd stop shooting at me."

A brief silence, until someone said, "Really, kind of ingenious."

"I know, right? Who's ever going to look hard at a nonprofit handing out money all over the state?"

"Especially this state."

There was a brief, uncomfortable silence. "Exactly," Kate said. "Alaska, in spite of its ideal location for an operation of this kind, is seen as a bastard child by—" she shrugged "—I was going to say the rest of the nation but really by most of the world. And you'll notice, Bannister mostly gave in poor communities off the road system or otherwise isolated, generally with no or very slow Internet access. Some of them are still working on getting cell phone providers to come into their areas. Most of them don't have a permanent law enforcement presence of their own and they never see a fed. Who will ever show up to ask them how much money they really got? And they'd certainly never complain about getting less money than had been reported, because, a, how would they know, and b, why would they care? In the Alaska Bush cash in hand will always trump every other concern."

Kate drained the bottle and screwed the cap back on. "In the meantime, the bulk of the 'donated' money is electronically transferred, as might be expected, to various offshore accounts, all numbered."

"We'll get on that," Mason said.

"Yeah, good luck with that," someone said *sotto voce*.

"We did find the same name in three different places in the Bannister records," Kate said, "but only three out of fifty-plus."

"Who's that?"

"Not who, what. A law firm called Cullen and Associates."

Mason sat upright. "In Chicago?"

She nodded. "You'll remember last year we found evidence that Erland Bannister and the Chicago Outfit had Cullen and Associates in common."

"I do," he said grimly. "And Eugene Hutchinson?"

She shook her head. "So far as I can tell he was only Erland's lawyer. He may just have been collateral damage."

He waited, and when she said nothing further he said, "That's it?"

She looked at him. "You stopped an organization that was transshipping illegal drugs to Alaska. If that jet hadn't crashed you wouldn't have known a thing about it. Sure, you'll have to track down the distribution in the state and you'll have to follow the money out of the state, but as far as I'm concerned this is a good day's work." She stood up and pulled an envelope from her pocket and dropped it on his desk. "Our bill. You'll notice the biggest items are pilot hours and avgas, which is why I included a copy of the pilot's log book. Prompt payment would be appreciated."

His phone rang. He listened to the voice on the other end for a moment and hung up. "We have a warrant to search the offices of the Bannister Foundation. Would you like to join me?"

She thought it over. She found that, after all, she didn't really need to gloat in person at Jane's downfall. On the other hand, she wouldn't mind having a few blank spots filled in, and if Jane was in the mood to talk... "Sure."

Red and his co-workers were gone, along with the visqueen and the scaffolding. The security guard's jaw dropped when he saw Mason's identification and he made no move to call anyone. A rent-a-cop's loyalty only went so far. They rode up in the elevator in silence, and when it arrived at the top floor exited out into what was still an echoingly empty office space. No receptionist on the front desk, no one getting coffee in the break room. The lights were on but no one was home.

Mason's agents fanned out, opening doors into individual offices. There were no cries of outrage or demands to know what was going on. There was no one to make them.

Kate led Mason to the corner office that was Jane's, and was a little surprised to find Jane was there, sitting at her desk.

She looked up as they appeared and went very still. It was instantly obvious that she remembered Mason from his previous visit and that she knew very well why he had returned. Mason nevertheless identified himself again and displayed the warrant to search the premises. Jane nodded as if she understood but Kate thought she looked a little numb.

"Boss?"

Mason disappeared, leaving Kate and Jane staring at each other.

"I told him," Jane said. It sounded to Kate as if the words had been forcibly pulled from her mouth. "I told him it was a bad idea. I told him you'd never fall for it." A ghost of a sigh. "But he hated you so much. He would do anything, sacrifice anything or anyone for a chance at bringing you down, whether he liked to see it or not."

"When did he name me his trustee?"

Jane swallowed. "When he got the diagnosis that his cancer was terminal."

"Was I supposed to find out about the money laundering?"

"No."

She might not have, Kate thought, if Curley's plane hadn't crashed at Canyon Hot Springs. If Laurel and Matt hadn't been spending New Year's at the cabin. If Jim and George hadn't found that Ziploc bag full of fentanyl at the crash site. If Mason hadn't reached out to her about Curley. If the FBI hadn't already had the Bannister Foundation in the crosshairs. "What was supposed to happen?"

For a moment there was the merest trace of the old hostile Jane Morgan, Jack's resentful, revengeful wife, in the twist of Jane's lips and the narrowing of her eyes. "If you repeat any of this I'll deny it."

Kate rolled her eyes. "Of course you will. What was supposed to happen?"

Jane looked at the door but found the temptation to brag irresistible. She did lower her voice to a whisper. "After six months, I was supposed to discover that the check we are... we were about to cut for the Niniltna Public School was considerably less than the Bannister Foundation had granted them."

Kate remembered what Valerie Doogan had said. *Now that I think about it, I had to kind of force her to listen to what I wanted to do with their money.* And Jack had said that Erland had come to Val personally last year with the offer of a grant for the school.

"Upon investigation, I was to 'discover'—" Jane's voice put the word in air quotes "—that this had happened with many of the Bannister Foundation grants. After which, I was to go to the FBI with the files and tell them everything."

"What were you supposed to say about me?"

Jane said nothing, and any shred of sympathy Kate might have felt vanished in that moment. "I see. Was Eugene Hutchinson involved?"

"Gene? No. He was a friend of Erland's. He didn't even practice anymore. All he did was write the trust and the will."

Why they hadn't been able to find an office for him. "Got him killed anyway."

"Yes."

"What did you get out of it? Erland must have made the payoff pretty good for you to risk three to five to life." Nothing, and Kate, goaded, said, "Pretty clever, by the way. Backing up the books to your accounts with Amazon, Apple, and Google. Good to know all that free cloud storage didn't go to waste." Jane couldn't hide her surprise and Kate smiled thinly. "Oh, yes, we found them all. We even found the Dropbox backup through your Yahoo account. You really should have changed your password from the last time I hacked your finances. It's been, what, six years?"

Jane turned brick red. It was most unattractive.

"Were you the secondary trustee, Jane? If I had said no thanks, would you have carried on moving money around for these fucking death merchants as usual?"

Jane was by now the color of eggplant to the tops of her ears.

Kate, sickened by the entire mess and perhaps a little by her own spite, turned and left Jane's office.

Mason looked up and saw her. "Hey, hold up."

Kate paused. "I'm done here."

"I get it," he said. He looked around the offices. "There is no one here except her."

"There only needed to be her," Kate said. "You saw the Safescan in Curley's house. He received the pills, he packaged them, he sold them, he counted and banded the take when necessary, he deposited it." She snorted. "He had his own aircraft that could make Seattle in three hours, Portland in four, LA and Chicago in five or six. Whatever bank he deposited it in, it all showed up as donations to the Bannister Foundation's account from donors who aren't meant to be identified. The overseas take probably came in by wire transfer from Gary Curleys in Japan, South Korea, Russia, where the fuck ever." She shrugged. "All Jane had to do was manage the grant applications and send out the checks. With the two sets of books in hand you may be able to sustain a conspiracy charge against her, but none of it will matter a damn to the drug trafficking organization who reaped the profits if you can't track back the deposits."

Special Agent James G. Mason stuck out his chin. "We'll find them. It's what we do."

Good luck with that, Kate thought.

He straightened to attention. "Thank you, Kate," he said formally. "We would have got here eventually because it's what we do, but it would have taken us longer without you, your skills, your connections, and your local knowledge." He sighed. "It won't stop them, of course. There's too much money in it. But it'll slow them down for a while, and you never know, maybe this time long enough for us to get out ahead of them for a change." He held out his hand. She took it. "Thank you," he said again.

She almost smiled. "Prompt payment will be appreciated."

He laughed, and let her go.

And Jane, she thought as she rode down in the elevator, still hadn't said one word about Johnny.

# Twenty

A N UBER DROPPED KATE AND MUTT OFF AT Merrill where they picked up the Forester and drove back to the townhouse. The neighbor was spreading de-icer on his steps when she opened the front door to grab the mail. He wore the same ratty old brown bathrobe he always did. "Hey," he said.

"Hey," she said, and paused in case he wanted to say more, but he finished the steps and went back inside. She been staying in this townhouse while she was in Anchorage for over a decade and she still didn't know his name. Apparently he liked it that way.

She wanted to go home.

She called the housesitter to let her know it would be empty again tomorrow, and to instruct her to call someone to replace the window. There wasn't much in the way of food in the house but she didn't feel like going out to shop.

She nuked a frozen package of moose stew meat for Mutt. There was a bunch of fresh asparagus left in the refrigerator and a package of Top Ramen in the cupboard. She opened the ramen and put the flavor packet back in the cupboard, good for a hot cup of bullion on some future cold day. She sliced the asparagus on a diagonal into short pieces and put water on to boil. In a small bowl she whisked a large glop of mayonnaise with mustard, rice vinegar, sesame oil and soy sauce. When the water boiled she added the cut-up asparagus and set the timer for three minutes. When it dinged she added the noodles and set it for another three minutes. When it dinged the second time she drained the contents, returned them to the pan, and tossed them with the dressing. It passed the taste test and she took the bowl and a fork out into the living room along with a can of Diet 7Up she'd found hiding in the door of the fridge. It was a little stale but not bad. Probably best not to look at its sell-by date. She turned on the gas fireplace and sat down on the couch and propped her feet on the coffee table.

She ate slowly, watching the light fade from the sky and trying and failing to ignore the hole in the window. "Good girl," she said to Mutt, whose bark had put the shooter off his aim. Although the curtains had been drawn that night so he was shooting blind anyway. Had it been only a warning, or had he been trying to kill them? He'd killed Hutchinson right after, so she thought the latter. She wondered if it was the same person who had taken a shot at them when they came out of the bank. He'd come a lot closer to success that time, and she remembered that Mutt bumping into her was why he hadn't. "Really good girl," she said. Mutt raised her head, yawned, and laid it back down again. Kate only wished she was as good at staying in the moment.

Entirely too much shooting about their persons of late. She wondered if other PIs got shot at as often. She wondered if she ought to up her computer skills so she could start doing less fraught work like background checks on prospective employees. And how boring would that be?

She finished her noodles and thought about hitting the Coastal Trail. She was still thinking about it when her phone rang. It was an Unknown Number. She answered it anyway. "Hello?"

"Kate Shugak?" A young man, very polite.

"Speaking."

"Would you hold one moment, please, for Mr. Smith? Thank you," he said without waiting for her to reply. "Mr. Smith? Ms. Shugak is on the line."

"Thank you, Jared," an older male voice said. A click as Jared exited the conversation. "Ms. Shugak?"

"Speaking," Kate said again. Something in the timbre of Smith's voice made her sit up. Across the room Mutt raised her head. "Your name isn't really Smith, is it?"

"I can't tell you what a relief it is to deal with intelligent people. It saves so much time."

"Why did you kill Hutchinson?"

A sigh. "Given his friendship with Erland, it was felt better safe than sorry." A pause. "He did call you just before he died, after all. Three times. It argued a certain… sincerity of purpose, shall we say."

And how had he come by that piece of information? She tried to picture Detective Branson as inside snitch for anyone and failed utterly. "Your sources of information are frighteningly good."

"Thank you. We try to keep abreast of the news. Do you have any idea what he was so determined to communicate?"

"If I did you would be the last person to know."

"Pity."

She knew a burning desire to shake him out of his complacency. "Did you know that Erland Bannister had set a plan in motion to reveal your entire operation and hang it on me six months following his death?"

A brief silence. "No," Mr. Smith said slowly. "No, I did not." He sighed. "It is always a mistake to allow one's personal feelings to enter into business dealings."

"Speaking as someone who could have ended her days in federal prison had his plan succeeded, I am forced to agree with you."

He chuckled. "I may owe you a debt of gratitude, Ms. Shugak, for extricating, however unwittingly, our organization from a matter that had the potential to inflict a great deal of damage to it."

"No gratitude is necessary, Mr. Smith, I assure you."

"Oh well done, Ms. Shugak. Just the right touch of sarcasm without abandoning good manners."

"Thank you." She remembered the angry bee sound of the round passing too close to her ear in the parking lot outside the bank. "Is your gratitude enough to get the bullseye off my back?"

"My dear Ms. Shugak." He actually contrived to sound wounded. "For all intents and purposes, our operation in Alaska is blown. The pursuit of petty vengeance after the fact is a waste of both energy and resource. I am not Erland Bannister."

She caught herself, barely, before she apologized.

"But to the point of my call." The tenor of his voice remained exactly the same; polite, informative, not a hint of menace, even a trace of apology, mixed with sorrow. Lord, what fools these mere mortals be. "You have twice now interfered in our affairs. I'm afraid we would be quite displeased if that happened a third time."

She found herself on her feet without knowing how she got there. Across the room Mutt was up as well, her ears back, teeth showing, and a growl on low boil. "Stay the hell out of my state and it won't."

"I appreciate your directness. Allow me to be equally frank. Our business is global and universal. It takes us everywhere. Simple opportunity may bring us your way again."

"Your business is killing people, Smith."

She could almost hear his shrug. "We offer a consumer good for sale, at a reasonable price made possible by bulk manufacture and distribution. If people want to stick a needle in their arm or shove powder up their nose—or pop a pill, or ten—it really is none of our business. Let them go to hell their own way."

"So long as you make a profit on it."

He tsked. "So judgmental, Ms. Shugak. I thought better of you. This call is merely to advise you that it would be best for your health, and the health of your loved ones, if you, shall we say, averted your eyes going forward? That is a very handsome dog you have, by the way. Half wolf, am I correct? She looks very comfortable there in front of the fire."

He ended the call.

Kate clicked the phone app on her phone and then Recents. She tapped Unknown Number and it wouldn't even ring. A second later, the call vanished from the list.

She sat back down on the couch, and looked up at the window. The hole was still there, still patched with a cross of silver duct tape.

She got up and pulled the drapes, keeping as far out of view through the window as she physically could.

# Twenty-one

## SATURDAY, JANUARY 19
### *Niniltna*

JIM, KATE, JOHNNY AND VAN WERE BACK AT Bobby's, who was sprawled on the couch with Dinah curled up next to him. Katya sat between Mutt's paws, where she was narrating the action of *The Snowy Day* out loud with great animation. Mutt was following along with apparently deeply felt interest.

"So, you going to help Vanessa with video footage for her little online Park Inquirer or not?"

"Sure." Dinah's smile broadened. "So long as she spells my name correctly in the credits."

"Might maybe figure out a way to work Park Air into the mix, too," Bobby said thoughtfully, and Van brightened.

"Did you really get Pete Heiman to sponsor the Treviosos for fast-track citizenship?" Bobby said.

"I did," Kate said.

"High five right there, woman." They smacked hands. "How the hell?"

Kate smiled.

He shrugged. "Keep your secrets. I'm all about the happy ending." He looked across at Katya and Mutt playing Story Time. "Sometimes I think—"

"What?"

The oven timer dinged and Dinah got up to get the coffee cake out of the oven.

"What, Bobby?"

He sighed and sat up, elbows on his knees, looking tired. Not physically tired, Kate thought, but mentally, emotionally, spiritually tired. Tired right down to his soul. "Sometimes I wonder if we'll ever get it right in this country. If we'll ever stop seeing people who don't look like us as other. As disposable. If those kids had been white, how different might their story have been at that border crossing in Texas?" He was watching Katya. "You know why I always wear cutoffs in Anchorage? Because if I'm pulled over driving while black, the cop sees my prostheses and assumes I'm a vet. Half of them are vets, too, and all is well. That getting shot while breathing because you're black shit is not something I want to be dealing with every goddamn day. I may be the Park's token black, Howie Katelnikof might call me 'that nigger' when he has too much to drink, some of the old farts may tell me to go back to where I came from—"

"Tennessee?"

He smiled, at least a little. "All that may be true, but people know me here and they leave me alone to live my life."

He looked at her. "Sorry, Kate. I know I don't have to explain this to you."

"No."

"I'm praying that things get better before Katya has to go out there among them English. Otherwise I might as well lock her in the barn and keep her there for the rest of her life."

She looked at Katya, too, who had inherited more of her father's black as ebony than her mother's white-as-you-can-get-without-bleach. She hadn't learned yet that white can be the enemy.

"Let's eat!" Dinah said. Jim picked Katya up and tossed her in the air. Kate noticed that he winced a little as he did so, the healing wounds inflicted by Auntie Vi's enthusiastically fired shotgun still making themselves felt. The little girl with the Hershey's chocolate skin and the flyaway dreads shrieked with laughter.

Over the lump in her throat Kate said, "You don't have a barn."

"I'll build one."

They ate, and then they went to the gym and mourned for the Topkoks and for Auntie Edna, too. Jim noticed that Maria Jose Trevioso came with her children. They were all wearing new, much warmer clothing, and Ms. Trevioso cleaned up pretty good. He also saw Park rats taking notice of the fresh meat in their midst—already proven fertile, too—and made a mental note to spread the word that this woman and her children were under his protection. He doubted it would even slow down the hornier among them but he had to try. And he could always sick Kate on them.

In February Johnny went back to school. Van went with him, committing to one more semester, and that only because it was paid for, and then she'd see. In the meantime Jim got busy buying Herbie Topkok's shop. The Topkok kids okayed the sale of the house, too, and Jim hired the same carpenter who'd built his hangar to come out from Anchorage and remodel both into something approaching a school and a dormitory. He thought about buying Auntie Vi's B&B, too, but Auntie Vi wouldn't hear of it. She was back home, and Ms. Trevioso, David and Anna were living with her now to take care of her. Old bones take the longest to heal, and she would need help from now on if she wanted to keep on living at home.

Annie Mike put together an advisory board for his school, consisting of herself as president, Valerie Doogan as treasurer, and three more women from around the state: Bobbi Quintavell, Tara Sweeney, and Jeanine St. Jean. Bobbi was the president of a Native association in Nome,

Tara was helping to run the Bureau of Indian Affairs, and Jeanine ran a shipping company responsible for bringing in half the consumer goods sold in the state. Annie had summoned Jim and Valerie to NNA headquarters for a Skype introduction and it became immediately evident that the three were none of them shy people. They'd flirted with him for five minutes just to loosen him up and then asked a whole lot of questions that in the end left him questioning his own motives in starting the school, after which they were gracious enough to allow as how it might be a good thing, maybe, possibly, even, at a stretch, probably. They decided the school should be incorporated and should apply for nonprofit status so other people besides Jim could donate to it, even if he did have more money than any one human being should have and he didn't even have to work for it, either. They picked the school's accountant and attorney. They decided that despite his protests he should be on the board and put him there as a member without portfolio, like he even knew what that meant. They chose one additional board member for a quorum of seven, and they picked her, too, because evidently he had nothing to say about it. Deciding on a date for their first board meeting in person would have been easier with access to the Cray computer at UAF but they managed it, eventually.

"What are you going to call it?" Bobbi said.

"Gotta have a name," Tara said.

"Something local," Jeanine said. "A name that means

something to the people who live there, that the students will be proud to say they graduated from."

All he'd wanted was someone to annual his airplane and now he was starting a school and making himself answerable to a board of directors that had dominatrix written all over it.

"Speak up," Bobbi said, "we don't bite."

"Speak for yourself," Tara said.

"We promise not to break the skin," Jeanine said.

Annie and Valerie mostly sat back and looked amused, damn them. Jim gathered up his courage. "Herbie Topkok could fix anything you brought him, from a toaster to a Super Cub. It's his shop that will be the school and his house that will be the dormitory. I'm hoping it's going to graduate students who can fix anything, too. So I'd like to call it after him."

"The Herbert Topkok Vocational School," Bobbi said.

"The Herbert Topkok Academy," Tara said.

"The Herbert Topkok Polytechnic," Jeanine said.

"Ooooooh, fancy," the other two said, and then the screen was filled with the sounds of tapping as they all googled the word polytechnic on their phones to make sure it meant what they thought it meant.

Jim squirmed a little. "Could we call it Herbie, not Herbert? It's how everyone here knew him."

"Why not?" Bobbi said, and then asked him if he knew how to make a fireball. In spite of a feeble protest that he was already taken, somehow he found he had a date with the three of them at the Roadhouse when they flew in for his first board meeting. He quaked to think of what Kate would say.

She laughed, was what she did, loud and long, when he staggered home that afternoon and blurted out the whole horrible story. "I've heard of all of them," she said. "Not only are you going to get your school, it will be extremely well-run, never over budget, and will meet its student quota, with a waiting list, every single semester you are in business. Well done, Annie!"

He was glad to see her laugh, even if it was at his expense. There hadn't been a lot of laughter around the house during the last month. She'd told him about the phone call from Mr. Smith but she'd been threatened before and he didn't think that was it, either. Kate didn't scare easily. There had been many times when he wished she did and, he had no doubt, would be again.

The phone rang. It was Kurt. "They found the shooter, and his driver."

"Really? Who were they?"

"Local talent, and Branson says not all that bright local talent. They were hired over the phone and paid through a wire transfer into their bank."

"Let me guess. Untraceable?"

"Branson says so, but Tyler says he'll take a crack at it."

"He still winding up things in Fairbanks?"

"He showed up this afternoon in a robin's egg blue 1961 Ford Econoline van crammed with laptops and hard drives and battery packs and enough cable to reach high earth orbit. And one plastic Safeway bag filled with clothes." She heard him shudder. "We had to stop by Walmart to buy him some clean underwear. And a giant-sized tube of Clearasil."

"Just how old is Tyler, Kurt?"

"Almost nineteen."

"How old was he when you recruited him?"

"He bought a house off the Old Seward near Rabbit Creek. Five acres, teeny-tiny house. He likes his privacy, does Tyler. I left him instructing a locksmith on how many and what size locks he wanted installed on the doors and the windows. I imagine he'll be online and at work shortly."

Jim made her dinner, caribou steak with loaded baked potatoes and canned green beans fried with bacon and onions. Afterward they sat on the couch and she read a book by John Sandford that she claimed had Amur tigers and a pickle factory in it. A likely story. He contented himself with a biography of Winston Churchill so heavy it put his legs to sleep if he let it rest on them for too long. The fire crackled in the hearth and Mutt snoozed on her quilt and he kept thinking it ought to be snowing again but it still wasn't. He wondered about the wreck up in the mountains. He wondered how many Ziploc gallon bags full of homemade fentanyl were scattered around. He wondered if the wildlife would get into them. Not a pretty thought. About as pretty as some yahoo Park rat stumbling across one and making it his own personal stash. He was going to have to make regular trips to Canyon Hot Springs between now and breakup to check on the scene. He hoped his sled didn't break down before he graduated someone from Herbie Topkok Polytechnic who could fix it. "Hey," he said.

She peered at him over the top of her book. "What?"

"I didn't think to ask the last time we talked about it. You ever want kids?"

"I already have about two thousand of them."

It surprised a laugh out of him and she set her book on the floor and crawled down to his end of the couch. Kate didn't snuggle often, so he set his own book down and made room. She tucked her head into his shoulder and he put his arms around her and wanted for nothing else in this world, and was faintly surprised at himself for thinking it.

"Martin is sober," she said.

"I saw," he said.

"He's renting a house."

"I saw that, too."

"He's got a *dog*."

"Yep."

"And Laurel's going to give him a job?"

"I hope so. Otherwise how's he going to pay his rent and buy dog food?" She didn't laugh and he angled his head to see her expression. "Are you okay? You've seemed a little off, lately, and I don't think it's only about Martin Shugak."

"I have been a little off lately," she said, "and it isn't about Martin Shugak. Didn't realize you'd noticed. Sorry if I've been sulky."

"No need. But tell me."

Her breasts pushed against his chest on a long sigh. Sue him for noticing but there they were. "We live in this, this enclave," she said. "Everybody knows everybody else. It's like Bobby said. Nobody's going to shoot him in the Park for driving while black. Nobody's going to go up the hill and beat the crap out of Oscar and Keith because they're gay. Nobody's going to get mad at Willard Shugak because they saw him steal a Reese's Peanut Butter Cup from Binkley's because everybody knows he's FAE and they understand, so they pay for the damn candy bar themselves and forget about it."

"I like that about us, too," he said cautiously. "I was raised in the middle of way too much civilization and I didn't love it. Why I came looking for something else. How I ended up here."

She moved against him restlessly. "So much that is good in the Park was Emaa and the aunties. We've had drugs in the Park but not like other places in Alaska. Bernie keeps the booze out the road. People just, I don't know, get along. We know each other so we tolerate each other. Emaa and the aunties drew the line and then they held it, and led by example, and the rest of us fell in behind." She sighed, thinking. "Maybe it's insular. Parochial, even. Certainly Park rats spend enough time picking lint out of our own navels. But most of the time, at minimum we manage to co-exist without too much friction.

"Now Emaa and Auntie Edna are gone, and Auntie Vi and Joy and Balasha probably aren't far behind them." She touched his lower lip lightly, tracing it with her forefinger. "And the wider world has come crashing in, and it doesn't feel like much can stop it. The Suulutaq Mine. Demetri and his anti-mine PAC. Now this plane crash and suddenly we have two illegal immigrant children, the same kids in cages we're reading about in the news every day, made the victims of sex trafficking, something else we're reading about in the news every day. And we find out some asshole has been transshipping drugs through our airstrip for distribution in Alaska, Russia, Japan, South Korea, who the hell knows where else. Niniltna! Our town! Our Park! It's something you read about in the media. It's not something that happens here."

"Until it did."

"What I find hardest to take is that it was one of our own. Erland didn't just open the door to it, he laid down a welcome mat and invited it in. He was born here. He'd lived here all his life. He was one of us. And yet..."

"And yet," Jim said.

They lay in silence for a few moments, listening to the crackle of the fire. Two bald eagles had taken up residence in adjoining spruce trees at the edge of the yard and were conversing in the high-pitched, multi-toned chirps that sounded so odd coming from something that looked so fierce.

"'The world is too much with us,'" Kate said.

Her voice was so low he could hear her. "What's that?"

"'The world is too much with us.'"

"Aha." Gotta be a poem. Kate read poetry sometimes. When he'd asked her why she'd said because she liked it. He couldn't even. "Where's that from?"

"'s a poem by Tennyson. Or Shelley. Coleridge. One of the Romantics. 'The world is too much with us; late and soon/Getting and spending, we lay waste our powers.'"

She sounded exhausted. He ran his hand up and down her spine in slow, lazy strokes, enjoying the feel of the tension leaving her body, the way it seemed to heat up and elongate and achieve more mass against him as it did so. "Have you ever taken a vacation?"

The question seemed to startle her back into wakefulness. "What?"

"A vacation. Weeks, months even, spent in a place not your own, preferably exotic, definitely warm, not working, not anyone's beck and call girl, just being."

A brief silence. "Jack took me Outside once. Arizona and New Mexico. So different than here in every respect."

"How long?"

"Two weeks."

"Did you enjoy it?"

"It was hot." Her voice was getting drowsy. "And there were snakes."

"Did you see any?"

"No. But I knew they were there. Waiting for me."

He ran his hand up and down her spine, up and down. Her breathing began to slow and deepen.

No snakes in Hawaii, he thought. "And I could teach you to surf," he said. What could be more romantic than that?

She answered him with a snore.

*So they were staying here in this village in the middle of this place called Alaska, where there were big white bears like in the movie about the boy on the train, and other kinds of bears, too. There were big brown animals called moose that they saw on the way to school sometimes, and spotted, short-tailed cats with long legs and feet the size of tortillas, and round brown animals with needles for fur, and eagles with white heads and tails. It was everything he could do to keep Anna away from them, she wanted to pet them all. Too many Disney movies.*

*The swearing woman they knew now to call Tía Vi had come home, and Mami and David and Anna were living with her and taking care of her until she could care for herself. She might never be able to do that because she was so old, but they would stay with her as long as she needed them. David had made Mami promise.*

*They were staying in three bedrooms in the downstairs in the back, David and Anna next to each other and Mami across the hall. All three had locks on the insides of the doors and none on the outside. At least that was where they were supposed to be staying. For now they were all sleeping in the same bed in Mami's room. If Tia Vi knew she didn't say anything. She wasn't getting downstairs much anyway.*

*They had been told that there would be no return to the border, or to Tegucigalpa. Someone very important was sponsoring them to become Americans, and everyone acted like it was already done. It sounded too good to be true and David wasn't quite sure he believed them, but he didn't say so to Mami and Anna.*

*In the meantime David and Anna were going to school, walking up the hill every day. The pretty girl who found them had made sure they had the right clothes to stay warm outside, and other presents appeared from time to time, like the two big round plastic disks with handles used to slide down hills. David got dumped into snowbank after snowbank but Anna loved them, flying down the slope and screaming all the way, so David took her to the sledding hill behind the school every Saturday morning whether it was snowing or not.*

*They studied English every night for an hour. Anna was picking it up the fastest and David, his pride stung, shouldered in until he caught up. Even Mami was overcoming her shyness, able to shop at the grocery store and to talk to the dark-haired woman with the wolf when she came to visit. Even the wolf seemed to understand them, but then that seemed to be how things worked in this new and strange and, David had to admit, fascinating place. The black man with the missing legs, Bobby, who lived on the other side of town, promised he would teach David how to fly once his legs were long enough to reach the pedals, and Dinah, his very white, much younger wife, was teaching David how to make movies on his new phone, and Katya, their daughter with the braids, was already Anna's best friend. An older white woman, a friend of the wolf lady—David hadn't screwed up enough courage to call her by her name yet—named Ruthe was going to teach him how to shoot a rifle.*

*Or maybe that was only what he thought she had said, because he couldn't quite believe that, either. Or any of it. For now, it took everything he had to believe that they would always have enough to eat and a safe place to sleep, and no bad men coming to the door.*

*And if they did, they had locks. And Tía Vi.*

*There was a counselor that flew into the Park once a month to talk to him and Anna and Mami about how they got here and what happened to them along the way. She was a nice lady and she spoke Spanish but she had been born in* el norte *and she didn't understand. David was reluctant to tell her everything. He didn't want to tell anyone everything. Mami might, and Anna, too, and he was willing to believe that it would be good for them to do so.*

*But not him. David was the man of the family now. It was his job to look forward, not behind. It was his job to be alert, and strong, and wary. Because the bad men were always out there, at home and in* el norte, *in uniform and out of it. It was his job to protect Anna and Mami from them from now on.*

*So he would.*

# Acknowledgments

S O I STARTED A NONPROFIT. AND THEN, because this is what crime writers do, I immediately tried to figure out how to pervert it to be used in evil ways.

With the help (again) of Der Plotmeister, it was alarmingly easy.

Disclaimer: No actual nonprofits were harmed in the writing of this book, nor does the Bannister Foundation resemble any nonprofit in real life.

At least I sure as hell hope not.

My thanks to Barbara Peters for identifying all the gaping plot holes so I could backfill them in. A good editor's price is far above rubies.

Kate's thanks to Joyce White for sharing her fry bread recipe.

My thanks to Pati Crofut for the story about the night landing with the snow machines lined up along the runway.

Well. For all the stories, really.

My thanks to attorneys Andy Haas and Terri Spigelmyer for defining the responsibilities of a trustee.

I wish there was too little information out there on sex trafficking but the agony is that there is too much. There are articles on mainstream media everywhere, from the *New York Times* to *USA Today* to the BBC. The FBI and the US Marshals both have multiple posts on their websites, as do the United Nations and the European Commission.

There is every bit as much information out there on the opioid plague, from mainstream media to local, state, national, and international law enforcement websites.

The day I wrote these words I googled "how to make fentanyl" and got 11,900,000 results.

Goody.